T0017432

McKEE OF
CENTRE STREET

HELEN REILLY (1891-1962) was a pioneering author of American Golden Age mysteries and considered to be one of the first women to write in the police procedural subgenre. She wrote over thirty novels starring Inspector Christopher McKee, of the fictitious Manhattan Homicide Squad. Most of her writing was published under her own name but she also published several novels under the pseudonym Kieran Abbey. A member of the Mystery Writers of America, she served as president of the organization in 1953.

OTTO PENZLER, the creator of American Mystery Classics, is also the founder of the Mysterious Press (1975); Mysterious-Press.com (2011), an electronic-book publishing company; and New York City's Mysterious Bookshop (1979). He has won a Raven, the Ellery Queen Award, two Edgars (for the *Encyclopedia of Mystery and Detection*, 1977, and *The Lineup*, 2010), and lifetime achievement awards from NoirCon and *The Strand Magazine*. He has edited more than 70 anthologies and written extensively about mystery fiction.

McKEE OF
CENTRE STREET

HELEN
REILLY

Introduction by
OTTO
PENZLER

AMERICAN
MYSTERY
CLASSICS

Penzler Publishers
New York

Published in 2023 by Penzler Publishers
58 Warren Street, New York, NY 10007
penzlerpublishers.com

Distributed by W. W. Norton

Cover image: Andy Ross
Cover design: Mauricio Diaz

Paperback ISBN 978-1-61316-499-0
Hardcover ISBN 978-1-61316-498-3
eBook ISBN 978-1-61316-500-3

Library of Congress Control Number: 2023918641

Printed in the United States of America

9 8 7 6 5 4 3 2 1

INTRODUCTION

HELEN REILLY (1891–1962) began writing mysteries at the urging of a family friend, the noted author William McFee, and honored him by naming her series character McKee. Reilly's books usually feature New York City police detective Christopher McKee, who went on to become the head of the Homicide Squad, and were among the first American novels to stress police procedure.

It was common for female American Golden Age writers to lean toward writing in the "had-I-but-known" school of romantic suspense that made Mary Roberts Rinehart the best-selling mystery writer in the United States for decades from 1910 to the 1950s. Reilly, however, was virtually unique in writing police novels as a woman in the 1930s, though she gradually slipped into the woman-in-jeopardy genre, sometimes coming perilously close to producing HIBK stories.

Several writers strongly influenced Reilly, notably the wildly successful S.S. Van Dine, whose early Philo Vance novels were all the rage in the 1920s and early 1930s. It was clear that Anthony Abbot also was deeply influenced by Van Dine and served as an additional model for Reilly, whose series character McKee, like Thatcher Colt but unlike Vance, was a New York City policeman. While McKee was not quite as erudite as Vance, he was a challenger, as was the early Ellery Queen.

Several elements connect all four writers, though Van Dine and Queen have endured as popular writers longer than Abbot or Reilly.

All are New Yorkers. All are pedants (McKee less than the others but, still…).

The two cops and the two amateurs have friends within the justice system, whether police officers or district attorneys, from whom they either receive help in solving a case or are consulted and provide it. Recurring characters, in addition to the protagonists, are featured in most of their books, helping to give them depth and the pleasure of other voices. In the McKee series, the policeman relies on his close relationship with District Attorney John Francis Dwyer.

In the tradition of detective fiction since Edgar Allan Poe took pen to paper, the hero crimefighter has an assistant who takes the role of the readers' surrogate by not quite understanding what the great man is thinking and requires explanations, as the reader does. In Reilly's case, McKee's associate is his friend and fellow bachelor Todhunter, the highly effective "little gray man" cop who works for him. He is not alone, however, as McKee, in true procedural mode, has a large team of police who assist in a multitude of tasks that could never be accomplished by a single policeman. They handle background checks, engage in disguise and impersonation for undercover jobs, visit crime scenes, and question possible eyewitnesses.

An element of a McKee investigation that is unlike anything attempted by Van Dine, Queen, or Abbot is that we are with

McKee every step of the way, sharing McKee's thoughts, theories, discoveries, and deductions throughout the case, instead of the more common denouement when the detective hero explains everything to an awed collection of suspects and law enforcement members at the very end of the book.

Reilly's early work, like *McKee of Centre Street* (1933), was set in the Depression era or its immediate aftermath and featured the people who were most likely to be affected by it. Unlike Queen and Van Dine, who solved crimes among the upper levels of society, among lush homes, servants, and enormous wealth, McKee's work is accomplished in shabby apartments in poor neighborhoods populated by people worried about having enough to eat and keeping a roof over their heads.

Unlike the lower classes in the work of Dashiell Hammett, Cornell Woolrich, and most pulp writers, who are mainly criminals, the people in Reilly's books are mainly honest, hard-working people struggling through tough times. And McKee is a good, honest cop who genuinely wants to help civilians get a fair shake.

McKee had appeared in two earlier books, *The Diamond Feather* (1930) and *Murder in the Mews* (1931), but it is in *McKee of Centre Street* (1933) in which he becomes a fully developed character involved in a genuine investigation—the essence of detective fiction.

The Centre Street in the title, with its British spelling, is the location of the headquarters of the New York City Police Department, and the narrative opens with a detailed description of the radio room, giving readers a realistic view of the less-than-glamorous venue in which McKee and his colleagues work.

It is getting close to a century since the book was written but, in many ways, the set-up of the police headquarters is not very different from today. Sure, technology has become a good deal more sophisticated than the radios that were the cutting edge of modern communication in 1933 but having a room that serves as the center of the nervous system that reaches every corner of the city still exists.

For the action that sets the novel into motion, Reilly precisely notes the time when McKee enters headquarters (10:03), finishes getting a report (10:05), and a nearly minute-by-minute account of the activities performed until 10:16, when he arrives at the speakeasy where a woman has been killed.

Meticulous attention to police procedure follows throughout the investigations as various members of the department scour the crime scene for clues, interview everyone in the bar, some of whom were then shadowed, and employ the forensics that were available at the time. This approach to solving a crime may lack some of the pizazz of a dying clue or footprints on a ceiling, but it gives readers an accurate, realistic illustration of the life and times of ordinary New York City police and the citizens they were hired to protect.

How Reilly was able to so accurately describe the world of the lower middle class is somewhat surprising, as she came from an upper middle class family. Born Helen Kieran, she was the daughter of Dr. James M. Kieran, president of Hunter College. Her brother John was a famous naturalist and erstwhile panelist on the famous radio show *Information Please*. Another brother, James, also wrote a mystery: *Come Murder Me* (1952).

Helen was married to the artist/cartoonist Paul Reilly, with whom she had four daughters, two of whom, Ursula Curtiss and Mary McMullen, became successful mystery writers.

After living in Westport, Connecticut, for many years, Helen moved back to New York, where she had spent her early years, when her husband died in 1944. In 1960, she moved to New Mexico with the Curtiss family but, as Ursula wrote, her mother "always missed New York. She was a born and bred New Yorker."

Reilly wrote more than thirty novels about McKee in addition to three non-series books under the pseudonym Kieran Abbey. A major contribution to her ability to describe faithfully and accurately police procedure was that she had become one of the few "outsiders" to be given access to the Manhattan Homicide Squad's files.

In 1941, the great mystery scholar Howard Haycraft praised the McKee novels as "among the most convincing that have been composed on the premise of actual police procedure."

Otto Penzler
New York, July 2023

CHAPTER I

THE WEATHER prediction for May twenty-first was "clear and cooler." As a matter of fact it was hot and rained on and off all day—which didn't make any difference in the end.

McKee went up the last flight of stairs in the long gray building on Centre Street that night fishing for a minnow. He caught a whale. No sign of it then. It was exactly ten-three when he opened the last door and stepped inside.

The radio room was an inverted finger bowl of dull gold. Light flowed back from the rounded walls, stopped at a patch of sky dark above the ventilators. In the middle of the floor three big tables formed a hollow square at one end. The top of the tables was a map of the five boroughs divided by colored cords into little red sectors and bigger gray ones. Scattered over the red sectors were numbered brass disks representing the green scout cars carrying two uniformed men, one to each red division and, moving about the gray ones, the unrecognizable master cars loaded with detectives, machine guns, tear-gas and smoke bombs. There was a microphone at the far end of the room; at right angles a short distance away, the sending apparatus.

There were two operators inside the square, keen young men

in blue broadcloth shirts, head sets on, watching the movement of patrols with intent eyes. A third man, Lieutenant Balcom, sat at a desk thumping a typewriter. When the head of the Manhattan Homicide Squad came in, Balcom jumped up, his hand out. He said to the tall lean man in smoky tweeds:

"Well, this is a pleasure, Inspector. What can I do for you?"

McKee smiled. "I've been out of the city on a case—just back." And put his request: A man the patrol had picked up in Brooklyn the night before. "He's a Negro, twenty-one or -two, probably done time, probably gave a false name, also. He's a fellow I'm after as a witness."

"Right, Inspector, I'll run through what we've got if you'll wait."

That was at ten-five. While Balcom went through the turnover for the last twenty-four hours stabbed on the file on his desk, McKee picked up the Annual Police Report, skipped the picture of the mayor, and began to read the commissioner's summary of crime, with his customary morose expression:

"Crimes of violence decreased 2.6% as compared with the year 1931. There were 11 less murders and manslaughters committed than in the year 1931. Of the 478 cases of murder and manslaughter reported, 118 of those killed had criminal records. There were thirty-two less homicides committed with the use of firearms than in the year 1931. Felonious assaults were 4.3% higher than in the year 1931. Burglary cases reported were 9.7% lower than in the year 1931. Grand larceny cases . . ."

Balcom turned, flourishing a sheet of paper. Behind his shoulder the minute hand of the clock jerked forward. Six minutes after ten. Balcom said: "This may be the fellow you're looking for. Call came in last night that a haberdashery store in south Brooklyn was being broken into. Broadcast the message to cars in that sector. When they got there, a smashed window—nothing else. They let us know. We then sent a general alarm through the entire district. A car a half-mile away saw a Negro lurking in a doorway. He might have been all right, then again he mightn't. Our men hopped out to look him over. The Negro ran up some stairs. They followed. He had a big box under his arm. They asked him about that, and he said he'd been shopping. It was three o'clock in the morning. They opened the box. Six shirts, a flock of ties, B. V. D.'s, a dozen pairs of socks. They brought him in. He gave his name as Harold Kraft. His yellow sheet's got plenty on it. I'm afraid——"

Then and there Mr. Kraft ceased to be of the slightest interest. A phone rang. The other men were busy. Balcom picked it up and listened. McKee listened, too, half absently at first, scarcely recording. In the still air of the golden bowl the voice of a man at the other end of the wire was distinctly audible, high, breathless, and edged thinly with hysteria: "Police Headquarters? Police . . . She's dead. Right before our eyes . . . on the Sanctuary floor . . ." The voice stopped. Something banged, there was a muffled cry, a pause filled with silence, then a click. Balcom jiggled the hook up and down and swore. He said into the mouthpiece: "Operator, operator, Police Headquarters. I've been cut off. Trace the call that just came in. Hurry!" and turned to the inspector with a groan. "A woman dead in a church, and there are only two thousand, eight hundred and nine of them in the city. That's all."

McKee didn't answer. He tossed aside the report he had been reading with satisfaction, thrust his hands into his pockets. His gaze touched walls, floor, ceiling. The "Sanctuary". . . somewhere . . . recently . . . at his elbow the operator's voice was nasal out of black rubber. "Sorry, Headquarters, can't locate that call for you. Dial phone."

Balcom slammed the receiver back on the hook and stared helplessly. If he'd gotten the location of the church the radio car would be on its way there now. The inspector went on thinking: "Sanctuary, Sanctuary!" The picture began to fade in. A chair, a lamp, a magazine. Telfair's place, sketches in a magazine, a new weekly printed on good paper, "*Bab . . . Babylon!*" He said quietly:

"The Sanctuary is a speakeasy on Thirteenth Street between Sixth and Seventh avenues. The number is 604."

Balcom was across the floor in three strides. A quick look at the map for the number on the brass disk covering the location, at the microphone then. He reached up, pulled a lever. On the opposite side of the room, lamps in the transmitter were a blue glare behind wire netting. Crash and bang as though a bomb had dropped, above it, high, thin, electric, an owl's hoot to let the men in the cruising cars know that an alarm was about to be sent out. Balcom put his face close to the bronze disk, said slowly and distinctly, "Car 253, Car 253, Sixth precinct, 604 West Thirteenth Street, Code signal 30, Time 10:09 P. M." He stepped back.

McKee was already at the desk, crouched negligently over the department phone. Six words to the Telegraph Bureau next door: "Homicide, speakeasy, 604 West Thirteenth Street." Six words alone were required for all concerned to report to the scene of the crime, medical examiner, district attorney on homicide duty, his stenographer, fingerprint men, photographer, district and borough commanders, the assistant chief, and the police commissioner himself, every one of them available at any hour of the day or night. This done, he pushed the phone away, picked up another, got his own office, and said, his voice unhurried and sure: "Hello, Steve. The inspector. Who's doing night duty? . . . All right. Send them down to the Sanctuary." He gave the address, put the receiver back on the hook, turned away, felt for a cigarette, didn't light it, fell into a dreamless slumber on his feet, tall, slouching; cavernous eyes fixed, wide open. Who had a line on the speaks in the neighborhood? Hughes, the taxi starter at Twenty-third Street, for whom he'd done a favor, was thoroughly familiar with the lower West Side. He got the number and waited.

The radio room couldn't wait. Calls coming in now—fast. Crime fermenting in the darkness, patience wearing thin, endurance ebbing. Bang and jar of the transmitter, steel flash, high whine of the signal. A man was trying to climb in a second-story window on 56th Street, a dog had been run over on Atlantic Avenue, a woman had taken iodine in a drugstore on Sutton Place. A hit-and-run driver. . . . McKee got Hughes and put his question: "Hello, Hughes, Inspector McKee. Who runs that speak called the Sanctuary on Thirteenth Street? Gus and Louis? . . . Citizens . . . I see. Fancy crowd?. . . Thanks. Yes, sometime soon."

Already Balcom had reversed the little brass disk on the red sector bounded by Twelfth Street on the south and Seventeenth on the north. As McKee went past him with that deceptively languid stride, the lieutenant grinned and saluted.

"Luck, Inspector. Our men are probably there now."

McKee nodded, waved a hand, opened the door, closed it behind him. He was in the Telegraph Bureau. In a shabby glare khaki-shirted men in black ties were ranged either side of a long switchboard, their faces moon ovals beneath eyeshades. Behind glass in a corner, another official commanded receiving and sending teletype machines. The Policewoman's Bureau, the stairs. Down and down through the silent building, past the chief surgeon's office, the line-up room, into the lower hall with its information booth; wall on the right hung with bronze tablets where one could only be inscribed with honor by being dead, through the revolving door to the street. Pete, policeman chauffeur, behind the wheel of the Cadillac, waiting. Thirty seconds later, with the blue plate in the windshield, the car was flashing north, its way cleared, past lights, through the dark labyrinth of the chill night streets.

Meanwhile pandemonium raged, discordant, ugly behind the grilled iron doors of one of New York's smartest speaks. The Sanctuary was crowded that night. Bankers, brokers, artists, writers, men about town, women who should have known better, young people out on a bender, a sprinkling of social registerites, sightseers, sitting at small tables in soft light, perfumed with the odor of flowers, of wine, and of food, were shocked into cold sobriety in the twinkling of an eye. At one moment everything was just as usual. The long room was full of the tuneful wailings of the sax, the plucked notes of a violin, murmur of voices, figures shadowy above white cloths, people moving cautiously in gloom, cigarette tips glowing, glasses suspended in air, all eyes fastened with almost hypnotic compulsion on the slender gleaming figure in the middle of the dance floor. At the next, no one seemed quite to understand exactly what had happened, except that the delicately molded shaft of ice and glitter, arms extended, stopped whirling in full flight and tumbled, with a thud you could hear above the music, to the floor. One long-drawn shocked breath and the restaurant was a shambles of china and glass and incoherent babble. "What happened? . . . A stroke? . . . She's dead.

. . . Did you say she was dead? . . . A doctor, better get a doctor! . . . Heart, I guess. . . . Let's get out of here!"

A doctor and the proprietor stampeded through the press. The spotlight, motionless on empty boards, had been turned off, the lamps on full. The doctor knelt, peered, sought for a pulse, didn't find one, laid his head against silver lamé, took it away again, turned back an eyelid, and looked at the proprietor, who acted with a speed and decision surprising in a man of his bulk.

"Ladies and gentlemen . . . an accident . . . most regrettable . . . If you will all step into the inner dining room?" His voice was hollow out of colorless lips in a face exuding moisture. No one had the slightest desire to remain in the garden. There was a concerted rush for the door at the far end. Even the doctor went to have a brandy in the bar when he saw he couldn't be of the slightest use. That was at ten minutes after ten. At ten-sixteen the radio patrol rolled up.

The police were just in time. The doctor, warmed by liquor to a regard for his civic duties, commandeered a couple of waiters in an attempt to hold the doors. Another moment and the clamoring crowd would have broken bounds. Some sort of order was at once restored. Detectives from the local precinct entering the speak at ten twenty-two were a help. Sergeant Halloway was in command. He shoved excited guests back into the inner dining room under guard. Another man took up a position at the foot of the stairs leading to the ladies' room on the second floor, a detective went into the garden, and a uniformed man was assigned to the dark areaway to see that no one slipped past. That was the only entrance or exit.

CHAPTER II

McKee got out of the Cadillac a few doors east of the Sanctuary and approached it slowly, absorbing the atmosphere. Very few people were, about. The street was dimly lighted, lined with high-stooped brownstone houses of another era, as like as peas in a pod and devoted to the same usage: speakeasies in the basements, upper floors let out to roomers. The rain had stopped. Overhead May stars pierced the sky with tiny pin pricks of liquid silver. As he paused in front of Number 604, three other cars converged from different locations, drew up with a squealing of brakes.

Laconic greetings exchanged, the casual offerings of cool collected men who meet only on such occasions as this that brought them together tonight. "Got a job here. . . . Some woman killed? . . . How's the chief? . . . Cold, isn't it?" In a solid phalanx, moving easily, the New York Police Department crossed the pavement, went down three steps without hurry or confusion. A precinct detective opened the door.

McKee went in first, vibrant, attentive, without an ounce of spare flesh on his bones; then Lieutenant Donaher, a puffball of a fellow, nicking the regulation height by a hair; Johnny Tannin, slim and brisk (these three from the Homicide Squad); Sergeant Drake, a fingerprint man in an overcoat too big and a hat too small, spectacles drooping down his nose, an elderly and benevolent crane; a photographer, Dalligan, a dish-faced eager fellow with a big black suitcase; and the assistant medical examiner, Dr. Fernandez, bored and alert. Not much to look at in the way of what men will wear, but advancing with a directness that was a little appalling.

In the hall McKee looked about him quickly. At first glance the Sanctuary was not impressive. A flight of steps slumped sideways with age, a cloakroom like a slit on the right, a long mahogany table with a handsome gilt mirror above it, a hat-check girl on her feet, white-faced except for lipstick freshly applied and hair that could have done with more or less blondine; folding doors to the left, closed now. From behind these doors Babel seeped, thin, high, like waves rising and falling. The precinct man wiped his forehead. "Got the crowd in there, Inspector. Some of them are kicking up a row. Couple of drunks. They all want to beat it. Sergeant's got their names and addresses. Dame's dead. Dead when the radio patrol arrived."

"All right. We'll have a look."

The detectives led the way through a door at the back of the hall that gave on a small vestibule lined with waiters' hats and coats and with brooms and mops in one corner. It was not meant for the use of patrons. This in turn gave on a kitchen, a long whitewashed apartment with a *cabinaire* for the chef at the far end and almost directly in front of them the door leading into the Sanctuary garden. Before going through this door, McKee glanced around. In order to get into the garden, guests had to cross the kitchen from the bar, and would, therefore, granted the men weren't busy, be under the observation of both the bartender and the chef. He turned to Tannin: "Go find out what the situation was in these rooms when she died."

The garden then. Just inside the restaurant proper, perhaps five feet beyond the door, a mahogany barrier with service tables in front of it and topped with ferns and flowers, cut off their view. They rounded this, and McKee stood still, the others glancing curiously from behind. A long and wide room crowded with little tables and threaded lengthwise with two aisles. The place was a gimcrack paradise simulating the worst features of a baronial hall, a walled garden, and the smoking room of a cabin liner. It felt stuffy and at the same time dank. It smelt of fish and grease and perfume and cigarette smoke and the dregs of wine. Apparently nothing had been touched. A pair of gloves left behind here, a crumpled handkerchief there, a discarded corsage of orchids, an umbrella (some careful commuter). Overturned chairs, crumpled napkins, smashed glasses added to the confusion. The table lamps were out, and a huge bulb in the ceiling shed a garish and dusty light over marble that was cement, grained wood that was iron; even the flowers lining the walls looked faded and weary, as though they could no longer keep up the pretense of blooming in Eden. In the middle of the room, surrounded by tables, was the dance floor.

And in that open space, a little offside, lay a woman, nothing from that distance but a shimmer of green and silver and twisted limbs. McKee started along the aisle, gave way to Dr. Fernandez. They fetched up, the lot, three feet from the motionless huddle of silk and flesh, staring down in the involuntary silence that death commands.

The dancer was beautiful. It was not an attractive face. But her features were almost perfect. A Grecian head lovely in its sculptured simplicity, its sure blunted grace. But there was greed in the square jut of the chin, sensuality in the curve of the lips, and cruelty in the white-lidded, heavily lashed eyes. A fisher of men . . . most assuredly. Death could not subdue the springing curves of her body, high small breasts, rounded thighs, delicate limbs, reverting now by an inexorable process into the end of all things.

She was lying on her side, one arm flung back over her head, and, except for those wide-open eyes gazing up at the doubtful oak of the Sanctuary rafters with a surprised expression, the grace of her posture might have meant a fainting fit or sudden sleep. Only that in addition there was a strawberry splash on white flesh and silver tissue seeping into a jagged splotch near the umbilicus.

The medical examiner got down on his knees. Sergeant Drake, after a clicking sound, began to unpack his paraphernalia. Dalligan, so young and so anxious to do a good job that he could take a little thing like this in his stride, was looking around for the best location for his shots. McKee murmured a direction to Donaher and turned to Halloway. "Now then, Sergeant."

Consulting scribbled notes, Halloway produced what he had. The dead woman was Rita Rodriguez, a dancer, hired by Gus Evans at a theatrical agency. She had been performing at the Sanctuary for about seven weeks. She came on each night at eight, at ten, and twelve. Her dance took about fifteen minutes. Tonight everything was just as usual except that she was about ten minutes late arriving at the speakeasy, had gone immediately to her dressing room "back there"—the sergeant waved towards the barrier at the rear of the garden. "We looked it over, nothing there." At any rate, Rita took off her street clothes, changed into her costume, did her act, went back to her room, stayed there until ten, came in again, punctually this time, had been doing her stuff for about—— "I know," McKee said, "eight or nine minutes." "Yes. All of a sudden, without any warning, nobody heard a sound, she didn't cry out or anything, she dropped to the floor. By the time a doctor who was eating here got to her, she was dead."

"Bring me," McKee said, "the proprietor."

His glance was thoughtful and withdrawn. Out in front the medical examiner threw over his shoulder without turning: "This woman was shot, Inspector. One in the breast and another bullet in the abdomen." He stood up. "Better get the pictures first and then I'll give you what I can get."

Dalligan, who had been moving around on the far side of the room like an acolyte preparing the ground for some strange festival, called "Watch your eyes," pressed a switch, and roto floodlights filled the place with an incredible radiance, blue-white, blinding. The French camera was brought into play, that famous wide-angle lens whose twin, the only other one of its kind in the world, reposed in the Sûreté in Paris. Again and again and again, from different positions, he recorded the dancer's body, before photographing the room itself. Drake's turn then. He took the dead woman's fingerprints, each one on a separate piece of paper, making sure not to get them mixed before they were pasted on the fingerprint blank, began to scrutinize the results. Nothing unusual, loops, whirls, deltas, islands—no scars. In the middle of this the proprietor arrived.

Gus Evans was a big man with a body run to fat, a stolid face, little sharp eyes. He and a partner named Louis Verrili owned the Sanctuary. Louis was away that night. Mopping cheeks and forehead with a gray silk handkerchief, although it had turned colder, he repeated the story he had already told Halloway. McKee interrupted with a question which the sergeant answered. "Yeah, she lives at a hotel on Thirty-seventh Street. I sent a man over." Gus proceeded to relate with passion that he knew nothing of the dancer's private life, that she never ate or drank with anyone; didn't have any friends who came to the Sanctuary, concealing in a dribble of words a detail that the Scotsman pounced on. Rita was terminating her engagement that night.

"And she told you that—when?"

"She was late getting in, see? I went back to talk to her. She said she was quitting. It was after—after she had done her turn at eight." He was lying. Contemplating cupidity ill concealed behind scanty lashes, McKee couldn't at the moment see the point of this lie. . . . He went on to elicit more detail.

"What happened after Miss Rodriguez collapsed? Are all the people in the Sanctuary now who were here at the time?"

"Yes. When we found she was dead I got them all into the dining room inside and—and—called the police." Again he was lying. His was not the voice that had come screaming into the golden bowl at the top of Police Headquarters. The inspector nodded approval, his voice bland.

"And is this room now just as it was when Miss Rodriguez was shot?"

"Shot?" Gus quivered all over, panting.

"Yes, shot with a gun with a silencer on it. Is this room just as it was then?"

"Except for . . . the lights and . . . the people."

"What about the lights?"

"They were off except for the spotlight on the dancer.

"The spotlight?"

"Yes. Up there in the back room."

Gus exuded a fresh crop of moisture on a bulging forehead not stuffed with brains. McKee turned. The Sanctuary garden was two stories high. Built out into the back yard, its inner wall was the old outer wall of the original house, and it was through the middle window of three on the second story that light was directed on the dance floor. It was essential to get at the roots of Gus's unease—his misstatements. Was he shielding someone? Absently, his gaze on the room which was being fine-tooth-combed by detectives, McKee dismissed the man; sent Tannin for the electrician. The guests were all in the inner room milling around. He wasn't ready for them yet. Had anyone left the place since the shot was fired?

Stutz, the ballistics man from headquarters, had already arrived. He was standing at the edge of the dance floor. McKee joined him as Fernandez turned the body over. A small heavy object came out of a blood-stained fold of silver cloth. Stutz swooped and picked it up. "Oh, great," he said, "a spent bullet." He scrutinized the lead closely. "Fine, Inspector, very nice indeed. Now we have something to work on." It was true that even to an untrained eye the lines of the boring and barrel rifling were clearly impressed on the slug, but McKee was not jubilant. For the dancer had been shot at the particular point in the dance when she was whirling on her toes—impossible to tell which way she was facing or from what distance the bullet had come. He listened morosely while the men began to discuss the orifice of the wound and the angle at which the bullet had entered the body. Entrance and exit, entrance—no exit. "We'll get that in the autopsy. Yes." McKee turned away. Tannin was advancing down the aisle with a man in tow.

It was Williams, the Sanctuary's handy man and electrician. Williams looked frightened and then ill when he saw the body. Tannin began shooting routine questions at him under the inspector's negligent gaze. The moment Williams spoke, McKee knew his voice. Undoubtedly Williams and not Gus was the man who had called Police Headquarters. And what had happened was at once plain. The electrician, directing the spotlight and familiar with every movement of the dance, had realized more quickly than the spectators that something serious had happened. He fled to the phone. Gus, on the floor underneath, saw the light sag, rushed upstairs and snatched the receiver out of his hand—a second too late. Why was the proprietor so anxious to delay the arrival of the police?

He asked Williams that, quietly. The man's teeth chattered, and he looked over his shoulder. Tannin brought his hand down heavily on the gray flannel of a work shirt. "Lost your tongue, have you?"

"Gus . . . Gus didn't . . . He came upstairs. Then we both came down. He didn't know I was telephoning to the police. He wanted to do it himself."

McKee was calculating. The call had come in at ten-nine. Allow a minute. Rita had been killed at ten-eight. The radio patrol had arrived at ten-sixteen. Donaher, checking up, had already emptied the hall and bar of spectators immediately after the killing, for the hat-check girl, bartender, and chef had all rushed into the dining room at the outcry. Williams's story put him on the stairs in the period that followed. The Scotsman said, his voice mild:

"On your way down here, Williams, did you see anyone going out?"

And then it came, the flaw in an otherwise perfect set-up, prompt arrival of the police, bottling up of exits, detention of all persons at the scene of the crime. For the electrician, frowning, first thought, and was then absolutely sure, that as he was running towards the stairs he had heard voices in the lower hall, followed by the clang of the outside door.

CHAPTER III

Voices meant two people. For certainly no drunk, however far gone, would have been engaged in conversation with himself on that extremely expeditious flight from the Sanctuary, just after the dancer was shot. It was absolutely necessary to find out who these two people were. But there are more ways of killing a cat than by choking it with butter. Guests do not come to a speakeasy without eating and drinking; it isn't encouraged by the management. The checks were reposing on the file in the bar. They should provide a fairly accurate tally. McKee sent Tannin to investigate this angle while he went on a little tour. The electrician's cubbyhole, the ladies' room on the floor above, all the rooms down here, were being quietly searched for a weapon. The Scotsman started for the dancer's dressing room.

Four feet of space behind the mahogany barrier at the back of the garden. He stepped into the narrow corridor. Two telephone booths in the near corner, a small door at the far end, the rear wall roughly paneled in pine, green linoleum on the floor. McKee skirted the linoleum carefully in order not to destroy tracks, for the flooring here had not as yet been examined, opened the little door, closed it behind him, and looked around.

The room was small, square, contained a dressing table, a chair, a closet, and a washbasin behind a screen. There was linoleum on the floor here, too. The walls were gray. There was no window. McKee lifted the screen aside. The shelf above the basin held various cosmetics, creams, powders, rouge. McKee sniffed at a satin-covered box and got, in a cloying wave, the same odor that clung to the dancer's body, a sweet, lingering, and heady perfume of Chinese lilies. It was like the woman/herself, a distilled essence of that ivory skin touched with henna on cheeks and lips, numbing, soporific.

He went on with his intense scrutiny. The only thing of interest behind the screen was a little heap of gray ash, such as might fall from a cigarette burning unheeded. Two things were at once evident: In spite of Gus's assertion to the contrary, Rita had had a visitor here, for it was certainly not the proprietor who had stood behind the screen. The space was too narrow. Equally certain it was not the dancer herself. His first glance at the woman had told him she was not a smoker. Just as he had figured her age roughly from the tiny gum-line fillings showing beneath the scarlet arch of her upper lip. The edges of these fillings showed not the slightest trace of stain, showed in addition that she was not as young as she looked. That type of cavity becomes prevalent as a general rule after twenty-five and nearer thirty.

He turned his attention to the rest of the room. At first glance it said little or nothing. Simply verified the story that she had come in here; had taken off her street clothes—green duvetyn dress with white collar and cuffs, brown pumps, beige stockings, a tan tweed coat with a fox collar, and chamois gloves, and had changed into her costume. There was one thing that McKee missed, searched for in the pockets of her coat, didn't find, and continued to be annoyed. Where was the dancer's purse? Certainly not in the dressing room. He snipped the label from the coat, the laundry mark from her dress, picked up one of her shoes. To stand, astonished, turning the slipper over in his fingers.

It was made of expensive brown calf, with a turned sole and a slender heel, but the fact that the dead woman had a beautiful foot was not what brought the sudden gleam into the back of the Scotsman's cavernous brown eyes. The leather itself, just above the sole, bore a faint wavering line of moisture which was still damp to the touch—the spike heel had within a very short time been plunged into earth, fragments of which made a dull smear on its shining surface.

Gus had said, and his testimony—Tannin had gone into that—had been backed up by the check girl and the man on the door, that the dancer had entered the Sanctuary at ten minutes after eight. The night was fine then, with merely the threat and smell of rain in the sultry air. To the best of McKee's knowledge the sudden showers that had deluged the city, stopping at four, hadn't begun again until around nine. How, then, if Rita had remained in the speakeasy, had she gotten her shoes wet?

Putting the slipper beside its companion, he left the dressing room and strode along the corridor towards the telephone booths at the far end. He pulled the handle of the first door which was not quite closed. The door stuck, then slid back. McKee stood still. Crowded into the dark interior, a woman faced him in dimness. Her arms were hanging at her sides, her shoulders flat against wood, her eyes closed. As he stared, she opened her eyes.

The inspector said softly: "Can I—be of any assistance to you?"

Her voice was collected enough. "Thanks very much. I'm afraid I fainted. Stupid of me." Refusing McKee's hand, she stepped out of the telephone booth and walked, unassisted, past the mahogany barrier and into the main body of the dining room. He pulled out a chair. She sat down.

She was young, perhaps twenty-five or -six, slim, with a pair of long gray eyes whose brightness hardly suggested physical collapse. She accepted the room, the garish light, the presence of the police without any attempt at surprise, turned her head, saw the silver-and-green huddle on the floor with Stutz and the medical examiner still busy over it, put the back of her hand across her eyes with a quick breath, took it away again and looked at McKee.

"Is she—dead?"

"I'm afraid so. Yes."

"You're a—a policeman, too?"

"Yes." Somewhere, sometime, he had seen this girl before. That wasn't what engrossed his attention. How was it that she had remained in the telephone booth unseen for so long a time? Granted that the door was not quite shut and the light in the ceiling not therefore on, her face and hands should have been visible to the precinct man who had given the place the once-over on his arrival. Unless she had deliberately concealed herself. As though she guessed his thoughts, she said:

"You will want to know things, of course. I've been in the booth for hours. Perhaps I'd better begin at the beginning. My name is Judith Pierce, and I was dining here tonight with a friend, Mrs. Gerald Gair, when—it happened. They told me we couldn't go. Mrs. Gair was worried. The last train leaves at eleven, and she wanted to get out to the country. I decided to call a friend of mine who has some influence, but I had trouble getting him, and then the memory of . . . of the dancer falling . . . and the heat made me feel faint. The next thing I knew you were there. Is that—all right?" She smiled. McKee remained grave. The young lady was too ingenuous.

Rita Rodriguez had been shot at around eight minutes after ten. They themselves had arrived at a little after half-past. It was now about a quarter of eleven. The girl had been in the booth for over half an hour.

He said: "You know the dead woman, Miss Pierce?"

"Knew her? Why—I'd seen her before, of course—dancing. I often came here. That's all."

He asked: "Mrs. Gair, with whom you dined, is still inside?" and she answered: "I suppose so." Yes, decidedly, eyes, lips, voice under too careful control. And the booth was only a short distance from the dancer's dressing room. He merely said:

"Odd that your friend hasn't come looking for you."

Her "Yes, that's rather worrying me. If that's all, may I join her now?" was a cool murmur against a movement of rising from her chair.

He let her go, watched her walk down the aisle without haste, crossed to Drake, who was beginning to assume a fretful expression at the size of his fingerprinting job, borrowed a magnifying glass, and returned to the shadowy corridor behind the barrier. But before proceeding with his task he called the Weather Bureau. A curt voice at the other end of the wire confirmed his earlier guess. Showers had begun at eight fifty-seven, sweeping across Manhattan under a south wind blowing at the rate of forty miles an hour. Which left the riddle of the dancer's wet slippers exactly where he had found it.

Crossing to the door of the dressing room, he got down on his knees and began to subject the linoleum to careful scrutiny. The chance of finding the girl's prints was slim, for the flooring,

although resilient, was clean, and dry shoes would not ordinari-
ly leave any trace. Kill two birds with one stone. Rita's had been
damp. Torch in one hand, glass in the other, he crawled forward
inch by inch.

Once again he was startled. A queer case, with discrepancies
that were almost meaningless. No trace of Miss Pierce at all, but
of the dancer. . . . The only entrance to the corridor the opening
from the garden, opposite the booths at the far end. Rita's tracks
began midway along its length, proceeding in an unbroken line
to her dressing room. But how in the name of blazes had she
reached the middle of the corridor without putting her foot to
the ground?

McKee bent lower to the smooth green surface, his glance
avid now. Two minutes of study gave him the following facts:
Of Gus, the Pierce girl, the precinct man who had first examined the dressing room, no trace at all. For the rest, two men had
walked to the middle of the corridor, and their feet and those of
the dancer had left very definite traces in the strange marriage of
prints close to the rear wall. One of these men was undersized
and thin. He had fallen arches. The other was tall, wore rubber
heels, had been a sailor, was obese, or afflicted with some bodily
infirmity, for his line of march was staggered off center.

And suddenly McKee knew for what he had to look, knew
the secret of Gus's attack on the electrician, his uneasiness, the
reason why the dancer's shoes were wet, had half known at the
back of his mind all the time, ever since Hughes, the taxi starter,
had said over the phone: "The liquor's swell. It's the real McCoy."

He went through the garden without a single glance at the
plodding activity of police routine, across the kitchen and into
the blazing and empty bar. Folding doors at the far end were

closed. Steadily rising clamor came from behind the doors. It didn't worry the Scotsman. Get the evidence straightened out first and then talk to these people later.

Tony, the bartender, with easy Latin grace was doing nothing behind marble. He detached himself from the wall as McKee came in. Their glances met. Nothing to be got from Tony; silence had been probably made well worth his while. The inspector looked over the shelves; two bottles of gin, one half empty, bathtub stuff, a bottle of Chartreuse two thirds gone, vermouth, fruit, bitters, and a lot of glasses. He said, lighting a cigarette, "Stock's pretty low, isn't it?"

Tony was all smiles. "Yes, sir, it is, and that's a fact. We're pretty near sold out. Can I mix you a Martini?"

But McKee was already at the kitchen door. As he entered the garden, Tannin advanced between some tables. He said: "There's no gun anywhere on the floor, boss; we've been over every foot of it."

The Scotsman's answer startled him: "It'll turn up. Never mind that now. Come back here with me." In the narrow corridor again, halfway along its length, he sought and found the thing for which he looked. A knot hole in paneling. Nothing particularly ingenious about the metal hasp inside. McKee pressed this down. The panel swung sharply out, flinging a sudden gust of night air into their faces.

CHAPTER IV

BOTH MEN stepped through the opening. They were in the back yard of the brownstone building which housed the Sanctuary—what remained of the back yard, three feet of damp cement running across the rear of the building in front of a high fence of gray boards from which paint was peeling and without a break. But there was a door at the far end—not locked. McKee pushed it wide and sent his flashlight traveling.

The yard of the house next to the speakeasy, clothes poles strung with sagging lines, a suit of underwear flapping dismally, a pair of socks, a basement door down three steps. This wasn't locked, either. He opened it with caution, closed it quietly. They were in a long, badly lighted corridor with clammy walls that needed attention and a carpet underfoot flat with grease. The air was used up, hung with the odor of a hundred unsavory meals. Tannin, his lips at McKee's ear, said: "Hideout for their stuff. Afraid of a liquor collar." McKee's voice was a thread: "Yes. Go back. Bottle up this place from the outside. I'll have a look."

The sergeant vanished as he advanced on the nearest door, easing it out of its frame, was in a disordered kitchen with some empty boxes standing around, left the kitchen, examined a bath-room next to it with distaste, retreated and opened a third door. Faint light seeping past him from the hall touched the outlines of a brass bed in one corner, a pair of run-down oxfords and black stockings, a rocking chair with a chemise that had once been pink flung over the arm. McKee switched on his torch. Against the sudden heave upward of a cotton comfortable with stuffing coming out in one corner, a woman screamed.

Before she could scream again, McKee said, as he dug a small black leather case from his righthand pocket and exposed the gold shield: "It's all right. I'm from headquarters. I want to ask you a few questions," and studied the woman sitting up in bed staring into his face. She was thin, scrawny, undernourished, clutched the cover to her breast, squeezed it with convulsive fingers, and answered his questions with the stammering evasiveness of a person who recognizes catastrophe without in the least knowing what to do about it.

Her name was Mrs. Bartell and she was the janitor's wife. Bartell was the janitor of the house. He wasn't at home, and she didn't know where he was, and she'd been in bed two hours and . . . "The entrance through the alley into the speakeasy next door?" She didn't know anything at all. She didn't . . .

McKee said pleasantly: "It's used to slip liquor through when a raid is threatened in the Sanctuary. I suppose the stuff they removed tonight is in this flat? Never mind that now, Mrs. Bartell. Just tell me what happened as far as that passageway is concerned, who made use of it this evening, either coming or going."

"I don't know. I can't tell you nothing. I've been mostly in the kitchen with the door closed. Anyhow I been in bed since nine o'clock. My back ached. I——"

Reaching sideways, the inspector put the palm of his hand on the chemise, took it away again. "You were wearing that garment not more than five minutes ago."

His steady gaze wiped away the last remnants of her composure. She told him the truth then, as accurately as a ten-year-old brain and a halting tongue would permit.

It was true that her husband had a deal with Gus and Louis to store liquor in this flat and to help take it out of the Sanctuary when there was any danger of the stock being seized. This had happened three or four times in the last six months. Tonight her husband had been at home playing poker with a friend— "Just a minute, Mrs. Bartell—his name and address?" She gave it, and McKee noted with satisfaction that the friend was a steward on an ocean liner, confirming his earlier guess about the footprints.

Well, anyhow, sometime along in the evening the bell rang. The bell in the hall outside connected with the Sanctuary bar. That meant that they had to hustle stuff fast. This they did, and when the job was finished they had gone out, telling her to go to bed and not answer the door. But she hadn't gone to bed. . . .

"You know that Miss Rodriguez is dead, Mrs. Bartell?"

She cringed back against the pillows, whispered "Yes," and then surprisingly, "I was afraid something . . ."

With delicate skill McKee urged the story from her. It was quite usual for Miss Rodriguez to come through the passage. Not so often going into the Sanctuary, but very often when she was leaving for the night.

"And sometimes she slipped away between the acts?"

"No, never before, sir. Miss Rodriguez was very careful of her looks. I went over once to mend a tear in her gown. She was lying back with cold cream on her face, and she didn't speak. She used to rest, sort of, with her eyes closed, but this evening she went out. I was surprised. I was washing the dishes——"

"That was about twenty minutes of nine?"

"Maybe. It was long after eight. I was in the kitchen. The door was closed. Bartell and his friend were in the front room having a game of cards. All of a sudden the door opens and she's standing there looking at me, only not . . . she didn't seem to see me, if you know what I mean . . . just stood stiff, kind of, and said: 'Where's the phone?' I wiped my hands on my apron and showed her. Then I went back into the kitchen. But I got to thinking about her. She looked so strange, set-like. When I got into the hall again she was just going through the front door.

"After that I kept watching. Then she came back. I was there, sir. I spoke to her. She didn't even look at me, didn't stop, didn't answer me at all, just went through the basement door at the back, left the door open behind her. I knew there was something the matter. So that when Bartell tells me she's dead, tells me to keep my mouth shut, I was scared. That's why I screamed when you come in."

McKee questioned the woman carefully, established that, to the best of Mrs. Bartell's belief, Miss Rodriguez had been away about an hour—perhaps less—and continued his probing. Neither Gus nor Louis nor any of the Sanctuary guests or help ever made use of the passage, but tonight a man had done so.

"It was," she said, "just before the bell rang." Mrs. Bartell didn't know this man, had never seen him before, could only say he wasn't very tall, not short, either, was muffled in a coat with the collar turned up, and had his hat pulled down over his eyes. Again she was the only witness of this subterranean flitting, the two men being still engaged with poker in the front room.

McKee made a rapid calculation. Rita dead on the floor, the guests hastily removed to the inner dining room, the alarm. The janitor's wife was distressingly vague about how long before the bell rang this strange man had made so hasty an exit. She did, however, in an effort to be helpful, offer a fresh and startling piece of information: "Maybe, sir, it was that fellow in the yellow roadster. The chap that waits for the dancer 'most every night. I've seen him time and time again when I been out on the front stoop for a breath of air. If she knew about this way of getting in and out of the Sanctuary, he might have, too." The inspector, alert, attentive, agreed that he might and concealed satisfaction behind a quiet, "Go to sleep now, Mrs. Bartell. We'll take your statement later and talk to your husband when he comes in." He left the room. Rita with a boy friend in a yellow roadster, not time yet for him to turn up—that was, if he hadn't already appeared. Quite possible it was this man who had entered the speakeasy and, mingling with the guests, had pulled the trigger of the gun that killed her, making his escape immediately afterwards by this route of which he must have known. Talk to Gus, the check girl, the waiters, but first squeeze this passageway dry.

Ten minutes of careful work got him nothing but a few crumbs of earth near the front door, similar in texture and color to the ones he had picked up from the linoleum in the Sanctuary, and a little farther along a tan tweed thread where the dancer's coat had caught on a rough sliver of the baseboard. Directly below this spot there were two thin silvery objects of about the thickness of broom straws.

Standing motionless under an almost spent bulb, McKee examined them curiously. Blue spruce needles. Blue spruce is one of the most expensive of evergreens. Self-evident the conclusion that in that brief journey away from the Sanctuary she had been among trees in a garden. But where in New York . . . Central Park? Rita didn't look like a woman with a passion for exercise on a rainy night. And there was the telephone call she had made. He was still thinking this over when Tannin reentered from the street. He had nothing to report. Among the private cars drawn up there was no roadster at all. Leaving a uniformed man in the flat to await the arrival of the janitor and take him around to the precinct for questioning, both of them returned to the Sanctuary.

The scene was comparatively unchanged. Drake was still making a round of the tables. Dalligan, the photographer, had finished. The medical examiner was through, too. He and Stutz were discussing the case. McKee fetched up at their chairs, intent gaze ranging the garden. The barriers at either end, tables in serried ranks surrounding the dance floor. If they could only narrow the thing down, determine the general direction from which the shot had come! He put this question. Was met by a slow shake of the head from Stutz.

"Oh, but surely," the Scotsman urged, "from the depth of entry, the orifice of the wound, the bullet's impact, the lacerated condition of the flesh—you can tell at least the distance . . ."

The ballistics man shrugged. "We can tell you that the gun was more than three or four feet away because there were no powder burns. Outside of that—this guy was shrewd, Inspector. She was whirling on her toes, the place in darkness except for the spotlight——"

Here there was an interruption. It began at the doorway at the end of the garden. Heads turned, a murmur ran through the garish disorder. Men straightened all over the room. "The commissioner—here he comes," Tannin said in an undertone to Dalligan. "I knew he'd roll on a case like this," and stood stiffly at attention.

Carey came slowly down the aisle, slim, spare, steady-eyed, oblivious of the hush. Thirty-five years of experience was behind his casual survey of the premises, his appreciation, contained in a turn of the head, of the outcry the guests were making at being detained inside. He came to a stop at the edge of the dance floor, looked down at Rita's body, distaste etching sensitive features, then turned to the little group beside him, said to Fernandez, "Hello, Doctor," and to McKee as ranking officer, no sign of their friendship in his crisp tone, "Well, Inspector?"

The Scotsman gave him, curtly, a résumé of what they had discovered. She was shot while she was dancing. The room was in dimness. The gun had not yet been found, if it was on the premises at all. The police had succeeded in bottling up the Sanctuary, but it was possible that three people had slipped out before they arrived. McKee ended with: ". . . a man or woman takes up a certain amount of space. It may be possible to . . ."

"Oh . . . I see what you mean. A little sum in arithmetic." They looked at each other. Stutz stared, and Fernandez stared, too. Carey merely said: "Let me know how it comes, Inspector. I've got a lot of things to do, but you can get me through the Telegraph Bureau at any time." And without further instruction or admonition he turned away.

And as he strolled up the aisle, each officer in the room knew—and this knowledge was heartening—that Carey would follow and direct, if necessary, every resource known to the department, until, and in spite of New York's multitudinous affairs, this crime had been solved. His upright figure vanished behind the barrier. Tension eased at once. But not as far as McKee was concerned. They were coming now, in the Sanctuary itself, to the last act. He was impatient. He had a job to do and had been interrupted. He was interrupted again. For the second time the door at the far end of the room opened and the assistant district attorney and his stenographer walked in.

CHAPTER V

ADVANCING TO meet him, McKee said: "Hello, Armstrong, our first tonight." And Armstrong nodded and followed him to the dance floor. The assistant D.A. neither drank nor smoked, had a bad digestion, a sound legal training, plodding brains, very little imagination, and a suspicious nature. He suspected everybody: the police, of negligence in the pursuit of duty; and the rest of the world, of every sin in the decalogue. His sons gave him trouble. He looked with disgust around the room, at the cluttered tables, the empty or half-filled glasses, the lovely huddle of green and silver on the floor at their feet, his face expressionless, and murmured out of the corner of his mouth, "Well, what could you expect in a dive like this? Wonder it doesn't happen oftener. What's the dope, Inspector?"

McKee gave it to him, a little wearily. He was very anxious to get on. In the cleared space beyond them a uniformed man was busy scribbling the dancer's name, her address, the Sanctuary address on what looked like a baggage check. He got down on his knees, tied it round a slender blue-veined wrist beginning to stiffen a little. McKee's glance was morose. For the dead woman the end was in sight. She would be borne away to the morgue.

Her clothing would be removed by a woman operative, each article placed in a sealed envelope and handed to the property clerk. (It engrossed his attention at this point that she wore no jewels, imitation or otherwise.) The officer first at the Sanctuary, in this case the radio man, would be on hand the next morning to testify that Rita's was the body he found on the dance floor and, failing a relative, Gus would have to appear to certify that the woman shot in the Sanctuary was Rita Rodriguez, all this in order that no possibility of error might occur and that a proper *corpus delicti* be established.

After that Fernandez would go to work with his nice shiny scalpels, a stenographer in attendance, every particle of evidence would be wrested from that inanimate figure, helpless to protest against indignity, on an enamel table in the basement of the big dark building on First Avenue.

The course of the fatal bullet or bullets would be traced, the point of entry so many inches from the heel, likewise the point of exit noted. Fernandez would be through then, until he was called upon to testify at the trial. But if there ever was to be a trial, the work of the police was just beginning. Had he himself overlooked anything?

Overcome by the doubts which always beset him at the scene of a crime—and no man could be more thorough—McKee got down on his knees for a last glance. The body had been photographed, and the medical examiner was through with it. To disturb it now would spoil no evidence. With careful expert gestures he straightened her head, explored her throat, smoothed folds of her gown across rounded haunches, examined slim smooth fingers that didn't tell him anything. Raising her arms, he lowered them again, pushed back crisp ruffles of organdie. . . . His voice was sharp against the rafters. "Dr. Fernandez."

"Yes, Inspector?"

"Take a look at this, please—this bruise on the right arm, just above the elbow, here on this side."

Fernandez stared. "I see. A bruise is right. Made possibly when she fell?"

"I think not, Doctor. The floor is flat. Whatever hit her here had an edge."

"Oh, I see what you mean. A lateral blow across tissues. Yes, that's right." Fernandez bent closer, reared himself after a prolonged scrutiny. "I don't know whether it's important or not, McKee, but that mark was made before death. Cold cream had been rubbed into it, powder superimposed. How long ago it was inflicted I can't say now. It's quite recent. Suppose we shoot a picture, watch the discoloration, and let you have the result later? Take her away now?"

McKee said: "That will be fine—yes, I'm all through," and glanced sideways at Armstrong, gazing down with marked disfavor at the dancer's ivory shoulder where her gown had slipped a little. The district attorney nodded sourly. Two men came forward with a stretcher. As though she were a bundle of flax the dancer was lifted, placed on canvas between poles, borne away. An inaudible breath of relief ran through the room.

Armstrong turned impatiently. "I suppose I'd better begin with the guests. No use taking them round to the precinct. It seems to me that the proper procedure is to weed them out first——"

"Just a minute." McKee told the district attorney what it was he wanted to do. Armstrong shrugged. He disliked drama in any shape, but these people would all be his afterwards for questioning. He was grimly certain of being able to get at the truth. McKee called Tannin, gave an order. It was while they waited in that curiously still and breathless garden that a plainclothesman, one Saunders, entered the room. Saunders was the detective who had been sent to the dancer's hotel, the address of which Gus had furnished. And Rita Rodriguez no longer lived there. Had left it some five weeks before. The management didn't know where she had gone. The inspector was digesting this, matching it up with the yellow roadster and the care she expended on her appearance when the first contingent of that flood in spate broke on the silence. Guests began thronging into the garden.

Voices fell instinctively as men and women rounded the barrier, started along the aisles, singling out their places, Women's faces were white, men's grim and angry. There was some little confusion. Distaste, fright, in some cases horror, were expressed in furtive glances, covert observation of the police, low-toned questions. All crowds are more or less alike with a certain drifting, sheep-like quality. This one was no exception in spite of the preponderance of well-dressed people, used, in other circumstances, to bearing themselves with assurance.

Certainly no one there that night had any desire to single himself out from the throng by a decisive movement.

It took two or three minutes to get the waiters and musicians into their proper positions, the last wavering guest seated. When this was accomplished, McKee detached himself from the wall where, withdrawn in the shadow of some palms, he had been an interested observer. He walked, in a hush that was profound, between tables out into the middle of the dance floor.

Motionless as figures carved in wax, they all sat and looked at him. His voice, pitched low, carried into every corner of the room. "I'm sorry to subject you to this ordeal, but a serious crime was committed here tonight. I appeal to your patience, ask your coöperation in helping us to bring the perpetrator to justice.

I am going to have the scene reënacted, just as it was before, during, and after the shooting of Miss Rodriguez. If any of you see any difference in the position of any person—and by person I mean both guests and the staff—please say so at once. Ready? Now then." He stepped aside, waved his hand.

Instantly the top light which had been on when they entered the garden was switched off, the table lamps glowed instead, exotic jewels that plunged the restaurant, in a golden gloom four feet above white napery at small tables crowded with people, faces unnaturally set in stillness. The Scotsman was only a voice, the more impressive because he was no longer visible. He said: "We will suppose it is ten o'clock." Above in the little cubbyhole the electrician pushed one switch, pulled another, and dimness except for a single shaded bulb in the middle of either wall engulfed the entire room, a dimness which made it difficult in those first moments to see anything except the brilliant circle of blue radiance, ghastly now, focused on the empty floor where the dancer should have been. There was nothing there now but a small dark stain on honey-colored boards.

A breath rustled through the garden, someone moaned, the moan was covered with a cough, a woman cried, "I can't bear it!" And her rising sob was buried in snuffles. Then, as eyes became more accustomed to the shadowy spaces and the nerves steadied a little, heads began to turn, people conferred in whispers, and the tiny babel spread, feeding on itself. It was not an atmosphere of trust. Each table was a spy on its neighbor. And they were all united against the waiters. For a half-minute nothing happened, and then the break was like an explosion.

At the far end of the restaurant, close to the mahogany barrier in front of the kitchen door, a woman jumped suddenly to her feet. Her voice was shrill, her outstretched arm a sword. "Those people weren't at that table. They weren't there when the dancer was killed. There was no one there. That table was empty!"

Pandemonium then, almost a reproduction of the murder itself. Chairs pushed back, people leaping to their feet, excited questions. McKee's order overrode the uproar. "Anybody who has anything to say will please remain here and tell the police. The rest may go into the other room, where your statements will be taken by the district attorney, after which you may all leave."

The temper of a mob is a peculiar thing. An instant before, they were all curious, engrossed; now the dominating emotion was a desire to get away. In the twinkling of an eye the aisles were jammed, the doorway choked. As for the Scotsman, he took plenty of time. Scattered groups here and there were being challenged, but what interested him most was the fact that among the three people at the table who had been so publicly accused was the girl he had found in the telephone booth.

CHAPTER VI

ACCUSER AND accused. Donaher and Tannin were engrossed at the far end of the garden with another group. McKee walked slowly down the aisle. Routine first, questions asked and answered, identity established. The lady who had made the dramatic announcement was still on her feet, large hands clasped tightly around her purse, as if it were a shield and she expected at any moment to be run through the body. Her name was Florence Carraway, and above a mannish suit and pique stock her large formidable face glared at the inspector as she told her story. It revolved around a no less momentous thing than curried lamb. She related in competent detail her discovery that the chef had omitted Worcestershire sauce, her search for this condiment, her discovery of a bottle on the table in question, and finished up with: "There was no one at the table. I took the sauce. Just as I started to mix the curry with my fork, the dancer fell. I never did get to eat it."

"Now, Miss Carraway, this must have been about seven or eight minutes after ten. Was there anyone at the table before that?"

"Yes. Those two women were there. That girl and that other

woman. But the man who's with them now wasn't there at all. I saw them when they came in. They were alone, and I noticed that . . ."

The Scotsman thanked her firmly, escorted her, still talking, towards the door, turned back. Paused for a moment to light a cigarette and behind the match studied, out of his eye corners, the little waiting group. They were curiously contained, smiling faintly, looking rather bored. They were waiting for him. He stopped three feet away and looked from face to face. The Pierce girl, a woman in her early thirties who would have been pretty except for her nose which was swollen, and for a scar across her chin (she was quite obviously suffering from some sort of skin poisoning); and a man of forty-five or -six, big, broad-shouldered, with a heavy underlip, cold blue eyes, and blond hair beginning to recede from a high broad forehead. He looked ill-tempered, obstinate, and clever. They murmured their names, produced driving licenses and cards: "Mr. and Mrs. Gerald Gair."

Gair did most of the talking. Putting his wallet back into his pocket, he said in a rather disagreeable voice: "Now that's out of the way, may I inquire what all the rumpus is about? I wasn't aware that it was a crime to meet one's wife in a public place."

The Scotsman explained with noncommittal patience what he was after. It was necessary to reset the scene of the crime. Their effort now was to find someone who, unobserved, could have fired the gun that killed the dancer. A process of elimination. He smiled. Gair glowered.

"Very well, Inspector, if I understand you rightly, you want each of us to say where he or she was when the dancer collapsed. That's quite simple. I was at a table at the other end of the room. I had made an engagement to meet my wife here late in the evening, but arrived much earlier because the man with whom I had an appointment was unable to keep it. My wife and Miss Pierce, coming in at about half-past nine and not expecting me, took this table close to the door. The place was crowded. It wasn't until after the accident that we met."

McKee let this statement go unchecked for a moment and turned to Mrs. Gair. She said: "You mean why wasn't I sitting here at the moment in question? For the simple reason that I'd just seen Gerry on his feet at the very end of the aisle—"

"Going, Sue, to phone Judith and find out why both of you hadn't turned up."

"I know, darling. I'm just trying to explain to this man . . ." Mrs. Gair had a beautiful voice, a little too controlled for the tight look at the back of her velvety brown eyes. Both of them moving around in what was almost absolute darkness in the crucial interval! . . .

"And you, Miss Pierce?"

Was the girl's small insolent smile a cover for something else as she drawled: "I thought I'd bared my soul to you, Inspector. Must I do the stripping act all over again? You're being very unkind."

"I don't think we covered this point, Miss Pierce."

"Really? You won't hang me if I tell you the truth—about my legs, I mean. There was a draft blowing on them. While that woman was dancing, I went out into the hall and got my coat."

The picture was crystal clear in the Scotsman's mind. The dancer dropping in the middle of the floor, guests jumping to their feet, bar and hall empty, check girl, bartender, and cook rushing into the garden. He said gently:

"Oh, but you were back in this room before she fell." And eyed her coat. The pocket was capacious, could easily hide a pistol, its length thrust down between cloth and lining.

"Was I, Inspector? All I remember is a woman screaming, people milling around."

McKee went on asking questions, thought racing swiftly behind his expressionless face. All three of them denied categorically knowing the dancer. They were simply, at this stage, individuals who might, from their positions, unchecked by witnesses, have shot Rita. And yet behind their calm faces, indifferent bearing, he felt the surge of some emotion intimately bound up with this room and what had taken place in it. He hesitated. As always, in cases of this nature, there were various offshoots of the main thread, people with things to hide which had nothing to do with the actual commission of the crime. But there was nothing to hold them on. Gair's story was still to be checked. If he had been sitting in a certain place, the guests near him would be able to . . . Suddenly a very interesting situation arose.

The room by this time was almost empty. Minor discrepancies were being cleared up by Donaher and Tannin. Just as two groups, finally exonerated, swept up the aisle and McKee put the question of Gair's position, the big blond man, sitting forward, an unlighted cigarette in his fingers, leaned sideways a little and said in a low voice:

"I'm afraid I'm going to have some difficulty getting my alibi, because that gentleman down there who's telling your man that he was seated at the table with the woman who's with him is lying."

The Scotsman started to turn, didn't complete the motion, looked at Susan Gair instead. She was staring at her husband, and just for an instant there was an expression of horror on her face. It faded, leaving her very pale. Oh, decidedly these people interested him. He merely said, moving forward: "Better come with me, Mr. Gair, and get this matter cleared up."

An angry man confronted them at the end of the aisle. He was a Colonel Waring, and a luckless waiter had already raised a question as to his position. Faced now with Gair, he said with open exasperation: "I consider your interference entirely un-called-for, sir," and to McKee: "This is all very stupid. To the best of my knowledge and belief I was either at this table or I had just left it. How do you expect us to remember silly details after what we've been through? This whole procedure is an outrage!"

McKee answered mildly: "I'm sure you can clear it up if you'll give the matter a moment's thought." His manner propitiated the colonel, who turned to his dinner companion, still seated, head and shoulders outlined against the dark wood of the barrier behind. She was a woman of perhaps forty-eight or -nine, small-boned, holding herself stiffly, her face a mold of white distaste under ash-blonde hair in the shadow of a wide hat. Waring said: "Can you remember, Claire?" And in an aside to the Scotsman, "This is Mrs. Philip Barcley."

Mrs. Barcley spoke without making the slightest movement of head, hands, or body; even her lips didn't open very wide. "I'm afraid . . . weren't you going to speak to Judge LeMarr, Colonel? He was on the other side of the room. I think perhaps you had already gotten up when——"

"Yes. Yes. Of course. You're right." Obvious relief put geniality into the colonel's voice. "I'm sorry, Inspector. That's exactly what happened. I remember now clearly. We'd sent for our check, and as the dancer was already on the floor I started round the room instead of crossing it. I suppose I was somewhere about the mid-dle when—it happened. I'll let this be a lesson to me. This is our first visit to a place of this kind. Unfortunate that we should have chosen this particular night."

All of which, after a few more questions, left exactly five people in the net, Judith Pierce, Mr. and Mrs. Gair, Colonel Waring and Mrs. Philip Barcley, any one of whom, alone in the darkness, might have pulled the trigger of the gun that had sent the whirling figure crashing down. He let them go, watched with a thin smile the haste with which they left the garden. A little joker, in the shape of the assistant district attorney and his stenographer, was waiting in the outside rooms. Now for Gus and some information about the man in the yellow roadster who waited each night for the dancer outside the Sanctuary.

But before he could take a step one of the waiters dashed along the aisle like a runaway horse, frightened, stammering thickly: "Cop . . . look . . . Look what I got. Look!" He needn't have been so emphatic about his demand. Like a chip caught in an eddy, he was immediately surrounded with big observant men who stared down at the thing he held in his hands. It was a pistol with a black cylinder protruding from the barrel, and it had been concealed under a napkin on one of the service tables just inside the door leading to the kitchen. "Drop that!" McKee's voice rang harshly but it was no suspicion of the waiter, no fear of smudged fingerprints that put controlled rage into his command. It was a sudden devastating conviction that the discovery had been made too late. They would never know now whether the gun had been there all the time or whether it had been concealed by one of the guests reentering the room an hour after the shooting was done. If the first were true, the whispering voices that the electrician had heard, the man who had made his escape through the house next door, would be involved. If, on the other hand, one of these five people had taken this swift and clever method of getting rid of it . . . Too late now.

He flung himself with renewed vigor at obstacles, sent men scurrying, emptied his mind of extraneous detail, and, pacing the aisle, head bent, lighting cigarettes, putting them out, summed the available evidence. They were doing everything possible. It was only a question of time until . . . and then the break came. Donaher flung into the garden, his voice preceding his hurried stride: "We've got something, Inspector. Take a look at this."

"This" was a soft gray fedora hat of excellent quality. Inside the leather band below silk lining, two initials were stamped in gold letters: G. A. The lieutenant explained: "It belongs to a guy named Archer, a young swell, comes here every night, and the hat-check girl told me on the Q.T. he was gone on the dancer. He came in here tonight, just after ten, bunned to the ears, and he's not here now because I took the check-girl through the crowd and she can't find him."

The man in the yellow roadster! It leaped to the eye. No time wasted, then. He dug Archer's address from the frightened but reluctant proprietor. Two minutes later, leaving Donaher behind in the Sanctuary, he, Tannin, and a man named Peters from the local precinct were speeding north through the darkness of the May night.

CHAPTER VII

TRAFFIC NOT so heavy now. The stars were gone, and a ground mist obscured the pavement. Tannin was jubilant. "We're hitting on high now, Inspector. Looks like this guy Archer musta been in an awful hurry to get out of that speak when he left his hat behind him. I'll bet you a dollar he shot her from behind that mahogany barrier at the back of the room, went in and grabbed her purse, made a getaway through the basement of the flat next door!"

"The gun," McKee said dryly, "was at the other end of the garden."

"What of it? In the jam after she was bumped off he could easily have planted it there without being seen."

This was true. McKee went on thinking, hat pulled down over his eyes. He wasn't pleased. The medical examiner had a body to dissect, Stutz had a slug and the pistol from which it had (possibly) been fired. The Missing Persons Bureau at headquarters had a laundry tag from the dancer's gown. Nevertheless . . . it wasn't good enough.

The precinct detective was thinking, too. It would be a feather in their cap if they broke the case. He posed his difficulty in the car's dim interior: "But, Inspector, if this guy Archer we're on our way to see was so crazy about the dancer, why did he shoot her?" They crossed Madison Square. High up somewhere a clock chimed twelve. Against the trailing echo of the last stroke, McKee answered dreamily: "Mr. Archer may have had a lucid interval. It does happen sometimes."

The Cadillac freed itself of a crisscross of streets, shot round a trolley past the park where slouched figures, shapeless in gloom, cumbered the benches, swung into the wide lighted expanse of Fifth Avenue. McKee shuffled theories in his mind, making patterns of them. Certain things were—out. The crime had about it none of the earmarks of a mob's work. No subtlety about those babies, no skilled calculation regarding anonimity in a crowd, the deadening of attention, all eyes and ears focused on one spot. If the dancer had been involved in an underworld affair there would have been an abrupt entry, a harsh command, the explosion of a sawed-off gun, and a quick retreat to a waiting car with the engine running. All of which brought these personable men and women he had managed to isolate into interesting prominence.

He let the Gairs, Judith Pierce, parade through his mind. Mrs. Barcley . . . with her air of being deaf and dumb, though she spoke when pressed . . . rather an odd place to find so modish and aloof a woman. The Ritz perhaps, or Pierre's . . . Colonel Waring with his authoritative manner. Waring. Waring! He said aloud: "Who's Waring, Tannin?" And the sergeant, rousing himself from slumber with a guilty start, said briskly: "The bozo with the high and mighty dame? I was thinking that myself, boss. I've seen him some place. Say . . . wasn't he in that Trembath crowd, mixed up in that stock deal? You remember Seebrook's inquiry last year? Trembath and his friends beat the rap by the skin of their teeth. Oh, say, I forgot, Inspector. Just before you called me from headquarters tonight a fellow was trying to get you on the phone. Seemed pretty anxious to locate you."

"Who was it, Sergeant?"

"That big lad I've seen you with a couple of times. Telfair, his name is. Yeh, that's right, Telfair."

McKee said slowly: "Jim Telfair? That's rather odd. It was because I recognized some drawing he'd made of the Sanctuary for a new magazine that I knew where the place was when the call came in."

"Gee, that's quite a coincidence, ain't it?"

The Scotsman didn't answer. His silence hid conjecture faintly tinged with uneasiness. He didn't believe in coincidence. Not, that was, delivered in this shape. So often coincidence was unpredictable chance revealing a hard basis of fact. Mrs. Brown couldn't be seen by a neighbor in the Grand Central with Mrs. Smith's husband if they weren't together. He didn't believe in thought transference, either. It seemed queer that Telfair and he should have . . . He shrugged irritably and reached for a cigarette. Once during the war he had to go after a friend who had sold out to a woman. It wasn't an experience he wished to repeat. Giving a light to Peters, he drew smoke into his lungs, growled, "Filthy habit, deadens all the sensibilities," took a deep inhalation, and threw the match out of the window.

Night New York slid rapidly past. Thirty-fourth Street, hung with flashing signs, upgrade now between curving lights, the Empire State Building, its unseen glistening dome shrouded in mist; ponderous bulk of Altman's on the right—Tiffany's. Forty-second Street was a flood of taxicabs making for the station. It was quieter after that. Bowling smoothly along, they turned left at Fifty-seventh Street, rounded Fifty-ninth, ran east. Off to one side the park slumbered under the heavy sky, and out in front the square blazed, flanked with great hotels in whose shadow General Sherman rose gallantly, Victory at his stirrup, pigeons asleep over his head.

Tannin said: "Here we are boss," and the Cadillac stopped before a towering monument in marble and granite. The three men crossed the pavement. A revolving door was swept out of their path by a white-gloved hand, and they were in a long and wide corridor hung with paintings of the Sorolla school, flooded with soft lamplight above rugs an inch thick. At the foot of a flight of red-robed steps a polished slab gave on a small office.

McKee drew up at this, parked his elbows on the desk, and said to a languid and polished clerk, "Inspector from headquarters." At the flash of that brilliant insignia in its leather case the clerk's ease and placidity went away. He answered questions with a dazed air.

"Yes, Mr. Gregory Archer lives here. Yes. He has an apartment. A very fine young man with excellent connections. An accident perhaps? . . . Oh." Whether Mr. Archer was at home or not, he couldn't say. A well-manicured hand shot towards the phone—didn't touch it. Tannin growled: "No tip-off!"

Smiling at the sergeant's gaucherie in so select an atmosphere, McKee led the way into an elevator, which shot up swiftly. When they passed the twelfth floor, a peculiar gleam came into the back of the Scotsman's eyes. He fingered the spruce needles in his pocket with caressing fingertips. The elevator stopped, the door slid open, the boy in buttons said: "Mr. Archer is the only one up here, sir," and waved at a door on the right of a small square vestibule.

As the whine of the descending car died, Tannin crossed the floor and put his finger on the bell. There was no answer. The ivory panel remained obdurate in its frame. McKee wasn't interested in it. He was already at the only other door, had it open. He stepped through. The two detectives followed him, to stand still under the chill sweep of a northeast wind. Far below, above mist, the park was a vague blur in a sea of fallen stars. They were on the roof. McKee shone his torch.

Straight ahead an open space, guarded only by a cornice, on the right an iron fence, a grilled iron gate, a tall lantern. McKee opened the gate, moved nimbly down steps. They were in a garden. Standing still on broken flagstones patterned with moss, the sergeant said: "Well, b'gosh, what do you know? Pretty nifty, huh?" And looked around with admiration. Johnny Tannin was a great lover of flowers—and they might have been a hundred miles from New York. "Gee, this guy Archer must have tons of money. A penthouse, ain't it? And they cost plenty in this neighborhood!"

McKee looked around, too, his glance narrow, contemplative. If Archer was the man in the yellow roadster, Rita had made a killing. Laughter etched itself on his lean satyr-like face for a moment at the juxtaposition of the word and her fate. The walls of this bungalow in the skies were mantled with ivy. That wasn't what he was looking for. The faun peeping from a thicket of rhododendrons gay with buds didn't interest him either. But something else did. He held his swinging torch steady on the stately spears of bluish silver rising from rich earth in a wide border close to the foundations. Both the detectives were watching him intently. He murmured: "Blue spruce," and Johnny Tannin, quick on the uptake, drew in his breath and pronounced: "The needles that were stuck to the dancer's coat!"

"Yes. She came here tonight after her first turn, from the Sanctuary, during a shower. But . . . Johnny, if a girl was in love with you, would you expect her to come peering through your windows instead of walking into your house?"

The slim sergeant gave this question due thought. "If she figured I was mixed up with some other dame, maybe . . ."

McKee laughed. He told Peters to go back to the front door of the penthouse while he himself set about, with Tannin's aid, the slow process of substantiation. The simplest statement must have proof behind it. Clever deductions were very nice. They didn't go far with a jury. They found, after a short search, the things they were looking for. Round holes in leafmold, three or four inches deep, faint toemarks, unmistakable prints of Rita's slender feet in the boxes rimming the penthouse. The dancer had changed her position more than once, but she had remained between two pyramiding spruce trees either side of a leaded casement some five feet six inches from the ground. McKee frowned. Impossible to see through folds of monk's cloth with darkness behind. The police have wide powers in running down a murder, but breaking and entry are prerogatives of the criminal except under the most severe provocation.

Without any warning while they stood there, shoulder to shoulder, hunched a little against the steady wind, darkness went away behind the window, light sprang up. It didn't do much good. Apricot folds of thick linen were too heavy to reveal even a shadow. McKee's voice, a breath, was in the sergeant's ear: "Go round and ring the bell. Send Peters down to watch the back of this apartment house." Tannin was gone. The Scotsman waited, eyes and ears alert. Felt as much as heard, a few seconds later, the shrilling of a doorbell somewhere within the penthouse. The faint clamor died, was repeated more insistently. At the third summons the light went out.

Then, his patience exhausted, McKee went to work. A patent fastening on the casement held it securely in place, but not for nothing had the Scotsman studied locks and bolts from men who had misspent their lives conquering them. The hasp was free. He swung a leaf of the window wide, leaped the sill, was standing on his feet inside, his torch lacing walls, floor, and ceiling. The room into which he had made so sudden an entry was empty. A sideboard in walnut mocked him. Eight chairs ranged round an oblong table were so many exclamation points. But heavy velvet draperies across an opening beyond a tantalus and coffee table still swayed a little either in the sudden draft or as though someone had just gone through them.

The inspector was taking no chances. Tannin was at the front. That was blocked. Someone had turned the light on and off. That someone . . . He flung folds of velvet out of his way, was in a kitchen admirably blue and white, behind a swinging door which he pushed ahead of him. Refrigerator, cabinets, sink, stove . . . He wrenched at the lock of a door beyond an enameled table, charged into a gray cement vestibule with a service elevator at one side, the dark well of a staircase beyond it. The indicator above the iron shield was motionless. He dove for the stairs.

Down and down and down, flinging his body around relentless flights, corkscrewing. His head was perfectly clear. He reached the bottom unexpectedly. The stair gave on a rabbit warren of doors and passageways, in the bowels of the huge apartment hotel. One door was marked: "Seamstress"; another: "Laundry"; packing cases spilled straw in front of a third. The corridor doubled. McKee raced along its length, collided with a gentleman in an apron made of ticking, armed with a mop, who squealed and looked astonished. The Scotsman ignored him, went round another corner, saw the time clock on the wall, knew he was near the exit, saw it up a tunnel with a door at the top. He went through this and out on the street, came to a sudden stop.

An amateur would have barged wildly. McKee hugged the shadow of rising granite walls behind him, looking right and left. It was getting late. On the left entrance to the hotel, a handful of pedestrians along the pavement. On the right, the lighted portico of the Plaza, a man and a woman in evening dress mounting the steps, and, farther along, the back of a cab speeding towards the square. The cab was in second. It shifted to high, gathered speed.

The Scotsman's eyes shone behind short thick lashes. With the observation that was second nature to him, he had noticed just such a green-and-silver taxi pulling to a stop farther along the curb when they themselves had entered the building. The one putting the side street behind it now might or might not be the same cab. It was a chance worth taking. Action and thought synchronized. He sprinted along the pavement for the Cadillac. The driver behind the wheel was ready. The Scotsman jumped in, gave a curt direction, slammed the door, and went back against leather with a jerk as they accelerated. Lighting a cigarette, McKee closed his eyes. The man who owned the yellow roadster and who lived in the penthouse wasn't in. And yet someone had entered and left the place in a hurry. Interesting, to say the least.

CHAPTER VIII

THE EFFORTLESS functioning of a perfect police machine relieves wear and tear on the individual and permits each man to work at the highest degree of efficiency. Following the cab ahead was the chauffeur's business. But curiosity is an emotion that transcends expediency. After a moment McKee opened his eyes. The taxi swung left around a green light and up the now almost deserted lane of Fifth Avenue. He eyed its fleeing bulk speculatively. Where was its occupant going?

On the left, deep shadows beneath invisible trees; on the right, street lamps wreathed in drizzle. Tudor mansions, Norman châteaus, Elizabethan manors, Italian palaces which house the rich in an incongruous jumble, slid rapidly past. Sixty-second, Sixty-fourth . . . they were gaining on the cab now. At Sixty-sixth a lighted bus chugged away from the curb. The taxi, riding close, swerved and shot sharply across its bows. The bus shrieked to an indignant stop, barring the entrance to Sixty-eighth Street. The Cadillac piled up alongside; Pete, gripping the wheel hard, hurled a lurid stream of oaths. McKee glanced sideways. Nothing remained of their quarry but a red taillight, retreating rapidly along the side street. This vanished.

The Scotsman looked startled. As if to remove a certainty in his own mind, he glanced at the numbered plate on the tall iron stanchion close to the corner, then tapped on glass. "Never mind, Pete," he said softly. "Turn right at the next corner."

Sixty-ninth was a west-bound street dimly lighted in slanting rain. The Cadillac ran east along it, purring at a low direction to a mere walk. "Stop here." Their lights were off now. A man went by on the opposite pavement under an umbrella, a big gray limousine splashing rain slid towards Fifth, behind the limousine— McKee sat forward on the edge of the seat—the green-and-silver taxi with the aluminum fenders came slowly into sight, just visible against the diffused glare of Madison Avenue beyond it. It stopped a hundred feet away. A man got out of the cab. He was not alone. There was a woman with him. The man was carrying a bag. They crossed the pavement. Light was a bright rectangle in the face of a tall narrow house as the door opened. They went in. The rectangle vanished.

With a swift "Get that taxicab number, Pete, and watch the house those people went into until I come back," to the chauffeur behind the wheel of the Cadillac, McKee was out of it and loping east with a long steady swing that put distance behind him rapidly. He realized Tannin's predicament when he found the penthouse empty. But the sergeant would know what to do. Inside a telephone booth in a drugstore on the corner of Lexington Avenue, be got the Homicide Squad. He was right. The clerical man had a number at which he could reach Tannin. McKee said into the mouthpiece, "Have him grab a cab and get up here as fast as he can. He's to bring Peters. Tell them to meet me at the Park wall, Sixty-ninth and Fifth."

The sergeant made good time tumbling out of the cab before it had come to a full stop. Taking them with him, the inspector pointed out the location, gave orders, narrow-lipped, abstracted. "Peters, cover the back. Remember it's the third from the corner." The precinct man vanished in wetness, praying devoutly for an empty lot. Devil of a job waking people up and telling them you wanted to go through their back yards!

McKee advanced on the narrow house. As they moved towards it side by side, Tannin said in a low voice: "What's it all about, Chief?" And the Scotsman answered: "I'm going to pay a call on Mrs. Philip Barcley and find out who the two people are who left that penthouse in such a hurry and came straight here. This is the address she gave us down in the speakeasy. You cover the front." With a wave he mounted two wide shallow steps and put his finger to the bell.

The delay was overlong before the grilled iron door opened a very little and a man in a green uniform, with silver buttons glinting, thrust out a bleak, inquiring face. The inspector made the opening wider by the simple expedient of thrusting himself into it, stepped carelessly past the man into the soft illumination of a handsome hall with a marble staircase ascending to the left.

"I want to see Mrs. Barcley, please, at once." And against the fellow's amazed stammer that it was very late, that Mrs. Barcley had retired, "Tell her that Inspector McKee of the Homicide Squad is here. I won't detain her more than a few minutes."

The man went away. McKee moved, too; advanced noiselessly to the foot of the stairs and listened. Above him somewhere, after a minute, the sound of whispering. The man came back too soon to have gone as far as Mrs. Barcley's bedroom, which would be in a house like this, on the third floor. If the inspector would wait . . . ?

"Thanks. I'll wait upstairs. Mrs. Barcley won't have so far to come. You needn't accompany me. Stay where you are."

The fellow, rooted to the floor, stared helplessly at his ascending back. McKee paused at the head of the first flight and looked around. He was in a Directoire foyer opening through double doors (closed) into what was probably a library at the back. There was a drawing room on the right. The drawing-room door was open. The inspector went through it and looked around. It was a very beautiful room. The woodwork was glazed in antique turquoise, with three paintings—one a Boucher—let into it at intervals. The furniture, which he guessed as fifteenth- and sixteenth-century, included a grand piano, finished in gold and ivory, a Louis Fifteenth canape with curved legs, a fauteuil in mauve velvet, a petite commode in . . . there was a hat lying on top of the commode. McKee stared at it fixedly, his lashes together. The only thing arresting about it as a head covering was the fact that Colonel Waring, the man with Mrs. Barcley in the Sanctuary, had been holding it in his hand while he answered questions. The colonel must be in the house now.

With that motionless padding slouch that made him look like a leopard now and again, the Scotsman crossed black velvet carpet under chandeliers in crystal and silver, pushed rose-colored hangings aside, and gazed into the Georgian library. Charming. Whoever had designed these rooms had excellent taste. Odd in the first place, and constantly becoming odder, that Mrs. Barcley should leave surroundings such as these to seek diversion in the tawdry furbishings of the Sanctuary garden. Recessed shelves were full of tooled-leather books, Chinese porcelains. There were some Chippendale and Queen Anne chairs, a monk's stool, an Elizabethan trestle near the fireplace . . . His glance stopped at the fireplace. No cigarette butts in it, but something dully black against glazed black tiles.

The Scotsman turned his head. No sound of footsteps, nothing but the light patter of rain against the dull roar of the city beyond the walls. In an instant he was beside the hearth, down on his knees, still listening, his fingers moving swiftly. The thing on the tiles was a bit of charred paper. With the most delicate care he managed to get this up intact with the aid of a picture postal card his landlady's daughter had providentially sent him from Niagara Falls, and had just the fraction of a second to insert it into his pocket and make the drawing room in front of the sound of low voices.

Mrs. Barcley came slowly into the room, followed by Waring, pausing just inside the door. She was pale now, paler than she had been in the speakeasy, and her features were pinched above the blue negligee trimmed with expensive fur that didn't quite conceal the fabric of the gown she had had on in the Sanctuary and still wore. There were mules on her feet. They were pulled on over stockings; and, yes, tearmarks streaked powder on thin, sallow cheeks. They both tried to look surprised behind polite inquiry. The colonel succeeded. Mrs. Barcley didn't And as she stood there staring at him, her nose took a sharper edge, the outline of her thin lips became more defined.

McKee apologized suavely for his intrusion, and on top of that said, "But before I go any farther, may I trouble you to ring for your butler?"

She was frightened behind brittle composure, masked it with movement, crossing to a chair while Waring rang the bell. When the man appeared, McKee said: "There is a detective at the back door, one at the front also. Ask the man at the front to step up here, will you,"

As the butler left the room, Waring said: "But, my dear fellow, is this necessary?" smiling indulgently at the histrionics of police routine. The Scotsman was equally casual—and apologetic.

"Just the usual procedure, Colonel. We're not so brave as we're reputed to be. An officer never advances on a place alone, for two good reasons: He doesn't know what he's going to find (someone might try to slip away), and then there's got to be a witness to all testimony."

Mrs. Barcley was drawing her negligee carefully about her slim body, erect on the edge of the chair. Waring drawled: "But—eh—why advance on this house?"

Tannin appeared in the doorway. McKee didn't look at him but at their unwilling hostess, sitting motionless, ringed hands buried in her sleeves.

"Because we followed a man and a woman here from an apartment on Fifty-ninth Street, an apartment from which someone escaped by the back way while the police were at the front. We went there to get hold of a man named Gregory Archer. He was not at home. Can either of you tell us where he is?"

The room was very still. A clock ticked somnolently somewhere. Mrs. Barcley didn't move, and yet, sitting perfectly still, she looked suddenly much more dead than Rita Rodriguez on the Sanctuary floor. Every bit of color had vanished from under her skin, her teeth protruded, her eyes began to glaze. The colonel sprang towards her as she slid sideways. And holding her in his arms, he shouted angrily over her bent head: "Archer's her son, damn you! Ring for her maid. She's fainted."

CHAPTER IX

THERE WAS a great deal of confusion then. Bells rang, the butler appeared, running, an elderly woman was summoned, Mrs.
Philip Barcley was taken up to her bedroom, and the doctor sent
for. A silent witness of all this, Tannin was flabbergasted. To say
that McKee was surprised would be to overstate the case. He
was seldom surprised at anything. Profoundly cynical by nature,
he ascribed the basest motives to all men and most women as
a matter of principle. Questioning Mrs. Barely in the Sanctuary, he had detected fear in her contained speech, caution behind
Waring's frank answers. Just as, with that other group, the Gairs
and Judith Pierce, he recognized something that was also off key.

When the little procession filed out of the room, Tannin said:
"Archer got the dancer, sure as you're alive, Inspector, and Mrs.
Barcley beat it up to his place to get hold of some kind of in-
criminating evidence."

The Scotsman continued to look thoughtful. "They went into
the penthouse, certainly. Or rather the colonel did. I imagine she
remained in the cab—probably saw us going in. They'll deny the
whole expedition."

Which was exactly what happened. For when Waring came

back into the room he said that the entire proceeding was out-rageous, he would see a lawyer in the morning. McKee was exceeding his authority, that jumping the rails with this third-degree stuff might succeed with the riffraff with which he was no doubt thoroughly familiar, but that with an old reputable and honored family. . . . He was talking too hard, fuming too much, his steel-colored eyes cool behind a lot of angry gestures.

The inspector remained calm, waited until he ran down, then gave the information the colonel was fishing for. (Might as well clear the decks.)

"My dear Waring, you say you came straight here from the Sanctuary after being released by the district attorney. Do you know what's going to happen? All I need to do to establish your exact movements is to have a man call up the Plymouth Taxi Company and say: 'We want the driver working on cab 00-622 tonight.' And when the driver reports in to the garage he'll bring his trip ticket with him. We'll be there to look them over, to talk to this driver. He'll tell us that you drove to Central Park South from the speakeasy, left Mrs. Barcley in the cab, rejoined her after a short absence, and came on here. Where's the bag you were carrying?"

Waring denied the bag coldly, and McKee let it go. Suddenly the colonel capitulated. He became expansive, almost genial, acknowledged himself beaten. Would they have cigars, a drink? Ah, well, duty was duty. But it was so late, and both men must be tired. No? He lit a cigar himself, dropped into a chair and began to talk.

"The maternal instinct, Inspector, will always remain a mystery to me, I fear. Mrs. Barcley was a very young woman when Gregory was born. I'm his godfather. She's older now. A pity that when women reach the age of discretion they don't stay there.

She's always spoiled the boy. After her husband's death she married Barcley. I can't say, as far as Gregory is concerned, that Barcley has been particularly successful in the handling of him. Not an ounce of harm in Greg, understand me plainly, but—well—too much money."

"Colonel, why did you go to the Sanctuary tonight?"

"Well, the fact is, I heard rumors—a man spoke to me at the club—about Greg's infatuation for this dancer. Mrs. Barcley and myself were to have dined with friends tonight. I suggested the speakeasy instead. Didn't say a word to her, of course, didn't want to worry her but . . ."

They weren't getting any place. The Scotsman started abruptly for the door, interrupting the easy flow of uninformative words, turned on the threshold, surprised relief in Waring's face at the sudden termination of the interview, and asked curtly: "Is Mrs. Barcley's second husband in the land of the living?"

"Philip? Dear me, yes. He's been off on a little trip to Canada, I think, in search of one of his damned little bowls or jugs, but he's expected home at any minute."

On that they left the house. Outside, rain was falling harder now. The Cadillac was drawn up a short distance away. McKee roused himself from abstraction with an order that didn't bring any satisfaction to the sergeant huddled down into his coat. "I think you'd better plant here tonight, Tannin. If Mrs. Barcley comes out, give her a tail. I'll send someone to relieve you in the morning." With a wave of his hand he was gone. Peters had already reported back to the precinct. The sergeant took up his long, lonely, and wet vigil.

On the way downtown McKee meditated. What he craved at the moment, like Goethe, was more light—more information about these people. Someone who knew the Sanctuary well, who would talk. . . . Telfair shot into his mind. The very man. He was an habitué of the place, and speakeasies are like clubs frequented by the same people over and over again. Archer's affair with the dancer, however discreetly conducted—and care had most certainly been employed—could not have gone unobserved by a keen eye. And Telfair might know something about the rest of these people that he himself had succeeded in isolating from the throng crowding the garden when Rita was shot.

He wanted most particularly to get hold of the dancer's address, found the secrecy surrounding it more annoying each minute, wanted also to see what significance, if any, the burned sheet of paper had that he had retrieved from the fireplace in Mrs. Barcley's library. This last could wait. And he could call headquarters and find out whether the Missing Persons Bureau had traced Rita through the laundry mark.

Tapping on glass, he gave the cartoonist's address. Like himself, Telfair seldom went to bed before three or four in the morning.

But when he got to the little house that was a remodeled stable in the back yard of a red brick building in Grove Street, he found the door locked, the windows dark. McKee struck a match and glanced at his watch. Twenty minutes past one. He was just turning away when a step rang in the alley and the cartoonist appeared. Telfair didn't show any surprise when he saw the inspector. It was not the first time McKee had paid him a visit so late. They exchanged the casual greetings of men who are really intimate, although they hadn't seen each other in over a month. It struck the Scotsman that his friend wasn't in good spirits. Telfair fumbled for his key, opened the door, switched on the lights.

Once inside, McKee went straight to the phone, dialed a secret police wire, asked for news, didn't get any, left word where he was, put the receiver back on the hook, and turned around. It was then, as he stood there, yawning cavernously, that he saw the thing. A red chalk drawing of Judith Pierce over the bookcase under the stairs.

The Scotsman didn't betray the slightest interest in this really admirable piece of work—instead he abandoned his hat, confided his sinewy length to the doubtful embrace of an armchair with broken springs, and asked: "What do you know about the Sanctuary, Jim, and the woman who dances there, Rita Rodriguez?"

The cartoonist took his time about answering, tamping tobacco into the cracked bowl of an old briar. He was naturally deliberate, a big man, slow in all his movements, who hated to be hurried. "I know that she's dead, Chris———"

Before he could say any more the phone rang. Telfair handed the instrument to McKee. A man named Cannon from the Missing Persons Bureau talked. "That laundry mark, Inspector, came from the shop of a man named Smykowski, a Pole, who's got a small place over on the East Side. He serves a lot of those new apartments on the river. Owns his own place, I think, lives over the shop." Cannon gave the address. McKee thanked him, put the receiver back on the hook, took it away again, dialed the precinct in which the laundry man lived, spoke to the desk officer, asked for the detective wire and, settling his shoulders against red rep, made himself comfortable.

"Hello . . . that you, Doolan? Inspector McKee. Fine, thanks. . . . Yes, it was a nice affair. Want you to do a little favor for me. Send the man on night duty over to the shop of a man named Smykowski,"—he repeated the address. "He's in the laundry business. Wake him up and find out all he knows about a woman whose clothes bear the mark 098376, hand-lettered in black India ink. I particularly want her address. Call me here as soon as you can." He gave Telfair's number, put the receiver back on the hook, and resumed where he had left off. "You were saying, Jim?"

Telfair was using a lot of matches to set fire to his pipe. "I said that I knew Rita was dead. A friend of mine called me up from the Sanctuary earlier tonight. I tried to get hold of you, but you weren't in, so I went over there myself. A uniformed cop at the door not only wouldn't let me enter the place but had half a notion to run me around to the station house."

"Your friend is a girl named Miss Pierce? I talked to her. Known her long, Telfair?"

The cartoonist had his pipe going now. He said carelessly round the stem:

"Oh . . . couple of months."

"Know these people she was with, these Gairs?"

"Uh huh. They're swell. Gair's a clever bird, and Susan's a peach."

"Mrs. Gair has a charming voice."

"She was an actress before her marriage."

"An . . . actress? She's not pretty. Her skin is disfigured."

"Poison from make-up. She's very sensitive about it. But she's really good. Can play almost any part. Been crazy about the stage ever since she was a kid. Who shot Rita, Chris?"

"Ask me that forty-eight hours from now."

"Why forty-eight hours?"

"Oh, once the scent gets cold on a trail like this it's ten to one you're sunk. Tell me what you know about a man named Gregory Archer and Rita."

A shadow darkened Telfair's fine eyes. His voice was careless enough. "You mean a tall, weedy lad with light hair and no chin that they took out of the oven before he was done? If I told

you he was a half-wit the estimate would be too high. He——"
The phone rang again. Telfair grinned. "Make yourself at home.
Don't bother about me. Nobody ever calls me up except the jan-
itor about the rent."

The Scotsman hugged the instrument to his breast. This time
it was Stutz, speaking from the Ballistics Bureau at headquarters. Stutz said with solid Teutonic satisfaction: "The gun the
waiter found under the napkin on that table in the speak was
the one that did the trick, Inspector. Tried her out on the pistol
range. I'm just through. Test and fatal bullets are absolutely iden-
tical. This is foolproof. If you've any doubt come down and take
a squint. There's a . . ." Stutz relapsed into technicalities for a full
five minutes before McKee could detach himself. He shoved the
phone aside and turned back. "You were saying about Rita and
Archer . . . ?"

"That he's a prize sap and was there every night—every night
that I was there, anyhow. Always alone except for a bottle of
champagne, sitting at a ringside table. Didn't look like a solitary,
either. He was gone on Rita all right."

"You could see that?"

"I . . . someone told me—I forget just who."

With lightning certainty McKee knew this someone. . . .
He drew a bow at a venture. "Miss Pierce is an acquaintance of
young Archer's?"

"No. He spoke to her one night. You know what speaks are.
Say . . . wait a minute. There *is* something." Was it his desire to
deflect interest from the girl that made Telfair so helpful? He
knocked the dottle out of his pipe, refilled it from a handsome
silver humidor at his elbow, a present from his aunt who thought
it would tone up his shabby rooms, and over spilled crumbs continued thoughtfully:

"It was at the beginning of last week—Monday—no, Tuesday. I was working late, and after I was through I went round to the Sanctuary for a sandwich and a pick-up. I left just as Rita was through. It was raining that night, and I had a touch of bronchitis and a hole in my shoe. When I got outside there wasn't a cab in sight so I——"

Again the shrill summons. McKee answered it. Doolan was speaking from the uptown precinct. He said briskly: "Inspector, we located that laundry man, Smykowski, for you. He's here now—seems all right, willing to do all he can. This is the way he describes her: Tall, fair, beautiful figure, queer-colored eyes, Latin type. He says also that . . ." McKee sighed with satisfaction. Although Doolan had never seen the dancer, didn't know anything about her killing three hours ago, he proceeded item by item to give a perfect description of the dead woman.

"Where," he asked quietly when Doolan stopped, "does she live?" And when the detective gave him the address, he hung up and got to his feet, his eyes shining.

"Come on, Jim, you can tell me the rest of the story in my car going over. We know too little about Miss Rodriguez—yet. Her belongings, her apartment, may be more informative."

CHAPTER X

OUT IN the chill darkness of the wet spring night, the cartoonist continued his tale against the panorama of the city flashing past the windows, black patent leather highlighted with a thousand reflections from shops and signs in spite of the lateness of the hour. New York never really goes to sleep.

The substance of what he had to say was this: Waiting in the vestibule of the Sanctuary on that Tuesday night, he had seen Miss Rodriguez issue from the basement of the house next door, walk a little way along the pavement, and get into a yellow roadster parked along the block. This in itself wouldn't have attracted his attention. It was what happened afterwards. There was a taxi drawn up behind the roadster. When he himself first came out of the speakeasy, he had dashed for this, only to find the flag down and a man asleep in the corner—apparently waiting for someone. But the dancer was no sooner in the yellow car, which proceeded to move away at once, than the waiting taxi followed—at a discreet distance. "It was as plain as the nose on your face," Telfair concluded, "that the man in the cab was following her."

He had gotten this far when they arrived at their destination, a towering block of apartments a short distance from the river. As the Cadillac drew into the curb and McKee opened the door and leaped out, you could smell the sea. Telfair followed him across the pavement.

Lieutenant Doolan was pacing up and down in front of 1208, whose entrance was a well of light cupped in darkness. The two officials greeted each other. McKee introduced the cartoonist, and Doolan hid a stare. The Manhattan Homicide Squad doesn't generally go into action with amateurs in attendance. It wasn't his business, however. He said:

"This woman, Miss Rodriguez, lived on the top floor. This place is mostly small flats, medium-priced, a good many of them sublet. There's an elevator, one of those electric ones you operate yourself. Man on in the daytime, nobody at night. Superintendent lives in an apartment on the ground floor back. See him first?"

McKee agreed, led the way into the lobby, imitation marble and too much mirror, along its length to a door in obscurity at the far end. The superintendent was a sound sleeper. It took him a long time to get into a pair of trousers with suspenders dangling. Red-eyed, unshaven, he stared at the three men in the corridor. McKee said: "We're policemen. What do you know about a tenant in this building named Miss Rodriguez?"

The janitor echoed the dancer's name stupidly and didn't do anything more about it. The Scotsman eyed him narrowly. He had noticed in passing that the card in the mail box belonging to the top-floor apartment was blank. He said: "She told you not to talk about her to callers, I suppose? You'd better loosen up if you don't want to get into trouble."

At that a voice through an open door under a mound of blankets was suddenly shrill: "Don't be a fool, Benny. Tell the captain.

He won't bite you. Haven't you got any brains?" Admonished in this salutary fashion, Benny became more communicative. He didn't have much to tell, however. She didn't seem to have any friends. Didn't go out much except at night—to work, he thought. The voice interrupted him again: "Don't forget to tell the officer about the young swell in the tony car who sends her flowers and candy and comes to see her almost every day." Doolan looked hopefully past the man's shoulders. Find a gossiping woman and you have a gold mine. But Benny's mate had apparently exhausted her information, if not her curiosity.

"All right, Mr. Superintendent, come upstairs with your master key and open her door for us." The swift ascent in the electric cage was accomplished in silence. Rita's apartment was at the far end of a long narrow hail. This hall was lighted only in the middle, shadows lapping the rest. The janitor fitted his key and stepped back. Doolan said: "O.K., big boy, you can beat it now." And when the man had gone reluctantly away, he opened the door without making any noise. All three of them stepped into the small square foyer. Telfair, bringing up the rear, imitated caution instinctively and looked around when the light was switched on. The button gave a little click.

The dancer must have rented the place furnished, for there was no mistaking the trail of the interior decorator. Through glass doors on the right davenport, overstuffed chairs, radio, lamps, draperies were empty of meaning in a too facile artistry which——What the devil was up? Telfair stared in astonishment from Doolan to McKee. Both men were standing as still as though they were stuffed, and both moved at the same instant, lunging swiftly through a door at the back of the foyer into a suite containing bedroom and bath.

At the far end curtains fluttered before an open window, and rain splashed the sill. McKee was through this window like a shot. Telfair gasped—then realized that there was a fire escape outside. Doolan followed him. The Scotsman's voice came back, muffled, low: "Take the roof, Lieutenant—Telfair, you stay where you are." With his feet rooted to the carpet under the sill, the cartoonist watched him vanish down a square opening.

Telfair turned back. Even to him what had happened was at once plain. Somebody already in the apartment, hearing them enter, had just escaped through the window. But Rita was dead, and apparently she had lived alone! He gave it up with a shrug, tried to put himself in the inspector's place, and studied the bedroom with interest.

The usual furniture plus a wardrobe trunk in a corner, open but packed. It wasn't very neat. In addition a pigskin bag against the wall. This was open, too. Telfair leaned over and looked down. A swirl of yellow chiffon and lace, a pair of satin mules . . . standing there, his shoulder pressed hard against ivory paneling, he remained motionless. Sweat broke out on his forehead, made the palms of his hands wet—for he got, full in his nostrils, the faint, sweet, cloying odor of Chinese lilies—for the second time that night. And the first time was when Judith, in front of her apartment to which they had walked together after she was released from the Sanctuary, had opened her purse to take out her key.

A second later, stupid with shock, his gaze running round aimlessly, he saw the green suède purse lying on the floor between the foot of the bed and the wall. It wasn't Judith's bag— hers was black and very much bigger—but the green thing had been inside Judith's bag; he remembered her ungloved fingers white against it in the gleam of a lantern above her door.

There was not a sound in the room—nothing—anywhere.

With the most terrific effort—for his body was stiff, his joints made of wood—Telfair stooped, picked up the limp green thing, thrust it into his pocket, had barely straightened and was still numb with the blow of his discovery when he whirled, fear rushing through him from head to foot.

Opposite the window, thirty feet away, at the end of the narrow corridor giving on the bedroom, there was a door leading presumably into the bath. This door had been closed when they came in. It was open now. And against all the whiteness, moving so swiftly, as he himself turned, that he doubted the evidence of his eyesight, the crouched figure of a man, formless, without detail, hurtled through the door into the hall and was gone. Just as the cartoonist started in pursuit, Doolan crammed his body through the window, dropped to the floor, saw the end of Telfair's sprint, and ran on to the foyer. Telfair was standing in the middle of the rug staring at the outside door like a man who has been hit in the head. When he didn't speak, Doolan asked impatiently: "What is it? What's the matter?" And the cartoonist answered slowly: "There was someone hiding in the bathroom. I ran out, but he was gone when I got here."

Quite obviously the detective didn't believe him. He made a perfunctory show of examining the corridor outside, listened at the head of the stairs, didn't see or hear anything suspicious, and came back wiping away a smile. (He wasn't entirely sold on this Bohemia type.) But when McKee returned a few minutes later and heard about it he didn't smile. Instead he looked very grave, went directly into the bathroom and subjected it to a long stare which included Telfair without seeming to do so.

There was nothing out of place but the rug, which had slipped sideways a little, and if the door was open the wind might have done that. Nevertheless Doolan was impressed by the inspector's thoughtful expression. Was it a coincidence that Rita's apartment had been entered in an attempt at robbery on the same night that she was killed?

Doolan said: "What are you looking for, Inspector?" And the Scotsman answered, "Trouble."

"You mean that there was a pair of them on the job? When they heard us come in, did one jump through the window and the other dash in here?"

McKee's glance slid round black and white tiles, tub, shower, tiny window high up in the wall with nothing between it and the street a hundred and twenty feet below. He shrugged. "This would be a rather stupid bolt hole. On the other hand, a rather good observation post. Take a look."

It was true that, with the door opened the merest fraction of an inch, almost the entire bedroom was visible and in addition part of the foyer and a section of the living room—behind glass doors. He went on slowly: "Taking the evidence we have now, I should predict two separate arrivals. The first person who came was interrupted and slipped in here, meaning to finish later. The second person was in the bedroom when we got as far as the foyer. They both got away. Better go and see, Doolan, whether you can find any trace of the man hidden in here." The detective did, only to return in a few moments with an expressive wave of his hands.

After that, back in the bedroom itself, Telfair leaned against the wall and watched a lot of things happen through the wrong end of a telescope on another planet. Doolan put cabalistic words along a private wire that summoned fingerprint men and other detectives through the darkness of the small hours of the morning. The Scotsman was going over the place with a fine-toothed comb. The cartoonist tried to follow.

The fact that the trunk was packed, the dressing table stripped, the lock of the bag forced, didn't say anything to him. Nor did McKee's slow, "Miss Rodriguez was going away somewhere," and Doolan's, "I was thinking that, myself." They removed the contents of the bag. The detective shook out folds of a yellow nightdress luminous as a veil, frothy underthings, threw them on the bed. The odor of Chinese lilies permeated the air. Doolan said: "Sweet smell, ain't it?" addressing no one in particular. Telfair pushed nausea away and didn't move from the spot where he stood.

McKee nodded. "Miss Rodriguez was a clever woman in her own line. Men have never properly understood that branch of sensory stimulation. It's more potent than any drug and less wearing on the system. Baudelaire's got an interesting passage on it in his *Les Fleurs du Mal*. Men dream dreams, go into trances under the influence of certain perfumes." And in the same tone and without turning his head: "What is it, Telfair? Anything the matter?"

Telfair answered with force. "Just that damn smell! It makes me sick," and a little too late obscured part of his face with a handkerchief and blew his nose resoundingly. This wouldn't do. It wasn't good enough. He had to get away and think. The green suède purse was burning a hole in his pocket. He had the odd conviction that McKee would discover it in another moment, even looked down to see whether a corner of it was visible. He took himself away from the wall with an effort, said: "If I can't be of any further assistance to you, I think I'll amble."

The Scotsman went with him to the door, said, standing there, his voice idle:

"You haven't got anything more to tell me, have you? Nothing here tonight gave you a lead that would help us out?"

Telfair put incredulity into his tired laugh. "I, Chris? Good Lord, no!" He realized that he was being too emphatic, went on more slowly in a quieter tone: "But then I only knew Rita in a public capacity, so to speak, dancing down there in the Sanctuary. However, she posed very nicely for me when I did those illustrations, and I'm interested. Can I keep in touch?"

"Do," McKee said affably. "Do." He watched Telfair into the elevator, listened to its departing whine, and didn't move. He was staring down at something small and whitish, tinier than a mouse and almost as active, something that drifted to and fro on the pebbled floor and then lay still. The nearest apartment was thirty feet away along the corridor, the elevator almost as far. Stooping, he retrieved the thing. It lay, velvet soft, in his palm. McKee's nostrils dilated. He raised his cupped hand and sniffed.

CHAPTER XI

WHEN MCKEE went back into the apartment with the flower petal in his fingers he played a queer game. Tossing it to the floor of the foyer close to the threshold, he had Doolan go through various maneuvers. Had him open and close the hall door a number of times, open the bedroom door, open the window, close it again. The detective watched these futile and childish proceedings until he couldn't stand it any more. "Is this a private fight, Inspector, or can anybody get in? What is that thing?"

The Scotsman said slowly: "It's a camellia petal, Doolan, genus *Ternstrœmiaceæ,* natural habitat tropical and Central Asia and the Indian archipelago; this particular species was named after George Joseph Kamel, a Moravian Jesuit of the seventeenth century . . . and the people who came into this apartment tonight all had keys."

Doolan had heard legends before of the inspector's odd learning; nevertheless he stared his incredulity. McKee laughed.

"Figure it out for yourself, Lieutenant. This is the top floor, nobody passing this apartment on the way to elevator or roof. Now take a look at this brown stain across the petal. Pressure from the lintel of the door where the petal was caught and crushed sometime earlier today. As far as this apartment goes, what do we know? That the dancer herself left it at about ten minutes of eight to go down to the Sanctuary; that there were two, at least two, visitors before we arrived ourselves. I found the petal a foot away in the hall. The bedroom window was open, and the east wind gave it an impetus that was not present earlier. I believe that it was on the floor of this foyer when we came in. Finding it made me look more closely at the knob of the spring latch on the door. There are no prints. The surface is tarnished. Hasn't been rubbed. Ergo, on each occasion the door was opened with a key. But that's not what's worrying me now. Where are they?"

"The guys that were in here and beat it away?"

"No, no, the camellias. They aren't here. They weren't down in her dressing room in the Sanctuary. Oh, well . . ." He dropped the petal into his wallet and turned his attention to as much of the apartment as they hadn't already examined. The remainder of the bedroom wasn't particularly informative—except for the labels on the trunk. There were three, and the way they overlapped, the tone and texture of the paper placed the dancer first in Barranquilla, then at the Hotel Angleterre in Havana, Cuba, and then traveling to New York on the S.S. *Wilson*. While Doolan went through dressing-table drawers, closet, and chiffonier, McKee turned to the black pigskin bag. The contents had already been emptied out, but he wasn't satisfied. This was a piece of hand luggage. Their search so far for something intimate, something more personal that would tie the dead woman to a definite background, had been curiously barren. Rita was evidently not a hoarder, disposed of things as she finished with them, and, except for clothes, she traveled light. And yet some place surely . . . He turned the black bag upside down, thumped it on the carpet—bent closer. Nothing as intangible as dust, grains of tobacco, tumbled out. Instead, a small leather case, scarcely bigger than the one that protected his own shield, fell to the carpet. It had apparently been wedged some place behind the lining. It was about two by two and a half inches long, black, shabby, and fastened with an ordinary snap.

McKee opened it. It contained two things: a round bit of greenish stone about the size of a five-cent piece with serrated edges, and a thin metal chain. He ran the chain through his fingers. Doolan said: "Silver? What was she carting that around for?" And the Scotsman answered, "Platinum, and there was something on this ring at the end."

"What's the stone nickel for, Inspector?"

"I imagine," McKee spoke slowly, handling the thing as though it fascinated him, "that this was a sort of talisman. Easier to carry round as a pocket piece than either faith or morals." His fingers kept on moving. He tore himself away from contemplation with an effort and followed Doolan into the living room.

Davenport opposite mantel, desk near the glass doors, windows at the far end of the room, radio cabinet to the left of the windows. . . . "By George!" The lieutenant turned at the queer note in the inspector's voice. "My brave young bucko had a fall—it's been coming to him for centuries." He pointed to a small bronze Mercury ignominiously prostrate, face down on the rug, the caduceus snapped off, lying some three feet away. As much as he liked this big gaunt head of the Homicide Squad, Doolan's patience was exhausted.

"So what, Inspector?" he said in a bored voice.

"There was a bruise on the dancer's arm, Lieutenant, received shortly before her death. That bit of statuary was knocked to the floor from the radio cabinet—see the impression of the base here in the dust on top? The edge of this cabinet is sharp. Rita was about five feet five inches tall. In falling or being shoved sideways while she was standing in front of these windows . . . of course, yes. Rita was late tonight at the Sanctuary. She had a visitor this afternoon—perhaps several, but one at any rate . . . she——" He broke off, his burning glance ranging the room, not seeing Doolan, seeing other things. At the expression on the Scotsman's face, in spite of himself a little chill ran down the burly lieutenant's spine. He thought "God! The inspector's gone bats." But before he could do anything, McKee said curtly: "I've got to get back to the office. Dump everything out of the desk, anything else you find in a bag. I'll send a man for it." And with a muttered "Good-night" he was off.

Meanwhile Telfair had gone home—had started for it, at any rate. McKee's chauffeur, returning from a cup of coffee swallowed quickly in an all-night stand around the corner, saw him come out to the pavement. Pete said: "Inspector coming?" And when Telfair answered, "What's that? No, not yet," the chauffeur good-naturedly drove him to the nearest subway station.

He had to wait a couple of minutes on the platform, but there were still people around and the place was brightly lighted. Similarly when he got out at Grove Street a quarreling couple also left the train. Their voices were loud, their recriminations annoying, and Telfair quickened his steps in an effort to shake them off and be alone with his crowding thoughts. It was after half-past two. Street lamps puncturing the darkness didn't do very much more than make the sidewalk visible. But he was on familiar terrain and he walked along, blindly trying to fight the black fog in his brain, so that when the marital misfits were still no more than fifty feet in the rear he bumped head on into a man coming briskly along the pavement from the opposite direction. He was disentangling himself with a muttered apology when the man laughed.

It was Enderby coming home from an assignment. Enderby lived in the apartment in front of Telfair's house. Enderby had a bottle in his pocket. "It's apple," he said, "come on up and have a drink. You look fierce. What's the matter?" The cartoonist didn't tell him, but he did go up, and had, not one drink, but half a dozen. It didn't help his brain processes any, but it deadened the furious clash of questions rushing round inside his skull. It also did something to his equilibrium, so that Enderby, a good-natured, weak-chinned fellow, saw him through the alley and into his own doorway. Waited, in fact, until he heard the click of the key before he went back to his own place and to sleep. That was at almost four in the morning.

It was after four when McKee went slowly between the green lights of the station house in which Manhattan's Homicide Squad is located, waved to the lieutenant behind the desk, went past the office of the local detectives and up the stairs to his own room. Three or four men sitting around outside waiting for squeals; it had been a quiet night on the whole, with the exception of the Sanctuary murder and a stabbing in Harlem. There, however, they had caught the perpetrator red-handed, in this case . . . Nodding abstractedly, he opened the door and found Donaher dozing in a chair against the wall.

The lieutenant opened sleepy eyes.

"Get this to the Telegraph Bureau." McKee shoved a piece of paper across the desk on which were scrawled the names of the hotels in Havana and Barranquilla where Rita Rodriguez had previously stopped. And when Donaher had done this: "Well?"

"Very little, Inspector. The D.A. finished up at the Sanctuary at around half-past one. I went over to the hotel where the dancer was located when she was first engaged at the speak. She left a lot of truck behind her when she went, but it had all been disposed of. But they gave me the name of a dame she used to chum around with, a Lily Henderson. Tracked the Henderson woman to a rooming house on West Twenty-fifth Street, but Lily keeps late hours. Show girl out of a job. There's a man on it now. What's that?"

For the inspector was delicately removing from his wallet the postal card of Niagara Falls clamped to an envelope with a rubber band. "It's a sheet of notepaper that Colonel Waring set fire to up in the library of Mrs. Barcley's house after the butler announced my arrival." He pulled open a drawer at the bottom of the desk. It was crammed with a welter of queer things. He took from it some tracing paper, a tube of paste, and several folded squares of cheesecloth, talked moodily half to himself, while he went to work.

"Gair was awfully anxious to drag Mrs. Barcley and Colonel Waring into the case . . . their hands are not clean, either." He spread the sheet of tracing paper evenly with gum, transfixed the burned sheet, by a process of sliding, to this sticky surface. Confronted with the result—buckled blackness full of tiny hills and valleys—he studied a word or two here and there standing out in moldy gray, couldn't make anything of these, got up, went to the sink in the corner and turned on the water.

"And what was the matter with Telfair tonight? He did quite a bit of walking after he took that Pierce girl back to her apartment. . . ." Donaher watched him anxiously. The reconstruction of carbonized paper is a difficult job at best and unless handled with the greatest care is rarely successful. But the inspector was a wizard with those narrow blunt fingers.

Still frowning, McKee saturated the gauze, wrung it out, and

returned to his desk, proceeded to erect a fence around his exhibit with an inkwell, a ruler, a couple of rubbers, a file on end—all
backed by books—stretched the cheesecloth over this structure
tautly, taking care not to let it come in contact with the paper
beneath.

"We'll never succeed in tracing the gun that shot the dancer.
That's why it was left behind. Quick thinking . . . clever thinking . . . Miss Pierce going for her coat—she was behind or near
the mahogany barrier when Rita dropped . . . Mrs. Gair midway
along the room . . . passing behind people who were all looking
at the dance floor . . . Waring on his feet, too . . . Mrs. Barcley
alone at her table in gloom . . . Gair just starting for the telephone booth . . . and Gregory Archer some place near the entrance to the garden. . . ." He drew back the gauze, threw bits of
wetness into the trash basket and then proceeded to flatten out
the now moist sheet of burned paper with the tips of his fingers,
working a tiny section at a time and using the most exquisite
care.

This done, he trimmed the firm base of the tracing paper
close, had now something he could handle freely and proceeded
to do so. "Pick up that lamp, Donaher—keep tilting it slowly.
That's right . . . a little more to the left. No—back farther. . . .
Hold it!" The words on the burned notepaper were now quite
legible, spidery gray on black. McKee read them aloud, tasting
each syllable, ruminating over it:

"'Claire—Don't worry. Everything all right. Back later.'"

"Claire—Mrs. Barcley, of course. 'Everything all right.'" Mrs.
Barcley had fainted when she found that the police were interested in her son! McKee put the note down, threw himself
back in his chair. The note was waiting for her when she got
back to the house with Waring. Someone had brought it, some-

one who——— "'Back later.'" McKee pressed a buzzer, and when the door opened and a detective thrust an inquiring face in, the inspector said: "Oh, Hickson. Go up and relieve Tannin at the Barcley house on Sixty-ninth Street. Pete'll take you, he's downstairs."

It wasn't consideration for the sergeant who had been going all day and all the previous night on a floater, found in the East River with a bullet hole in his head, that prompted Tannin's recall; it was the Scotsman's overmastering desire to know whether the writer of the note had fulfilled his promise. Primarily, the sergeant, obeying instructions, was only interested in someone coming *out* of the house or in Archer's going in. And Archer hadn't inscribed those affectionate words. This wasn't a drunken scrawl, and besides there was the heading, "Claire."

After that he sat tapping lightly on the desk with the end of a pencil for some time. Donaher was asleep again. Beyond the window dawn was coming up, a tremendous purple ushering in another day. It was very quiet in the little room. Quiet fled in front of the ringing of the phone. McKee took the receiver off the hook. The man covering Lily Henderson was at the other end of the wire. The inspector issued curt instructions. A minute later he and Donaher were on their way to the street.

CHAPTER XII

A GOOD many macabre legends cling to that big gloomy building on First Avenue, most of which are false. It isn't true, for instance, that a huge black Negress, without any nose, sews up the dissected bodies when the doctors have finished their work. A young girl does this, a young girl whose father was in the business before her. Certainly the atmosphere within the walls that house the city's unfortunate dead needs no aid from fiction to add to its gruesome sordidness. And a riotous night with the fumes of alcohol floating around in one's head is bad preparation for the things to be seen there, seen—and heard.

Lily Henderson, with her landlady on one side, Donaher on the other, went through the gates reluctantly. The back entrance to the morgue in the harsh gray light of early morning has about as much impressiveness as the approach to a brokendown livery stable. She faltered on the threshold, was swept relentlessly forward. In the basement, outside the door of the particular mortuary chamber in front of which they came to a stop, Lily tried to twist herself out of the grasp of her tormentors. "I can't," she cried hysterically. "I can't! Let me go. I tell you it's her all right. I knew she got this job in that speak. Let me go!"

The landlady said, "Hush, my dear!" with a shocked glance. Donaher said: "Take it nice and easy, sister." And McKee said: "Courage, Miss Henderson. It will be over in a minute." A businesslike attendant, with dull eyes above black handle-bar mustachios, moved the door out of the way.

Donaher supported Lily's hundred and fifty pounds of buxom flesh towards the slab where the attendant had already turned back the sheet. He eyed Lily sympathetically. He had always had a weakness for that particular shade of Titian hair. Financial difficulties attendant upon identification of the deceased were often a prominent feature of a relative's grief. He said unexpectedly in a confidential tone: "If the lady's worried about the undertaker, she'll keep. She's on ice. And if she don't have her friend embalmed it'll take twenty-five dollars off the——" Lily's scream cut him short.

"It's Rita, all right," she whispered. "Take me out of here. Take me out of here—quick!" Donaher obeyed McKee's signal. He was a tenderhearted man, and he had no wish to linger, himself. They got her into the little office upstairs. There the lieutenant said something in a low voice to the inspector, who went away and came back accompanied by another attendant. This man produced a flask. Miss Henderson drained reviving drops thirstily, kept the flask in her gripping hands. There was no need to urge her to talk.

"*Floradora* . . ." she cried with a queer twisted brokenness. "Oh, she was lovely. Only sixteen then. I used to recite 'The Wreck of the *Hesperus*' . . . Hyatt's parlor and the funny smell in it. And she used to dance and sing that thing from *Floradora*—'Oh, tell me, pretty maiden . . .'" Lily beat time with the bottom of her flask on a plump knee rigid under too much flesh.

McKee said gently, "You are talking of Miss Rodriguez?"

"Mrs.—Mrs. ? She was Rita Gonzalez then. She married that bum. He wasn't ever any good. God knows why she did it. Look, it was this way: We were both boarders at the same farmhouse in Dutchess County, six dollars a week and all the milk and eggs you could cram into you. Rita lived with an aunt in Brooklyn, a horrible old devil, widow of a cigar manufacturer. This Rodriguez she married was Rita's cousin. Rita always wanted to go on the stage. The aunt was very strict. My God . . . think of it, that's almost twenty years ago. Twenty years! And life is so short . . . and now we're old!" Lily began to cry. Donaher jogged her elbow, and she fortified herself against the world and time with another long swallow. McKee asked: "And you've kept in touch with her since her marriage—that would be about 1912?"

"No. I never saw her again after that last summer in Willow Brook until she turned up at Frascati's in London two years ago. You could have knocked me over with a feather when she walked out on the floor. Well, Rita'd made the grade. She was the star act in the cabaret. I went round to see her after the show. She told me her husband was dead and that she had to make her own living. I'm not telling you she was a little Alice Ben Bolt. Kind of disagreeable girl, but . . . Oh, I don't know . . . old times, I guess . . . anyhow, I kinda wanted to keep in touch. Not that she'd lend you a copper. She was in the money then. Some man. There generally was a man. You know the old saying, 'Neck 'em and nick 'em.' That was her. I lost my job there and came back to America. Before I left I gave her the names of some agents here in case she was thinking of making a change. And if it wasn't April Fools' Day when she turns up in that crummy little office over on Sixth Avenue looking as beautiful as ever! But I could see that she was on her uppers. The old hoof and horns that runs the dump got her a job right off with this speak called the Sanctuary. . . ."

Lily was beginning to ramble, didn't seem to be getting any place. If they could fill in that long gap between 1913 and now. "Didn't Rita have any other friends whose names you could give us?" McKee asked. Lily wiped a smudge of mascara out of an eye corner and winked at him. "There were only men—and they weren't friends." Watching her, McKee said, "Go on, Miss Henderson, please."

"Well, I found out where she was living through the agency, and I went to see her at her hotel over on Thirty-seventh Street, and I guess maybe . . . I shouldn't be surprised if . . ." Lily's glance sharpened . . . "Something funny happened there. Darned funny, now that she's dead. Rita was scared. It was like this: I wanted to borrow a little money from her, just an accommodation over the week-end, so I went to the hotel, but she wasn't home yet—she'd only been dancing in this speak about a week then, so I waited in the corridor outside her room. She came in about half-past twelve. And the minute she opens the door she goes kinda floppy and white and says: 'This room has been searched'—something like that. Of course you could see it with half an eye. You know . . . the way things are mussed up, bureau drawers pulled out and put back crooked, stuff sticking through . . . dresses off the hangers. The window was open, too. And she said it was closed when she left. There was a fire escape a few feet away. Anyhow . . ." Lily stifled a wide yawn composed in equal parts of fatigue, shock, alcohol. "I know she moved out of that place a few days later, and I haven't seen her since—not until tonight."

After that, McKee asked some questions, tested her with the bit of greenish stone, the platinum chain and the empty ring on the end of it, and didn't get any result. Consigning her to the care of her landlady outside in the corridor, motherly for a consideration, he told her to go home and to bed, that he would probably want to talk to her later.

Back at the office Tannin was waiting for them; red-eyed, jerking heavy lids apart to give the result of his vigil outside that narrow handsome house in the Sixties. Nobody at all had come out—the colonel was evidently spending the night—but a man had gone in. He drove up in a cab at one thirty-five. It wasn't Archer, because the sergeant got a good look at him in the flare of a match with which he was lighting a cigar while he crossed the pavement. He had a key.

McKee stretched a lean hand towards the phone, drew it back again, said softly, "Mr. Barcley, I think."

Donaher stared. "You mean it was the Barcley woman's husband who wrote that note you found in the fireplace? I thought he was out of the city."

"Waring merely told me that Barcley was away, had gone to Canada and was expected home. I think I see it—I think I see it now . . ." Then: "Tannin, go to bed; I'm going to need you later." And when the sergeant stumbled towards the stairs leading to the dormitory: "Donaher, here's what I want done. Take this bit of green stone up to Claubertson at the Museum of Natural History. Tell him I'm in a hurry. As you go out, ask them to send me up a cup of coffee and a sandwich."

There was a canvas bag on the back of the desk labeled, "Contents of Miss Rodriguez's desk," a smaller sack labeled, "Trash basket." McKee began to go through the mass of stuff. He interrupted himself from time to time to answer the phone, use it himself, rescind one order, issue another. A half-dozen major problems to be solved: Archer had to be found. Who was the buyer of the camellias, who the people who had rushed up to the dancer's apartment in advance of the police and why? . . . He kept turning over papers . . . eight o'clock half-past eight; outside, constantly rising clamor of New York rode swiftly into a new day.

It was at a few minutes of nine that Telfair woke up in the bedroom of the little house in Grove Street. He lay still for a moment, watched a fly moving across the ceiling, tried to resolve the fog inside his head and didn't succeed very well. He remembered the first part of the night with scorching clarity, seeing Judith home after the bust-up at the Sanctuary, McKee's visit, their trip to the dancer's apartment, but after that couldn't . . . there was something . . . He couldn't recall what had happened.

The room was full of diffused light seeping from behind drawn shades. His temples were pounding. Begin at the beginning and work forward. He had met Enderby as he was turning the corner, had gone up to the reporter's room for a drink. Damn Enderby's apple! Must have picked it up at a filling station. . . . Telfair went on laboriously unraveling. After he came back here . . . Oh, he was crazy . . . it was just the liquor. Everything was all right . . . and suddenly he knew that it wasn't.

Nine o'clock. Not quite—for the clock on the table outside in the hall was giving its first premonitory wheeze. It was an old clock and had to gather strength before putting its striking mechanism into play. One deep-bellied stroke, two . . . then Telfair knew what the trouble was. The door into the hall was open now and he had closed it when he stumbled upstairs at around four o'clock in the morning. That much was plain: a repeated vision of himself closing doors along an endless corridor as though he were trying to shut himself away from something!

Leaping out of bed, he started across the floor, caught sight of himself in a mirror, and stood stock-still. His body was blue silk, his legs red-and-white-striped madras, and he distinctly remembered that when he came up here last night he had thrown himself down fully dressed on the bed, too miserable to take off his clothes!

Suddenly like a streak he was down the stairs and into the living room. For it was coming now. The sound he had heard in the night! The sound of a window being raised. It was the window on the landing, and after he had closed it he had gone back to the bedroom and had automatically undressed, putting on the top of one suit, the bottom of another, and leaving the door open as a precaution.

Someone had tried to get into the house. He knew that now, knew also with heaviness in the pit of his stomach that that nocturnal visit had something to do with the green suede purse that he had dropped into the humidor just after Enderby saw him home.

He started slowly across the floor, stopped with a jerk when he was still in the middle of the room. There was someone at the door. He had to try twice before he produced a loud, "Who is it?"

And astoundingly it was Judith who answered, her voice muffled through the thickness of wood. Telfair pulled himself together with an effort and answered in an almost normal voice: "Give me a minute to get some clothes on. I'm just up—I'll unlock the door," and did so.

He was at the top of the stairs when she came in. She called up to him: "I'll make some coffee." Telfair went into his room and began to dress. When he came down, Judith was busy with cups and saucers on the table near the bookcase. She glanced at him quickly, reached for the sugar out of the cupboard, and said, her back turned: "You must have had a heavy night. Nine o'clock's late for you, isn't it, Jim?"

By this time Telfair had made up his mind. Anything was better than this uncertainty. And the sight of her standing there very trim and alert in a tweed coat and skirt, a soft white blouse open at the throat, a little hat crushed down on her dark hair, made last night a bad dream. He was putting too much on a single throw of the dice. After all, there were a lot of green pocketbooks in the world, hundreds, thousands of them, and the dancer didn't have an option on every Chinese lily in the universe. For all he knew they were selling the essence in drugstores. He said quietly:

"Never mind that now. Never mind the coffee for a minute, either. Listen, Judith, I want to ask you a question. I have a good reason for asking it, and I don't want you to be angry. Do you know anything about the killing in the Sanctuary last night, and were you—innocently, of course—I don't need to say that—tangled up with the dancer in any way?"

The pause was too long. The cheeping of sparrows came loudly into the little room against the muted murmur of the streets. The girl put the pitcher of evaporated milk down on the tray, turned round, and said very deliberately: "Jim, are you crazy?" There was amusement in her voice and on her lips but not at the back of her eyes.

Two pieces of flashing steel came together with a bang inside Telfair's head. He simply stood and looked at her, was incapable of doing anything else just then. She went on in the same light tone: "What in heaven's name makes you ask me that? How often have we been in that place together? If I had known her, don't you suppose I'd have said so long before this?"

She was lying. Stupid with shock, for it was as though the

ground had opened under his feet, precipitating him into strange subterranean depths where he couldn't find his way, he said slowly: "It was the first time you went there alone."

Her answer was patiently indulgent: "But I *wasn't* alone, Jim. I was with Sue Gair. She had a date to meet Gerry, and I took her around. You said a minute ago"—her movements were casual, lift the pot, pour the coffee slowly, put the pot down—"that you had a good reason"—sugar and cream?—"for asking. What was the reason?"

She was looking at him out of wide, clear gray eyes, brows raised in inquiry.

If he could shock her into telling the truth . . . "McKee's a friend of mine. You know that. He was here last night after he left the Sanctuary. He asked questions about you, questions about the Gairs."

"Did he really? How thrilling!" But her face changed, and he noticed with detached curiosity that the hand with which she put the cup aside was not quite steady. "Will it be a breach of confidence to tell me what his conclusions were?" She strolled towards the windows, stood there with her back to the room.

"McKee didn't tell me. But then, Judith, I couldn't really give him much information. I only met the Gairs last spring. How long have you known them?"

She said without moving: "Oh, ages and ages. We all drank out of the same christening mug." Telfair glanced past her small head at an acanthus tree just bursting into leaf, ugly and insipid against a brick wall. In its spotted shade Miss Fenwick's canary was chirping weakly at sparrows hopping around. The passion in the girl's voice, when she spoke again, startled him.

"And all this fuss about that—horrible woman! I don't know who killed her. I don't know anything about it. But the person

who removed her is a public benefactor. It was not murder—
it was an act of social surgery. Circumstances alter cases. Rita
deserved killing. It was justifiable homicide. Shooting was too
good for her. She should have been cut into little bits, roasted
alive. She should . . ."

"You seem," Telfair said when she stopped at last, "to know
quite a lot about her."

"Know? What do you have to know? Couldn't you tell by just
using your eyes?" But she was calmer now, turning round, moving towards the couch, picking up her gloves. Telfair continued
to wander around in blackness filled with ugly shapes, but he
was pulled sharply back to consciousness when Judith said a moment later, standing on the doorstep, pulling her hat down over
her hair, straightening the lapels of her coat: "Well, anyhow . . .
do see your inspector, Jim, and find out all the news. How about
dinner tonight? If you can make it, call me." Then she was gone.
Telfair went back into the little house, closed the door and stood
with his shoulders against it. So that was why she had come. To
find out what the police were doing. There was no longer any
doubt in his mind that the purse he had picked up in the dancer's apartment had been in Judith's hands earlier the night before. Beyond that he couldn't go. He knew, too, that he was concealing important evidence and that his integrity was seriously
involved. He glanced at the humidor but didn't move. The very
memory of that square green purse was like a blow; he couldn't
bear to look at—to touch—the thing. With an oath that startled
him in its reverberations through the room that seemed so empty now that Judith had gone, he went upstairs to work. The clock
struck half-past nine as he sat down at his drawing board.

At almost the same moment the telephone on McKee's desk
rang. The Scotsman pushed away Rita's checkbook with a bal-

ance of thirty-four dollars and twenty-two cents showing on the last stub and picked up the receiver. Hickson, the man who had relieved Tannin on the Barcley house, was at the other end of the wire. Hickson said, and he seemed in a hurry:

"I just put Mrs. Barcley and that guy, Waring, into a law office—Keely and Fancher—over there in the Stillwell Building. Want me to stick?"

And McKee answered curtly after a momentary pause: "Yes. Hold it down, give me a call if there's anything new." He put the receiver back on the hook. Donaher had just entered the room. The lieutenant repeated the names. "Keely and Fancher? Keely was the chap who got an acquittal for Two-punch Hunt last fall, has a lot of luck with criminal cases."

McKee nodded thoughtfully. "These people are beginning to interest me a lot, Lieutenant." He reached for his hat, stood up.

CHAPTER XIII

Sixty-ninth Street was a canyon of transparent blue shadow and bright gold where brilliant sunlight struck into it from the east. The morning had had its face washed and looked delightfully fresh and clean. McKee, surveying the narrow front of Mr. and Mrs. Philip Barcley's town house from a vantage point a little distance away, looked like a great gray cat who has strayed into the wrong neighborhood.

It had often been said of the inspector, even within the department itself, that he got the breaks. This wasn't true. It wasn't so much that he got them as that he took advantage of them when they came. That morning, Henry Links, the butler, went out to post a letter. He didn't quite close the big front door behind him, for the mail box was only fifty feet away along the pavement. Before Links had covered half this distance, McKee was in the shadowy hall, mounting with a cat's tread the gracious curve of the marble staircase. Nobody in the foyer, nobody in the drawing room but a voice coming from behind curtains that partially masked the entrance to the library.

"A milk ewer, painted faience, eighteenth century. Got that,

Miss Mason? Take this note on the bottle. The bottle has a spherical, elongated bag, or body, and an elongated narrow neck which usually . . ." McKee drifted nearer the archway. Philip Barcley, the man he wanted to interview, was sitting in a chair near a window. He was about fifty, going gray, with a distinguished profile and the deep-set eyes of a thinker. There was an untouched coffee tray on the table beside him, an empty packing case spilling excelsior on the floor, a number of pots and vases on the desk in front of the typewriter behind which the stenographer waited, her hands suspended over the keys.

It was the girl who saw McKee first. She tried to look meaningly at her employer, but Barcley merely said impatiently without turning: "If it's the barber, Links, I'm busy now; tell him to come back later."

The inspector went into the library, introduced himself. He decided that behind his involuntary host's surprised air Barcley had drawn himself swiftly together, was expecting him, had a bad cold and had injured his right hand. Barcley dismissed his stenographer: "Don't leave the house, Miss Mason, I shall want you again," then devoted himself to his neglected tray and listened in silence to McKee's curt summary of what had happened on the previous night.

At the end he merely said, in contrast to Waring's verbosity, "Gregory's a damn fool, Inspector, but he's not a murderer. I doubt whether he's got it in him. The woman richly deserved shooting, no doubt. As far as I can see, all you've got against him is that he knew this woman and was in the Sanctuary last night. Well, so were a lot of other people. I was there myself. I took him away with me."

McKee nodded. "I know that. The electrician heard you going

out through the hall. Why didn't you come forward and tell us that at once when you knew we were looking for Mr. Archer? And where is he now?"

Barcley put his cup down, lit a cigarette. "Perhaps I'd better answer your questions in order. In the first place I knew that he had nothing to do with the killing, because I had my eye on him at about the time the thing must have happened. I arrived home last night, from a trip to Canada, at about half-past eight. Mrs. Barcley wasn't here, but she had left word that she was going on to this Sanctuary and asked me to join her there if I arrived in time. I changed and went along. I entered the place, I should say, at about a quarter of ten. But I was too tired to stay, and a cabaret performer's dance didn't interest me."

McKee's thoughts raced behind impassivity. (Rather an odd request on Mrs. Barcley's part that at the end of a long and tiring trip her husband should join her at a speakeasy, particularly if she was—as Waring stated—in the dark about her son's infatuation for the dancer. Odd, too, that after going there Barcley should have left so soon.)

"Just as the dancer came out on the floor I left the room. I was almost at the door when I saw Gregory. You couldn't exactly miss seeing him."

(And yet Miss Pierce, passing back and forth across that space, had made no mention of Archer.)

"He had evidently just come in. He was leaning against the wall, and he was—to put it plainly—drunk. Naturally I didn't want his mother to see him in such a condition. It was as the hubbub began that I took him by the arm and marched him off. I didn't, at this time, know that a murder had been committed, heard nothing but chairs being knocked over and several women screaming. I thought it was just a brawl of some kind, knew that Waring was with my wife and that he would take care of her."

McKee's voice was tranquil: "Just a minute, Mr. Barcley. This affair between your son and the dancer has been going on for about six weeks. You say that both you and Mrs. Barcley were entirely unaware of it?"

Barcley's smile was thin. "You are moving from the general to the particular, Inspector, a mistake in logic. Gregory's always in love, it's a permanent state with him, we've got so we expect it, but it's seldom for long, and the affairs are not serious. His allowance is rigidly measured out to him, and for a fellow with his tastes it doesn't leave a wide margin for women who would do him any real harm. They come high."

"Then you don't think this entanglement with the dancer was serious?"

"Not unless she was a fool!" He continued his story: "Outside in the street I hailed a cab and got Gregory into it, meaning to take him to his own place and put him to bed. We never got there. He was too much for me. You know what men under the influence of liquor are, sodden one moment and the next violently energetic—and crafty?

"Without the slightest warning, when we were held up at a red light on Fourteenth Street, he wrenched open the door of the cab, leaped out, and took to his heels. By the time I managed to get to the curb, he had completely vanished. As to his whereabouts now . . . well, we are as anxious to know that as you are. I'll say one thing, however. I understand that the dancer was shot. When I first came on him, Gregory was absolutely pie-eyed, and he wouldn't have been able to hit the side of a barn at ten paces."

The Scotsman felt like applauding. The story was a workman-like job. No doubt it had been concocted during the night. All he permitted himself to say was, "You've injured your hand?"

"Yes. Opening the case when it arrived this morning."

Was Barcley lying? If you want to take a drunk somewhere, a knockout punch is one of the best methods of accomplishing this successfully. One thing was certain. His stepson was not a passion with Barcley. His glance, carefully level, took on real interest only when he glanced at the glass and pottery arrayed on the desk in a serried row. It was Barcley, of course, who had designed this admirable house. He would go to almost any lengths, probably, to protect and shield . . . Umm. And a murder case is *so* disrupting. You can't in decency continue to be absorbed in ewers and basins and books and stuff when . . . "Mr. Barcley, I understand that you didn't arrive back here until very late last night. Where were you from the time that your son so unfortunately escaped until you came in at some time before two?"

Barcley's shrug was tired. "Rather obvious, isn't it? I failed where you will probably succeed. I tried to find Gregory. I must have been in every dive in town. I knew some of the places where he . . ."

But McKee was no longer listening. Out of the tail of his eye he had seen what the other man couldn't see: the slow approach of Mrs. Barcley along the drawing room's length. And there was about her erect figure so triumphant an air that the vague shapes, the uneasy premonitions at the back of his mind, coalesced in a certainty of disaster.

She was alone. Hickson would have followed her back here. Which meant that Colonel Waring . . . He sat still with an effort. Certainly Mrs. Barcley's manner and bearing, a smile tucked round her lips, her head well up, that crushed-lily aspect completely gone, said something to Barcley, also. He jumped to his feet, concealed surprise and—yes, undoubtedly, apprehension—behind, "Claire. I didn't know you were out. Did Gregory . . . is there any news . . . ?"

Mrs. Barcley began stripping off her gloves. "None," she said tranquilly. "But it's such a lovely morning I feel sure everything's going to be all right. Besides, we went to the lawyers, and Mr. Keely assures me . . ."

Two seconds later McKee was out on the pavement, his only leave-taking an ironical bow of congratulation to husband and wife. What a damn, damn fool he had been! He knew that the colonel owned a house in the lower reaches of the city. At full speed then towards Gramercy Park, blue plate in the windshield, flying past lights. The square was quiet, almost deserted under trees brooding somnolently in the sunshine. As he sprang up freshly scrubbed steps towards a green door between shining brass rails, a clock somewhere struck eleven.

It was a few minutes after twelve when McKee went through the revolving doors at headquarters, answered the borough commander's genial greeting with an absent nod, brushed the advance guard of reporters out of the way, and ran on up the stairs. Armstrong was with the commissioner when he went in. The inspector told his story, pacing the rug, prefacing it with, "I was crazy not to have seen . . ."

Carey smiled. "If you had had prescience enough for that, Inspector, you would have known all about the murder before it was committed and there wouldn't have been one. You say the colonel lives at his club for the most part and when you got into his house in Gramercy Park the bird had flown?"

"Yes. There was no one there but a deaf old housekeeper. But

I found unmistakable traces of Archer. I mentioned in my report this morning the camellia petal I found at the dancer's apartment. Well . . ." He reproduced for them, then, a swift flash of Tannin, refreshed with five hours' sleep, locating the little flower shop, pursuing the thread in air spicy with carnations, sweet with lilies-of-the-valley, but not the flowers he sought. It wasn't the place where Archer had an account; it was a little cubbyhole around the corner from the dancer's apartment in the block of flats close to the river.

And the owner of the shop said that he sold a clump of camellias to a man answering Archer's description on the previous afternoon at about four o'clock. "This"—the Scotsman laid a tiny brown sagging thing on shining mahogany—"is one of the camellia buds Archer was wearing in his buttonhole from that time until he got to the colonel's after leaving the Sanctuary. It was in the trash basket under a lot of junk."

"And what do you think happened, Inspector?"

"Barcley took his stepson straight to Gramercy Park from the speakeasy, deposited him there, and went on to the Sixty-ninth Street house. Mrs. Barcley and the colonel weren't back yet. In order to assuage his wife's anxiety he wrote the note that I found later in the fireplace and to which Waring put a match when I was announced. After writing the note, Barcley went back to his troublesome charge."

"The housekeeper saw Archer?"

"No one saw him. They were all very clever, so clever that . . . I don't know yet. Anyhow, this housekeeper says that she was asleep when the doorbell rang. She went downstairs and admitted Barcley, who was alone. Barcley said he'd wait for the colonel and sent her back to bed. What he did, of course, as soon as she had gone, was to bring Archer into the house. Then, after he returned for the second time and had had a struggle with his charge—for his hand is injured—he got in touch with his wife and went home for a consultation."

"But wasn't there danger, in leaving Archer there for the night, that this housekeeper would discover him?"

"I looked into that. He was put into Waring's study, a big room on the first floor in back, which the woman enters only once a week to clean. This morning, after leaving Keely and Fancher's office with Mrs. Barcley, Waring managed to get out of the cab unobserved. He went to the house in Gramercy Park, sent the housekeeper on an errand, and while she was out of the way . . ." McKee waved a hand.

"You mean that the colonel has taken Archer some place? But look here, Inspector,"—the commissioners face was grave—"Keely and Fancher, whom these people went to consult, are smart. It's a reputable firm. They wouldn't advise hiding Archer. That would be almost tantamount to a confession of guilt!"

Armstrong, who had been listening gloomily, snorted. McKee said slowly: "I don't suppose for a moment they did advise it. But I don't suppose for a moment, either, that they were told the truth. Waring is one of Archer's guardians, was a friend of Mrs. Barcley's first husband. He and Gregory Archer are among the missing."

"Any ideas on the subject, Inspector?"

McKee smiled for the first time. "Plenty, but not much information—yet. Mr. and Mrs. Barcley, between them, own three country estates and a yacht, the *Catherine the Second*. I've taken care of that. Waring doesn't run a car. He'd scarcely make use of a cab, would figure we could trace that too easily. He probably hired a machine. We're going into that now."

"And if you get Archer, will you have enough to hold him on?"

McKee shrugged. Armstrong answered moodily: "As a material witness, yes. He went to the dancer's apartment yesterday, there was a quarrel—Oh, don't quibble, Inspector" (as the Scotsman started to say something) "this is no time for splitting hairs. The trouble is you can't see the wood for the trees. You've got this whole group of people on the brain. They can't all be guilty. Archer was whisked away from the Sanctuary by his stepfather right after the shooting. They hid him. What's the first thing they do this morning? Visit a firm of criminal lawyers! The time has come to put the screws on." Now it was the district attorney who was striding up and down the carpet.

McKee got out of his chair. "There are so many angles," he murmured. "A woman like Rita made so many contacts that won't bear sunlight. This Pierce girl and the Gairs . . . interest me. And who was the man followed Rita away from the Sanctuary last week, trailing her in the cab?" His questions hung in the air. There was one thing he hadn't mentioned: the whisky glass in Waring's study. It was standing on a tray beside a half-bottle of Johnny Walker, but there was no trace of liquor in it. An analysis might reveal something. The glass was in his pocket at that moment. But it might be a false trail.

The commissioner didn't say anything. Armstrong didn't, either. McKee said: "I'll keep you informed. I'm going over now to have a look at Archer's apartment and talk to his valet," and left the room. But for once the Scotsman was mistaken. For when he got back to his office, there was news of a very startling character indeed.

CHAPTER XIV

A GENTLEMAN had lost a hat and coat. Neither more nor less than that—and the whole case was thrown into the air. McKee understood a lot the minute he read the scribbled message in the wire basket to the right of a blotter on his desk—which was more than Donaher in the Sanctuary did. The lieutenant had gone back there on a final prowl.

McKee rang the Sanctuary and got Donaher at once. Donaher sounded unhappy. He said: "One of the waiters took French leave from this speak last night. He must have been the guy who beat it through the corridor of the house next door, because the janitor's hat and coat are gone and the janitor's putting up a howl. This waiter must have grabbed the coat off the hook at the back of the hall where it was hung, because his own coat is still here. I'd like to bust these dumb eggs in the jaw. They didn't even notice it when they went home last night or when they came back this morning. You know we lined them up right after the dancer was killed and asked whether they were all there."

The inspector said soothingly, "Yes, I know. Go on."

"Well, this waiter's name is Green, and he's been employed here for about three weeks."

"Got his address?"

"Yes. I found it on a rent receipt in his pocket. Place over on Seventh Avenue." Donaher gave him the number. "Meet you there, Inspector?"

"Yes, in fifteen minutes."

The sun was blazing down hotly out of an unclouded sky when McKee joined the lieutenant on the broken pavement in front of the third of an endless row of old five-story houses which had been a feature of the neighborhood since the days of horse cars and choleric men driving tandem. Almost two o'clock, and they had accomplished very little. When he jumped out of the car, staring right and left in the flood of uninteresting light, he stopped looking peevish and looked startled instead.

Donaher, detaching himself from a scrap of shadow beneath the awning of a wretched little candy store, said: "What's up?" But the inspector merely shook his head. They climbed some worn brick steps. The big Swedish woman, wisps of hair veiling her gaunt cheeks, didn't exactly welcome them in a hall that smelt of washing powder, sausage, onions, and people. She acknowledged vacantly that Green lived there, second floor, room at the back, didn't know whether he was home or not, crouched sideways over a soapy bucket as McKee, followed by the lieutenant, took the stairs at a flying leap.

In spite of their haste they approached the door without making any noise. It wasn't locked. Donaher pushed it away from in front of him, using warped panels, as a shield. There was no need of caution. The room was empty. In spite of the intolerable brilliance of the May afternoon, the cubicle into which they moved was steeped in a permanent dimness; walls, floor, ceiling, even the air itself seemed impregnated with the dye of poverty and despair. McKee said absently: "Fetch that woman. Don't scare her. She doesn't know anything," and looked around.

There wasn't much to look at. The bed was made. There was a picture of The Angelus on the stained wall above it, another picture of cows grazing, against broken plaster over the lopsided bureau. The Scotsman sighed. Not much disorder. But they were too late. Mr. Green had departed, probably for good.

Drawers were pushed back anyhow into the chest, a grass rug had been kicked sideways, but there were still garments hanging in the closet and an old duffel bag such as seamen carry was lying on the floor in the corner. Before he could examine these relics of the missing waiter, the woman came in. She bore the news of the departure of her lodger with a fortitude that was all she had to offer to the catastrophe of existence. "He bain gone?" began and ended her interest in him—perhaps because he had paid his rent to the middle of the following week and it was now only Friday. She had no curiosity and not much information.

Green had been lodging with her for perhaps a month. He had been out of work for a while and then had gotten work somewhere, she thought in a restaurant. He didn't get any mail. He hadn't any friends. The last she herself had seen of him was the night before, when he left the house at his usual time—six o'clock. He was a polite man. He held the door open for her when she went out. She was going out, too. Her description agreed with the one Donaher had already obtained from Gus and the others in the Sanctuary. Small dark fellow, dark hair, dark eyes, sallow skin. And his bed hadn't been slept in the night before. It didn't have to be made.

When she had gone, McKee crossed the room, ran the shade to the top, and waved at a vista beyond small dusty windowpanes with putty coming out in lumps. Donaher stared, didn't see any-thing but whitewashed backs of buildings, a wilderness of fences, a lot of fire escapes cumbered with things in violation of the fire laws, and said: "Well, I'll bite, what's the answer?"

"Have a look at that big building diagonally across from here, there to the left of the little house. You ought to recognize it. No? The hotel Rita stopped at when she first came to New York. Very interesting. Now then—let's have a look at what's here."

The first thing that fell out of the duffel bag was an owl edi-tion of the New York *Star*. The story of the Sanctuary killing was on the first page, low down, but as befitted that august sheet it was handled with gloves and without much detail. The lieu-tenant whistled. "So Green was out all night, was he? I guess he slipped in here this morning before anyone was up and beat it." The bag contained, in addition, a couple of denim shirts, a pair of greasy overalls, a white duck jacket with "S.S. *Santa Lucia*, Dace Line" lettered on it above the cuff.

McKee's brows went up. He said musingly: "Mr. Green was a traveler—and versatile. The overalls indicate a mechanic's job; we know he was a waiter, and he was also a steward." He turned his attention to the closet. There they found the waiter's coat and hat and a greasy full-dress suit. Mr. Green had evidently changed his clothes before he went, leaving his discarded skin behind him. But a brown coat, which had possibly been overlooked, at the back of the small dark space, was exceedingly informative. The first thing that Donaher pulled out of the breast pocket was a passport.

Both men studied the stereotyped form with interest. And Green wasn't Green at all. This was no shock. He was Salva-tore Eulalia Mendez, a citizen of Colombia, South America, his height was five feet three inches, his hair was black, his eyes were brown, his place of birth was Buenaventura. He was born in April, 1898, his occupation was laborer, and the passport was good for three months from date. It had already elapsed. It had been viséd in Buenaventura on December eighteenth of the previous year.

"This," Donaher said grimly, "will interest the Alien Squad. The fellow's in the country illegally right now." But McKee was fingering the garment he still held. Mendez, alias Green, had been fond of the brown coat from the condition of cuffs, elbow, and collar. He had worn it extensively as a private citizen. There was a tear in the lining. Between cloth and lining on the right side the Scotsman felt paper crackle. Something had slipped through. He drew it out carefully, crossed to the window with the result, and stared down with a distinct sensation of shock. Extremely odd how the thing kept turning up.

Telfair had builded better than he knew. For McKee held in his hand a page from the magazine *Babylon,* the memory of which had sent him to the speakeasy so promptly last night. There had been three sketches in all. This one was of the dancer. Slim, white, upright against twisted shapes in dimness, her body steeped in the brilliance of the spotlight, Rita Rodriguez stared out at them, dancing as she would never dance again, icy sinuous, head flung back, hands on her hips. It was an unmistakable likeness.

McKee folded the sheet, thrust it into his pocket. The link was now established. Until this moment the waiter might simply have been a man caught haphazard in a police net. He might, for instance, have been wanted for another breach of the law, and his flight from the Sanctuary at or about the time of Rita's death nothing more than a desire to get away from the scene of a crime where embarrassing questions would be asked. But not now. Not taken in conjunction with his flight, his selection of this cheap lodging house located close to the hotel Rita had been stopping at, and this picture of her tucked away in his coat. Moreover, he was sure of something else. Lily Henderson said that the dancer's room in the hotel across the court had been searched. The waiter had done that. The *why* still remained obscure. It troubled McKee.

Donaher was jubilant. This was something you could hang your hat on. He was leery of things like flower petals and people like the Archers and the Gairs. The two men went back to the office. And once there, the vast machinery for the tracking down of missing men was at once put into operation. By teletype, by radio, by telegraph, a description of Mr. Mendez, alias Green, was sent broadcast, not only to every police booth and precinct throughout the city and its environs but to private citizens as well.

Donaher departed for headquarters to see the head of the Alien Squad. Tannin took the white coat to the Dace Line offices, and McKee, moody and preoccupied, sat slumped behind his desk in rather a helpless mood. His common sense told him that this was simply fatigue. He had been on his feet for almost thirty-six hours. He forced himself up the stairs, found a smooth cot, threw himself down on it, knew that sleep was impossible, and woke an hour later, alert and refreshed.

And back in his office, meditating on the case, checking through reports, he knew that they had at last touched bottom, as far as the round-up was concerned. The preliminary work had been so thorough, Armstrong's questions, combined with their own, so precise, that there was no margin for error. All the men and women present in the Sanctuary had been checked and re-checked until the only ones not eliminated, from their positions in the restaurant, were the Gairs, Judith Pierce, Mrs. Barcley, Colonel Waring, Barcley and Archer near the door, and now the missing waiter.

News came in three separate installments. Hickson tele-phoned first. Sore at losing the colonel that morning, he had started out to find him. Hickson said: "First thing I did, In-spector, was to beat it up to Gramercy Park and canvass all the neighbors, but the only thing I could get was an old lady who saw a car, and she was sure it was a foreign car, drawn up before the colonel's house and a man get into it. She couldn't give me any description.

"I went around to a lot of likely garages. Found one in Vesey Street, couldn't get anything at the front entrance, but at the en-trance on another street I got a young Irish car washer going to a lunchroom (he's on the list to be appointed to the cops), and he gave me the low-down on Waring. That colonel is wrong, boss. Spends a lot of money on dames and booze. Always takes out the same big Hispano-Suiza. This is the number: 2708X."

Telling Hickson to report back to the Homicide Squad, McKee reached for the phone, called the Telegraph Bureau, gave the data on the Hispano-Suiza, and knew when he settled back in his chair that the radio cars would have it immediately and that it would be put on the teletype for the metropolitan dis-trict within a minute. He didn't, in spite of this, feel cheerful. The colonel had a long start. Wine and women! Two of the most potent stimulants known to man. But that didn't make Waring a criminal.

He was still thinking about this when the door opened and Tannin came in. The lively little sergeant looked tired. This case was running him ragged. He dropped into a chair, took off his coat, wiped his forehead, and told the story of his trip to the Erie Basin in Brooklyn, among those bags of coffee, barrels of oil, bales of fur . . . "and I never saw so much cat and dog food in my life, Inspector," with the pithiness of the trained police official.

"Had to chase the port captain over there. He showed me the *Santa Lucia's* manifold for the last three months. That boat never hired a man named Green, but they did employ a chap named Mendez, who signed on as a steward at Colombia for the full trip and deserted at Havana. And the dancer . . ."

McKee nodded, said: ". . . was engaged as a performer from last November until the beginning of March at the Hotel Angleterre. We had a cable." Difficult to associate an insignificant little man like the waiter with Rita, but there was some link between them.

Beyond the windows, the May afternoon faded. Just as dusk was sifting down over the rooftops and into narrow streets, slit here and there with the last gleams of the reflected sun, Donaher dashed into the office.

"It's a washout, Inspector," he said bitterly, standing still, the knob of the door in his hand. "Green wasn't Mendez either. Captain Peters of the Alien Squad got onto it. He knew just where to look. They had all the dope on that passport. It seems that Mendez, the real guy, got a three months' visa or whatever you call it in Spanish to come up here and see his folks. Well, he never left Colombia—died there a few weeks before he was supposed to sail. His family lives in Harlem. A brother-in-law who was with him down there put him under the ground all nice and tidy, so——"

"Our Mr. Green had his own photograph fraudulently inserted and left Colombia on the passport of the dead man?"

"Right. Doesn't it beat hell?"

"It does," McKee said without bitterness. "Your turn to get some rest, Donaher. Tannin and I have work to do. See you later." He pulled the phone towards him.

CHAPTER XV

DARKNESS SETTLED down over the city, but with its coming the roar simply increased, the tempo set at a faster pace. Lights now in a million windows in addition to the glare of headlamps in those endless streams of traffic. Down in his office McKee was ripping the case apart from the beginning, examining each separate fact with the most minute scrutiny, establishing all these people against their backgrounds, matching them with what they now knew of the dancer and, above all, trying, before he made another move, to solve several important questions. Who were the people who had entered Rita's flat after her death, and for what weighty reason had they gone there, and which man or woman had abstracted the pocketbook from her dressing room—and why?

He lingered over Mrs. Philip Barcley, with her pinched features and the air of invulnerability which unlimited money bestows. But if she didn't know of her son's intrigue with the dancer she couldn't very well have shot Rita. You couldn't get behind that at the moment. But Waring knew. Barcley? Quite possible. He had only been out of the city for three weeks in pursuit of his little pots, and the affair had been going on for almost six. He moved on to the Gairs and Judith Pierce.

Meanwhile Telfair returned to the little house in Grove Street after an interminable walk. Late in the afternoon, after forcing himself to sit still at his drawing board, he had flung charcoal aside and had gone out. But physical fatigue didn't help any. It merely narrowed the circle of those pressing thoughts. Judith, who was as open as the sun, whose reactions were as immediate and spontaneous as a child's, lying, plotting, scheming. Women were utterly unscrupulous. They fought battles like generals, regardless of any moral code, any ethical responsibility, without caring whom they sacrificed or how many lives they smashed as long as they won.

He couldn't forget, either, that he had found her drinking champagne with Archer at his table one night when he himself had gone away to telephone. She said at the time that she was bored and wanted to find out what was behind the playboy's vacuous gaze. That was what she had said! His footsteps rang heavily in the narrow alley.

Crossing the court, he took out a key that would have given him entrance to half a hundred places, so ordinary and standardized was its construction, opened the front door, closed it behind him, took the precaution of slipping the bolt, switched on the lights, and looked aimlessly around. He was stalling and he knew it.

For he had made up his mind to put the thing squarely up to Judith, tell her that he had found the green purse, that he knew she had dropped it in Rita's bedroom—and turn the thing over to McKee. The little house was very still. A cheap alarm clock on top of the bookcase beat a mechanical rhythm against the chirping of sparrows in the yard. Like a man forcing himself to go over the top of a trench alone and in darkness, Telfair moved slowly across the worn rug, past the Morris chair with broken springs, around the table, and then leaped back, colliding violently with the mantel, a galvanic shock running through him from head to foot. Something had brushed against his leg . . . something that moved.

The table was mahogany, its drop leaves extended, plenty of cover beneath it for . . . he drew farther back, doubled his fists, pulled his body into a crouch, stooped, and then laughed aloud, shakily. For he had glared down into green slits glaring back at him. The thing under the table was the janitor's cat. It must have slipped in somehow or other. His exasperation found expression in a hasty kick that didn't reach its goal. The cat miaowed, and Telfair went towards the phone. But when he took the receiver off the hook and dialed Judith's number, she wasn't there. It was Gair who answered, and the only thing in Gair's languid drawl that reached the cartoonist was that Judith was being followed. "Why don't you call your inspector friend off, Telfair? I call it a bit thick, if you ask me." Telfair slammed the receiver into place and turned away. So the police suspected Judith! His spirits already hovering around zero sank with a thud. That damned green pocketbook was the crux of the whole business. He circled the stand holding the humidor, hands in his pockets, glance fixed. And the old weariness settled down on him again.

Women! As soon as you got mixed up with them you got into trouble. He thought of his wife, a sweet girl with excellent principles (wretched equipment for matrimony) who had divorced him after two intolerable years. She had soft brown eyes, a gentle voice with a whine in it, and insisted on talking political economy over the breakfast table. Her mother stayed with them a lot, a lady full of probity, with an enormous number of teeth and a chin like a coal scuttle. A man ought to look his in-laws over before committing himself.

Judith never talked of her people. This reticence, which he had taken for tact, began to assume a sinister aspect. He kept on walking the floor in widening circles. The room was hot, airless. His feet, padding the carpet, didn't make any noise against the faint roar of the streets muted by the walls. The stillness began to get on his nerves. He had never seemed so much alone. But when a board overhead creaked, he came to an abrupt halt, shoulders back. It was nothing. The wind, perhaps.

He resumed his pacing. Judith wasn't like his first wife. She'd never whine. She had a devil of a temper. Strike back at you, perhaps—strike . . . As though the words were made fact by the sharpness of his reflections, something struck the floor of the bedroom above. Whirling, Telfair scowled at darkness veiling the hollow of the stairs. That damned cat again! Put the beast out. He rounded the table, began a yawn which never completed itself, and stood rooted to the rug.

Not ten feet away on the landing of the stairs, a man was facing him in dimness, figure indistinct against shadows, face and hands blurs of whiteness. The man was a perfect stranger. He was small and thin and dressed in rough clothes such as an artisan might wear. They stared at each other against two ticks of the clock. Then Telfair said coldly: "Who the devil are you and what are you doing in this house?"

The man on the landing spoke, and behind his liquid and unmoving gaze he was astonishingly self-possessed: "Where is it, señor?"

The cartoonist surveyed his visitor steadily. The man was a lunatic. He shrugged. "Sorry, but you're in the wrong pew. However, as I don't like people breaking into my house, I'm afraid I'll have to turn you over to the police." He began to back towards the phone—and found himself looking along the barrel of a squat piece of steel that was undoubtedly a revolver in good working order.

Sheer astonishment held the cartoonist absolutely motionless. In that first instant he was so appalled by the suddenness of this, there was about his visitor such an expression of calm ferocity, intensified by his economy of movement and his extreme quiet, that he himself didn't know quite what to do. Certainly the conventional command and reply didn't occur to either of them. Telfair didn't throw up his hands, nor did the man on the landing request him to do so. He merely repeated in that monotonous singsong:

"Where is it, the purse you picked up from Rita's bedroom last night? I have looked—I cannot find it."

As simple a statement as that—and their positions were at once reversed. The question hit the cartoonist like a deluge of icy water descending suddenly on his head. The shock of the impact left him groggy. He felt numb, helpless, then his brain began to function. There was only one person in a position to know about that quick furtive gesture while the police were out of the room, when, recognizing the green purse, he had thrust it into his pocket: the man hidden in the bathroom. This fact steadied him in the midst of chaos.

"So you're the chap who was in the dancer's apartment last night when the police arrived?"

"I am asking a question, señor. Do not waste time. Where is the purse now?"

Telfair didn't answer at once. He was standing between the

two bookcases that lined the walls on either side of the front door. The only illumination in the room came from a bridge lamp some distance away behind a chair. But the connection was plugged into a socket near him, and the long cord snaked along the baseboard at his right. If he could . . .

"You brought the purse back with you to this house last night."

The fellow was undoubtedly dangerous. Telfair gazed steadily at the pistol and at the face above it. "You followed me back here and tried to get in?"

"Yes."

This frankness was disconcerting. The only thing that appeared to interest the man was that damned purse lying at the moment inside the humidor not ten feet away. The muzzle of the gun raised itself the fraction of an inch. Telfair blinked into the small black hole, felt cold all over, thought, "I'll be damned if I do," and said languidly, with a discouraged droop of his shoulders: "All right. I guess you've got me where the wool is short. Put your pistol away." At the same moment, under a pretense of turning, he took a step, felt the cord under his toe, gave a quick jerk, and in the sudden and complete darkness dove for his antagonist's body in an attempt to knock the weapon out of his hand.

The two men met in the middle of the floor. Telfair struck out, connected with flesh, put his fist into it. They pummeled each other, wrestling fiercely between times. The table went down with a crash. A lamp toppled over. After that the stillness within the little room was broken by harsh grunts as each tried to get a stranglehold on the other. Somewhere outside a woman called, "Charlie . . . Charlie . . . supper's ready . . . CHARLES!"

Blood pounded noisily in Telfair's ears, sweat dropped into

his eyes. Get the —— over against the wall. Trip him up. Teeth clenched, head low, he lunged, felt cloth slide through his fingers, an arm twist out of his grip, and, unable to check himself, took the newel post squarely on his forehead, felt sick, opened his mouth for air, tried to pull himself to his feet, to turn round—and couldn't. He couldn't get any air into his lungs, either. Hands were at his throat, squeezing it as if it were a rubber tube. The relentless grip kept boring in. The pain was intolerable. His eyes began to bulge, his ear drums were bursting. Trickles of agony shot through his lungs. It came to him dimly in some withdrawn place that this was the end. His arms were wisps flapping. Then he stopped moving, thinking, feeling. His head was the *Graf Zeppelin* and it was traveling, released from his body, at an enormous rate of speed into the heart of the murmur you hear inside a shell, a murmur that was growing constantly louder, that was deafening, terrible. His head burst, spattering the stars. Consciousness went like a window being slammed on tumult that filled time and space.

When he came to, he was lying flat on his back on the hardness of wood. His lips were dry and swollen with caked blood, and a sledge hammer banged steadily at the base of his skull, but it was so glorious to breathe again that he lay still for a long time, drawing air sweetly into his lungs, before he summoned fortitude enough to assemble his limbs, get them in the right position, and stumble to his feet. The lamp had been smashed. He located the button in the wall after a half-dozen attempts and switched on the top bulb.

In its sudden glare the room was a wreck—and empty. Even the cat was nowhere around. He called her vacantly, his voice a hoarse cackle: "Here, puss, here, puss . . ." and listened. No patter of claws on the stairs. Of course, she'd gone out, as she had entered, with his visitor. Who in the name of blazes was the olive-skinned man with the gun and . . . The purse! He was across the floor to the little stand under the window in three strides. But even before he threw back the lid he knew what he was going to find. Did find it. The cedar-wood compartment was empty except for a few cigarettes. The green suède purse was no longer there.

CHAPTER XVI

IT WAS the newspaper that started the ball rolling merrily that night. Not bound by the same exigencies as tied the Detective Bureau hand and foot, the necessity for facts, evidence, substantiation, they sniffed out the detention for questioning of Mrs. Philip Barcley (New York, Newport, Palm Beach), hinted at a connection between Mr. Gregory Archer, Harvard man and polo player, and the defunct dancer, and touched lightly on the Gairs. Meanwhile, McKee, at the office of the Homicide Squad, had built up a picture of Rita's activities on the day preceding the night of her death.

She had had a visitor in her room at some time after five o'clock. (The woman in the apartment beneath had heard the thud of the falling Mercury. There were cigarette ashes—the dancer didn't smoke—*on top* of the caduceus which had broken off when the statuette crashed.) She had gone out at a quarter of six (a seamstress in a house across the street) to the Harriman Bank, where she had a safe-deposit box—this was arrived at through a study of her checkbook and papers—had taken something out of the box, and had returned to her rooms.

McKee himself had contributed to the late editions (they were charmed with this information so graciously given and with the bizarre note—it was better than the Wendel case) the story of the vanishing camellias. In consequence of which the Scotsman had a visit from a paper salesman at about half-past eight.

"My wife likes flowers—I took them home to her. I found them crammed down behind the wheel of my Ford parked near the river when I came back from seeing some people about our new bond—extra special and dirt cheap. Maybe you'd be interested for the department? It'll save you . . ." McKee said, affably, that he'd think about it and dismissed the paper salesman. Link by link it was coming.

The salesman's car had been parked within ten feet of Rita's apartment house. Archer had gone there. It was McKee's belief that he went no farther than the door and, opening it with his key, had heard or seen something that sent him stumbling to the street.

Who was the person with Rita?

Archer continued to be of grave interest, but the missing waiter engaged his attention, too. They had only one thing in common, a distinction which Colonel Waring shared: they had all vanished. And the vacuum they left behind echoed resoundingly with questions. Was there some indication of Archer's whereabouts in the penthouse? It was worth trying.

Hours had been consumed checking up on Lily Henderson's story of the dancer's early life. Rita's maiden name was Gonzalez. Her father had been a Spaniard in the cigar business. And undoubtedly she had been married in the Church of St. Ignatius Loyola in June, 1914, to Emilio Rodriguez. After that the couple dropped into a void. The aunt in Brooklyn was dead.

As to the bit of greenish stone that had been sent up to Claubertson at the Museum of Natural History, Claubertson telephoned. The thing was jade and very old. More than that he couldn't say. The man for the inspector to see was Mr. Parle, who had been connected on and off for years with the Thorndyke Museum in Baltimore. Parle lived in Harlem, was away at the moment but was expected back that night at around nine o'clock. It was a quarter of eight when McKee got his information. A few minutes later he and Tannin were on their way across town in the Cadillac.

A star-spangled night, cool, delightful, New York in her most propitious mood. But circumstances were not kind. McKee meditated, sunk in a corner. If he could explain some of the things that troubled him, eliminate a few of these people. That look, for instance, that Susan Gair had flashed at her husband, a mixture of terror and shock, when Gair had drawn Mrs. Barcley and Colonel Waring to the notice of the police down in the Sanctuary garden. And the girl, Judith Pierce, could scarcely have missed seeing Gregory Archer just inside the door behind the barrier, if he was there just before Rita was shot, as Barcley said he was. The district attorney was getting restless. He wanted the perpetrator. The Scotsman wanted the perpetrator, too, but first all these discrepancies had to be explained. But what really troubled him most was an obscure feeling that they hadn't touched bedrock in this case yet. Somewhere in all this welter of detail an essential clue was hidden. They hadn't found it. Would have to search until they did.

There were two detectives on duty at the towering apartment, one covering the tradesmen's entrance, the other the lobby. They had nothing to report except that Archer's valet had come in about half-past two, and that the yellow roadster was still in the garage over on Eighth Avenue.

McKee and Tannin went up in the elevator. This time the

door was promptly opened by a lean colored man in a white jacket, his sensitive features drawn with anxiety under the pressure of events for which he could find no answer but loyalty. Savages recognize one another. The Scotsman was a savage now, too, nose to the trail, determined to get the truth.

Henry James—that was the valet's name—said that he was alone in the penthouse. He'd been getting some dinner ready, hoping his young master would return to eat it. Both detectives followed him across the foyer and along a narrow corridor to the kitchen. He said that last night was his evening off, that Mr. Gregory thought a heap of Miss Rodriguez, that "maybe his ma wouldn't like it," but that Gregory's guardian, the colonel, might be able to fix things up. The colonel was a very nice gentleman. He kind of understood young folks. Mr. Barcley, now, Mr. Barcley was different. He thought that young folks ought to have old heads on their shoulders, which was against nature.

Tannin was restless, anxious to get hold of something tangible. McKee restrained him with a gesture, said, his voice lulling: "Mr. Archer's stepfather and his guardian disagreed about what Mr. Gregory ought to do?"

"Well, sir, if you know what I mean, the colonel is human. Mr. Barcley's always thinking about Mr. Archer's ma. But, shucks, a young fellow's got to——"

"Sow his wild oats, Henry, I know. Was Miss Rodriguez a wild oat?"

Henry James shammed facetiousness with: "She's a very beautiful lady, and her and Mr. Gregory is very much in love with each other. Be a good thing for them to marry and settle down." Henry evidently didn't know that Rita was dead, didn't read the papers. But he could read. A "Dream Book" to the left of the soup kettle on the shelf proclaimed that.

McKee took the valet's address and told him to go home. Mr. Archer was out of the city. He would be informed when to return. Troubled and uneasy, Henry was very glad to get away from the sergeant's frown. The two men began a search of the apartment, starting at the living room at the far end. It ran, foyer, two bedrooms connected by a bath, study, and, across the back, living and dining rooms.

A gap on the paneled wall above a desk between two hunting prints, a gap from which the colonel had undoubtedly removed Rita's picture on the night of her death. McKee sat down at the desk, turned over letters, a good many of which were unpaid bills, and glanced at a number of photographs. They ran back over a period of years. Gregory Archer—several of them were labeled—his father and mother on the deck of a yacht. He stared down at the long narrow young face. Archer wasn't bad-looking, but there were both weakness and obstinacy in the big soft chin cleft with a dimple, and vacillation in the loose mouth open in front of rabbity teeth with which even the most expensive of dentists could do very little. He pocketed two of the more recent pictures, stared for a long time at a shot of the yacht anchored in a wide harbor against a background of glittering white buildings with mountains towering in the distance, his eyes narrow, gleaming. Tannin said, "What's the dope, Inspector?" And the Scotsman answered: "I don't know—I'm not sure. But this looks like South America to me. We'll take it along and find out." Tannin stared. The waiter who wasn't Green and who wasn't Mendez had come from Colombia.

And then they came on something much more conclusive. Two tickets for Baltimore, useless now, on a train leaving the Pennsylvania Station that morning at eleven o'clock. The inference was plain. Archer and Rita Rodriguez had been going away together. Death—fortunately for the Barclays—had removed an undesirable daughter-in-law. But—how much did they know of all this? That remained to be proven.

The windows of the living room were closed. The endless song of the city was a murmur up here in this little house in the clouds. McKee finished his examination of the desk, glanced round to see whether there was any other likely source of information, started towards the dining room, and then, with the swiftness of a leopard pouncing, reached the switch, pressed it, and plunged the room into darkness.

Someone was coming into the apartment. The front door wasn't visible, but most of the foyer was, very still and empty at the end of the corridor. McKee put a careful gaze round the lintel of the open door behind him, the sergeant turtlewise thrust out his head. Mrs. Philip Barcley came slowly across the field of vision. She was moving cautiously. When she heard no sound, relief made itself manifest in the sag of her thin, erect figure under a black velvet evening wrap. She crossed the foyer and went into the bedroom on the left.

As soon as she vanished from sight, McKee and Tannin walked noiselessly along the heavy runner. Mrs. Barcley hadn't quite closed the bedroom door. She stood a little way inside, her back turned, staring around. Two things were at once evident: The room had been thoroughly searched. (And it had not been searched by the police—Mrs. Barcley couldn't know that, of course.) And this discovery was causing her intense distress.

A moan repeated twice broke the stillness of the big, handsomely furnished bedroom. Then she moved, still with her back turned, towards a walnut highboy to the left of a window seat against the far wall. Taking something from the wide sleeve of her evening wrap with one hand, she opened a drawer with the other. McKee stepped over the threshold and said, his voice pleasant: "Can I be of any assistance to you?"

She whirled around, her face above black velvet a clown's mask, patches of red on white chalk, mouth a red smear of fright. The thing she was holding in her hand was a pistol. The Scotsman relieved her of this gently, stood looking from burnished blue steel into her eyes and back again. "A weapon should have been here and isn't?" He said quietly, "You were going to supply the deficiency?"

Words were a rattle in the back of her throat, forced through stiff lips. "It's Gregory's. I thought . . . if the police found he had one . . . and it . . . wasn't here they might . . ."

"—jump to false conclusions, Mrs. Barcley? I see. . . ." He transferred his gaze to the open drawer, a pile of white silk handkerchiefs, a yachting cap, a pair of spurs, a box of cartridges . . . his glance sharpened. "Unfortunately you didn't select the proper calibre. This is a thirty-two; those cartridges are for a twenty-five."

Against Tannin's whistle (for the dancer had been shot with a twenty-five) and Mrs. Barcley's stillness—she seemed scarcely to breathe—he looked at something even more important than the cartridges, a yellow stain on the creaminess of silk. It was a camellia petal. And Archer had worn a camellia in his buttonhole; had come back here after a visit to the dancer's apartment, leaving the penthouse again to enter the Sanctuary at a few minutes after ten. The petal could only have dropped into the drawer when he opened it to extract the missing gun.

And Mrs. Barcley had read the evening papers, knew that the police were trying (so far without success) to trace the weapon that had been found in the speakeasy on the night of the murder, knew that he had had it when he went there.

It was then as the Scotsman turned back to her, thrusting away pity, that they all heard the sound. Something fell in the next room. Tannin leaped across the carpet, threw open the door. A girl was sitting on the edge of the bathtub. It was Judith Pierce. As they watched, she lit a cigarette she held in her fingers, got up, and strolled into the bedroom.

CHAPTER XVII

To McKee she said: "Sorry, I do turn up at the most unexpected times, but you did, too. I came in while you were talking in the kitchen." Slim, composed, her body without tension under the excellent lines of a tweed suit, her eyes bright in the shadow of a little hat, she turned to the other woman.

"You are Mrs. Barcley? I came to return your son's key. I found it on the floor in the Sanctuary after the dancer was shot, had just picked it up and was about to hand it to him when the outcry began. Afterwards I couldn't find him."

"You are very kind." There was bitter hostility behind Mrs. Barcley's thin smile as she held out her hand and the girl dropped the key into it.

"Most thoughtful of you, Miss Pierce," the inspector murmured. "The key explains how you got in. It doesn't explain why you searched this room, after your arrival and while we were at the other end of the apartment."

She gave it to him then with a smile, the lie direct, opening her gray eyes wide, "Oh, but I didn't."

He let them both go then, left himself after a quick survey of the remaining rooms. It was almost nine o'clock. Five minutes later both men were in the Cadillac on their way uptown to interview the archeologist.

Herbert Parle, A.M., B.A., Ph.D., lived with his sister in an unpretentious house on a quiet street in a decent, shabby neighborhood. The scientist was expecting them. And seated in a big room at the back of the hall, so full of objects that Tannin felt the sister's devotion must be boundless to permit such a bunch of junk on the premises, McKee looked around curiously. There wasn't an inch of space unoccupied. The walls were buried under a fresco of hundreds of photographs, maps, paintings. All sorts of objects littered the surfaces. Books were piled anyhow, on the floor, on chairs, and sheets of manuscript strewn broadcast added a final note of disorder to the confusion in the midst of which the doctor received them. He was a thin elderly man as bald as an egg, but with a beautiful sandy beard that would have made the fortune of a hair tonic.

Much of his ornamental and exceedingly verbose conversation with McKee was obscured by the vituperative screaming of a green parrot in a cage under the window. The sergeant, between looking and listening, was a little at sea. Such things as, "The first astronomical observatory in America with reference to the arrangements of temples, E-I, E-II, E-III, Pyramid E-VII, and Stella XX," a jaguar skin draping a rough mass of stone, a model of a queer building named the "Temple of the Dark Writing," confused his sturdy common sense. He concentrated on the doctor with an effort.

Behind the desk Parle was turning over the bit of jade between bony fingers the color of parchment, and listening to the inspector's story. He began to talk, and Tannin got hopelessly lost again. Maya and Inca civilizations tangled themselves in knots. He did gather at the end of a long and complicated narrative that the bit of jade was centuries old and part of a woman's betrothal ornaments. And to the best of Parle's belief had come from Costa de Muerte.

McKee's eyes gleamed behind squeezed-together lashes. Tannin stared. The liquid syllables rolled queerly back from the walls of this strange room. Parle translated: "In English, gentlemen, the 'Beach of Death.'"

Then it turned out that the beach wasn't a beach at all, but the bank of a river. "These alluvial stretches used to be used as burial grounds in ancient days. Successive deposits of silt when the river overflows in the rainy season have in most instances made them difficult to find. The Thorndyke Museum has made valuable excavations at Costa de Muerte."

"And where is this Beach of Death, Dr. Parle?" McKee already knew, but Tannin's eyes opened when the scientist answered. "In Colombia, about fifty miles away from the coast, thirty southeast of Bogota, high up in the mountains—a wild region."

"When were these excavations you speak of begun?"

"About five or six years ago, Inspector."

"What would a white woman be doing in such a locale?"

"Oh—she might be the wife of an engineer, or a man attached to one of our home industries, oil, bananas, rubber. The white population lives entirely in the hills. The coast is a marsh—full of fever." The doctor went on talking for some time. Although he had traveled extensively himself he had never run across Rita Rodriguez. When the interview was at an end McKee mentioned the waiter under both his aliases, Green and Mendez. The archeologist shook his head—then frowned.

"Green . . . Green. Curious! I seem to associate the name somehow with Costa de Muerte but not precisely in that way. Dear me, my memory's not what it was. If the connection comes to me I shall let you know."

The Scotsman thanked him, and the two men left the house. He was silent and abstracted on the way down through the city. Back at the office he threw away his hat, didn't pay any attention to the sheaf of messages from the Telegraph Bureau, the reports that had come in from men running down various angles, went out of the room, came back with a large thin book, dropped into his chair and leafed pages. Tannin crossed the floor and looked down. The book was an elementary school geography, and McKee had paused at an industrial map of South America. The sergeant's stupefaction deepened. They didn't even have their hands on the waiter who was wandering around loose in New York at that moment. How did McKee expect to . . .

Without looking up, the Scotsman said: "Exports," in a dreamy voice, and began to trace with a pencil various lines shooting out from the Colombian coast across the ocean to other parts of the world and labeled with the names of commodities: "coffee, mineral oil, gold, platinum, hides . . ." he stopped, looked away, looked back at the map ". . . and emeralds, Tannin," he said slowly, "emeralds."

The sergeant tried to take the implication—and failed. A dancer dead in a speakeasy in New York, mixed up with a young swell and a lot of other people doing monkey tricks, a shabby little waiter without a cent to his name . . . It was true that he had come from South America, true also that the dancer was carrying around a bit of jade that hailed from there, too, but . . . emeralds!

"She didn't have any jewelry, boss!"

McKee didn't answer. Looking pleased, he played a tune on some buttons at the back of the desk. The policeman-secretary thrust in his head. "Send someone for Lily Henderson. I want that check girl from the Sanctuary, too. Her address is in the files." And when the secretary withdrew, he fished a card out of his wallet with "Tiffany" engraved across the front, and beneath it a man's name and telephone number. McKee pulled the phone toward him and called this number.

"It was as big as the end of my thumb halfway down." The hat-check girl was very positive, sitting bolt upright on the edge of her chair, a little in awe of her surroundings. McKee glanced at the jewel expert, a slight man with a nondescript face, who knew as much about precious stones as any man in New York. Nixon said:

"Really? Then, my dear young lady, if it was genuine, it was very valuable indeed." There were four people in the room: Lily Henderson, looking a little gray (a defect she was on the point of remedying with a raspberry lipstick) above a hundred and fifty pounds of flesh shoved into a shiny satin dress; Nixon; the sergeant; and the girl from the Sanctuary.

As Nixon made this announcement, Lily held the tube of red paste motionless, awe in her voice: "You don't mean to tell me that that bit of brownish rock was worth anything? Sure I knew she had it . . . but in London it wasn't on the chain. More than once she said to me, and once it was while she was handling the funny-looking thing: 'I don't intend to stay in this business *all* my life.' I thought she meant a man, of course, but now—did the dirty louse who did her in shoot her for the stone, Inspector?"

McKee asked: "How much would it be worth, Nixon? She must have had it cut and polished since that time."

The expert shrugged. "Not having seen the stone myself, of course I wouldn't be able to give an authoritative opinion. But granting that it was a good color and without any cracks or flaws, even in the present depressed market it ought to fetch—say from ten to eighteen or twenty thousand dollars. You know the market is artificially controlled—that's what you've got to come to in all industry sooner or later. The supply is never permitted to catch up with the demand."

And that was that. Nixon went away, the room was cleared, and McKee sat staring down at his desk. The emerald was not on the dancer's person. It was not in her flat. It was not in her safe-deposit box. (This had already been examined.) Where, then, was it? The check girl had contributed, in addition, before she left, that Rita wore it the first three nights she was in the Sanctuary, and after that—never.

Of one thing the inspector was now convinced: the bit of jade, the emerald, were intimately bound up with her murder. The shrill summons of the telephone roused him from intricate conjecture. It wasn't news of Archer, or of the waiter, either. It was only Telfair, and he sounded furious. What the cartoonist said (in reaction from terror about the damn purse which had disappeared, leaving him free to move) was:

"Look here, McKee. You've got a man tailing Judith Pierce. Would you mind telling me the reason?"

The Scotsman gazed steadily at the wall, instrument loose in his hand. Keys. Archer's key. The girl had turned up with it in the penthouse. There must have been keys in the dancer's purse. The purse was missing. The girl had been hidden in the telephone booth. The telephone booth was near Rita's dressing room. Some one of those people might have seen her take it. A man watching her! He didn't say, "But we haven't"—instead: "Miss Pierce will be best able to answer that question. Suppose you meet me at her rooms in twenty minutes."

Leaving Tannin to wade through the mass of reports that had come in, he left the precinct.

CHAPTER XVIII

In the little house in Grove Street, Telfair put the receiver back on the hook with a groan. McKee's response to his call was more than he had bargained for. He didn't seem to be able to do anything right. And yet perhaps this was for the best. His reason told him that Judith couldn't possibly have committed the murder—or was it his reason? Wasn't it just the desire of a man to get a woman he loved out of a nasty mess?

"Circumstances alter cases. Rita deserved killing. It was justifiable homicide." That was what she had said early that morning standing at the window looking out into the court. He groaned again, pulled himself together, cast a last look around to see that everything was back in place, for he hadn't yet resolved whether or not to tell McKee about the attack on him, picked up his hat, locked the door behind him—a ridiculous gesture now—and, in the street, hailed a taxi and gave Judith's address.

And Judith wasn't home! Again and again in the familiar vestibule Telfair pressed the bell, impatience turning into rage. Gair had said she would be back soon. That was at about half-past eight. It was now after ten. What a fool she was to go traipsing the streets with a detective at her heels. He went slowly down the steps, paused on the sidewalk to glance up at her windows and came to a standstill. Her lights were lit. His fury evaporated as suddenly as it had risen. She had probably fallen asleep over a book. More than once at the tail end of a party she had gone to sleep like that, as suddenly and completely as a child, almost in the middle of a sentence. He mounted the steps again.

When McKee arrived some five minutes later he found the cartoonist, very white and grim, hurrying the janitor up the staircase to the third floor. His hand on Telfair's shoulder, McKee said, "Take it easy, old man, take it easy!" And to the janitor: "Open the door." The man did. "Now you can go away." The man went.

Telfair was already inside the apartment. Judith wasn't in the little living room, kitchen, bathroom, or bedroom. Racing through them in turn and not finding her, his heart pounding against his ribs, he refused to let himself think, stopped when McKee stopped, pushed down nausea and answered curt questions. "Yes, Gair said she would be home soon. Yes, Gair said . . ."

The inspector looked at his watch. The girl had left the penthouse well before nine, should have been back here in a short time. His face was heavy. He began to examine the place carefully. The tub had recently been used, was faintly warm, smelt of lilacs. The big sponge in the basket at the side was still wet. He squeezed a few drops thoughtfully, tossed it away. In the bedroom talc was sprinkled on the carpet and, what was much more disconcerting, the hat she had been wearing and the gloves were lying on a chair under the window. And in the closet—his gaze narrowed and drew down—the tweed coat and skirt depended from a hanger.

Deep brown eyes hooded, the inspector walked slowly into the living room. Beyond the walls an elevated train snaked past at the end of the block on half a hundred flat wheels. Against its thunder the Scotsman looked around. There wasn't cover, literally, for a mouse. Over his shoulder he shouted, "Noisy spot." And Telfair answered with elaborate reasonableness out of a dry throat, "It's cheap."

Outside a truck lumbered by. It turned the corner, seemed to take with it, when it went, the incessant din of the traffic rising and falling like surf, so that for a moment the little room was wrapped in the hush of one of those pauses that come now and again like an enchantment in the perpetual motion of a great city. Then the noise surged back again, a whistle blew, a taxi honked, but in front of the taxi both men heard the faint cry, a whimpering sound such as an animal in distress might make. And it came from somewhere close at hand.

Windows at one end of the room opening on the street, at the other a blank expanse of wall giving on the next apartment. This blank space was ugly, and the girl had broken it with a long piece of tapestry in front of which a bench was standing. McKee moved with the rapidity of light—almost. He flung the bench out of the way, dragged at the tapestry, pulled it aside. Behind it was a closed door. The key was in the lock; he turned the key, pulled the door open. Telfair was beside him. Judith Pierce tumbled out at their feet.

The girl as such was at first scarcely recognizable. She was unconscious. Her negligee gaped over a little flesh-colored nightdress; there were scratches on her throat. Dark hair hung in wisps over her face, which was distorted, lifeless, the features smudged. Her mouth was an ugly hole.

McKee stooped. "Put your hands under her shoulders, Telfair. Careful. Over there. Now that cushion. No, she's not dead. Go call a doctor."

The cartoonist stumbled towards the phone, remembered a sign in a window downstairs, raced out into the hall. In the living room McKee stood beside the couch looking down at the flattened figure. The girl was breathing all right. There was no sign of any wound. The scratches on her throat were self-inflicted. Her nails were broken, fingertips smeared with blood.

The doctor and Telfair arrived, the medical man in his suspenders and vest, carrying a bag. He was at once busy with aromatic spirits of ammonia, a glass and spoon, reassuring in the middle of administering this. The young lady had simply fainted. Charming girl. His wife and he had often noticed . . . Locked in the closet, was she? Ah, quite so. Lack of air and shock. Most of all, shock. Some people had a horror of enclosed spaces. Claustrophobia. She would be around in a minute now. Heart action was perfectly all right. "Open the windows wide, please, both of them. Thank you." He kept his hand on a slender blue-veined wrist, gazed at his watch, put it back in his pocket.

On the couch Judith Pierce stirred, her lashes fluttered, she opened her eyes. There was blankness in them at first, then terror, then, as she looked slowly from face to face—something else. The girl's strength was astonishing. She made a movement as though to struggle into a sitting position. The doctor nipped that in the bud. Telfair shoved a cushion farther under her head; she looked at him gratefully, colored rather suddenly, and said with a faint, smile: "I'd like . . . a cigarette, please."

Although the doctor demurred, Telfair gave it to her, was aware that McKee was at the telephone in the hall, heard him talking to his office. The Scotsman came back into the room.

"Now, Miss Pierce, if you please."

His first solicitude had given way to a manner that was not

indulgent. He didn't waste any time. "You came back here from the penthouse?"

She lay perfectly still, not looking at him, blowing smoke. "Yes."

"You still persist in the story you told there?"

Physical weakness hadn't changed her any. "Of course."

"What happened in these rooms?"

"When I came in, Gerry—Mr. Gair—was still here. I told him I was tired. He went away. I took a bath, was just going to bed when the doorbell rang. I thought it might be Gerry coming back again. I put on this,"—her fingers touched rosy silk—"and opened the door. A man pushed past me and came in. It was the detective who'd been watching me earlier in the day. I . . . he . . . that closet was open. I'd been putting winter things in camphor. He flung an arm around me, clapped his hand over my mouth so that I couldn't scream, pushed me into the closet and locked the door. I tried to get out. I've always been afraid of narrow dark places. I suppose I lost my head. Then I fainted. Then you came."

"Is this the man, Miss Pierce?"

McKee took the passport from his pocket, showed her the cleverly faked portrait of Mendez, which was in reality a likeness of the missing waiter.

"Yes, that is the man."

One thing was at once evident to the inspector's trained intelligence. The waiter couldn't have seen the girl abstract the purse from Rita's dressing room the night before. Because immediately after the murder (the exact moment was still in doubt, and this was one of the things that troubled him), at any rate before the alarm in the bar was rung, the waiter had fled through the corridor of the house adjoining the Sanctuary. Her theft had been accomplished when the garden was being emptied of the people, by which time the waiter must already have reached the street. How then did he know that she had possession of the purse?

He was satisfied in his own mind that Green, alias Mendez, was one of the visitors to Rita's apartment the night before. The girl therefore . . . He said: "You stole Miss Rodriguez's pocketbook, used her key, entered her rooms . . ."

Judith Pierce watched blue rings drift towards the ceiling. Telfair leaped to his feet, knocking over his chair, uttered something between a shout, a "No!" and a deep-throated curse. Without looking around, the girl pushed him away with a slender hand.

"Don't be a nuisance, Jim. Yes, Inspector."

"He knew you had the purse?"

"I suppose so."

Telfair said bitterly: "She's lying. She's lying all along the line. I found the purse in Rita's bedroom, took it home with me, hid it in my humidor——"

"From which I took it this morning when I paid you a visit. I found it while I was looking for a cigarette."

"I tell you she's lying—that man came to my rooms. We had a fight. He left with the purse!"

At the moment McKee was not interested in this love affair going astray. There were discrepancies. "Why did you want the pocketbook in the first place?"

"Because the key of the dancer's apartment was in it. I knew the police would go there. I wanted to get something out of her apartment before they found it."

"Did you succeed?"

"No. I was frightened away. When I first went into the bedroom I heard a noise like . . . the sound of the outside door opening. I went out and looked. I couldn't see anyone. I heard it again. This time the door closed."

McKee's thoughts were racing. If he was right, the waiter was the first arrival, Miss Pierce the second, and she was actually describing a third before they themselves . . . He said, "And then?"

"Then there was no mistake. After I'd been there for a while longer, I heard the electric light being switched on and thought it was time to go. So—I went, by the fire escape. I'm not afraid of heights, and it seemed the best way."

As simple as all that. Telfair sat like a man turned to stone. The truth was, he was not so much shocked by the moral implications as by the initiative with which she had acted, and the driving power behind it.

McKee was not shocked. There was no depravity with which he didn't credit a woman, particularly one as young and attractive as this. "What was in the dancer's apartment that you wanted to get, Miss Pierce?"

The girl blew more smoke, not rings now, a gray stream from the bottom of her lungs. "Letters. Rita had been blackmailing me for a long time." Her voice took on an almost conversational tone, remote, idle. "She wrote me a letter asking for money. I went to see her yesterday afternoon. I gave her the money. She said she'd bring the letters to the Sanctuary last night. I was glad to go there with Susan—would have gone anyhow——"

"Your interview with her in her apartment on the afternoon before her death was—stormy? I mean—the statue . . . ?"

She looked at him then with those long liquid eyes—McKee knew he had her. He pressed his advantage remorselessly. "You weren't up there in her apartment the afternoon of the murder, Miss Pierce. It's a nice little story, well put together—only it doesn't happen to be true. But I'll tell you who was . . ." Gaze fastened on the pallid oval of her face, he drew a bow at a venture and hit the bull's-eye. He could tell by the dilation of her pupils. "Mr. Gerald Gair was."

And then she was up off the pillows, seated on the edge of the couch, small bare feet just touching the floor. "I knew you'd find out. I knew it. I shouldn't have let Gerry go. I was in love with him once and he loved me. We're still—friends. I told him about Rita. He said he'd handle it."

The Scotsman's only emotion then was a sensation of pleasure. He had rounded out Rita's day. The explanation was complete. Gair had gone to the dancer's rooms as an emissary. Archer, with his sheaf of camellias on his arm and the bud in his buttonhole, had opened the door on that interview, a door for which he was provided with a key, had seen the two (Rita was insolent in her beauty) outlined in dark marble against the windows. And Archer had retreated, tearing one of the flower petals away as he closed the door.

As for the dancer, blackmail obtained, she had coolly put her visitor off with a promise to deliver the letters that night in the speakeasy. That was why Gair and the girl had gone to the Sanctuary. Rita meanwhile had paid a visit to her safe-deposit box, meant in good faith to return the letters, but, frightened by Archer's nonappearance, this minor affair had been thrust into the background. After the dancer was killed, the girl had taken matters into her own hands . . . but . . . there were spotty places—plenty of them.

"You took the dancer's purse to gain admittance to her apartment, Miss Pierce. Why, having done so, did you steal it from—eh—Mr. Telfair for the second time?"

"I—didn't get what I wanted—my letters. I knew—the dancer and young Archer were—intimate. I thought the letters might be there in his house. There were keys in the purse. I dropped it when I went through the window up in the dancer's apartment, was glad to find it again."

Her daring was admirable and easily understood. But he was investigating a murder. "Miss Rodriguez had a hold over you, Miss Pierce?"

"Yes."

"Will you be—more explicit?"

"I'd—rather not."

"I'm afraid I must insist."

A greenish ring of pallor round her mouth. The doctor leaned forward in his chair. Sweat glistened in small pearly drops on a white forehead. She brushed the drops away with the palm of her hand. "It was . . . in Paris a year ago. I was one of the hostesses at the International Exposition in our building, a replica of Mount Vernon. The . . . man I was with in Paris . . . was . . . afterwards with her. She took letters out of his pocket. I suppose that was part of her trade. I'm in love with him. You know what men are . . . he's married. If I were to cause him any trouble— he'd just hate me. Simple, isn't it?"

It was at this point that Telfair got up, very quiet for all his bulk, and walked out of the room. The girl didn't even turn her head. The silence after the door closed had almost the weight of an explosion. It scarcely registered with the Scotsman. Too bad, of course, but . . . "Miss Pierce, besides keys—Archer's, I presume, and Rita's own—what else was in the purse?"

He had to respect the way she rallied, answering him with the thoughtful simplicity of a child (the need for subterfuge was past):

"Money, a compact, and a handkerchief."

Profound disappointment engulfed him. No trace of the emerald. He kept on asking questions until the doctor stopped him. "She is ill. I really shouldn't advise . . ." They were all tired, on edge. The doorbell rang. It was a detective from the Homicide Squad. Obeying orders, he had scoured the neighborhood. His name was Tompkins, and he was a good man. He had searched the street thoroughly. He held out the thing for which he had been told to look, a woman's purse, which he had found in the gutter near the corner.

McKee turned to the girl and showed her the green suède purse. She nodded. He opened it. The purse—it was inevitable— held nothing at all.

CHAPTER XIX

CLOSE-KNIT POLICE work after that. Time was an important factor. The waiter had had a long start on them that morning; now he was just two jumps ahead. Whatever the pattern of the crime, it had reached its focal point in Rita's death, he had to be found. The description wasn't much good. Impossible to pluck him out of the endless tide of people among whom a small dark man shabbily dressed could be reproduced endlessly. Tackle it from another direction, figure out his objective, his line of march, forestall him somewhere along the path.

Ten minutes after he left the girl, McKee was back in the dancer's apartment, watching men go through it like a fire brigade. The place was literally taken to pieces and put together again. Cushions were stripped from couch and chairs, stuffing pummeled, furniture ransacked, draperies shaken, talcum and face powder dumped from boxes, bath salts flung into the tub (Donaher doing the same thing in the dancer's dressing room down in the Sanctuary). The result was a foregone conclusion.

There was no safe, no jewel box in evidence, and no woman (with a face like Rita's) would leave the emerald lying around loose. She had sold or pawned it. A discouraging reflection. It would take days to ferret the stone out. Unless . . . he returned to the purse. It had played an important part in the investigation so far. The girl said it contained a handkerchief, a compact, and money, besides keys. When Tompkins found it in the gutter it was empty. Why should Green be interested in . . . a compact was a metal case, enclosing various things, powder, lip-stick . . . capable of holding other things. A pawn ticket, for instance. Quite so.

Rita was a comparative stranger in New York . . . a tug whistled out on the river, long-drawn, mournful. She would want every cent she could get (that lovely mouth was greedy). How would she go about cashing in on the stone? In a neighboring apartment a radio turned on the saccharine cadences of a German waltz, "Zwei Herzen . . ." Ah, "Two Hearts in Three-quarters Time . . ." Archer? Had she asked Archer's help?

The Scotsman had already examined and thrown away the idea that Archer had the jewel. Rita was a cat lapping her own cream daintily, secretive. He veiled his gaze, let pictures flash across his mind. There was a lead some place—there had to be. She wanted clothes, then. Standing there, he didn't so much think of, as become, Rita. Money—I must have money.

She was no reader, didn't talk to strangers, was naturally cautious. The flash came then. A *Herald-Tribune* that the valet had placed on the table beside Archer's chair in the living room of the penthouse. A minute later he was out in the street. There was a newsstand at the corner. It began to be more and more possible. He turned pages, paused at a column low down on the extreme left. It was headed, "Public Notices." And it was there he found what he sought. Mr. LeGrande exchanged valuables for cash, and the Continental Agency bought, sold, and exchanged gold, silver, jewels (liberal allowance on false teeth).

LeGrande, most probably. However, it wouldn't do to slip up now. And it might be a matter of minutes. He called the office, gave curt orders, and was speeding across town to LeGrande's office in Fifty-ninth Street.

Darkness of a warm spring night. Store windows flaring, some of them blank. Plenty of people out and around. McKee dismounted from the Cadillac in front of a coffee house, walked fifty feet east. LeGrande's was a bookshop. Nothing as vulgar as three golden balls to advertise his sideline. Three worn steps to an area fitted, in front of plate glass, with a long table where a pasteboard sign announced about rows of battered volumes, "Stop! Look! Ten cents apiece. Three for a quarter."

McKee studied two people bending over the table, a stout woman in a gingham dress with a shopping bag over her arm, and an elderly gentleman with a dog on a leash. Neither one was the waiter. He advanced under the flare of a hundred-watt bulb through the doorway into slightly musty gloom of the long, dimly lighted shop itself. There were other things here besides books, old flat silver in a case, a nice Georgian tureen, some Colonial glass. A tall weedy youth, hair veiling an unattractive chin, was stowing an armful of Tauchnitzes on a top shelf.

He turned languidly as McKee said: "Mr. LeGrande?" and led the way along the aisles to a small room at the back of the store, jammed to the ceiling with English classics containing, besides, a carpet-covered rocker, a desk, a small safe, and a faded hyacinth on the dusty windowsill. There was a door on the far side. The youth knocked, yelled: "Gentleman to see you, sir," water gushed, a man answered testily: "Coming . . . coming," and the door opened. An elderly gentleman came into the room carrying a battered copy of Ovid and looking inquiry out of mild blue eyes above a pair of rimless glasses.

McKee didn't waste any time. Producing his shield, he put his query: A woman named Rita Rodriguez who had pawned or sold an emerald weighing approximately ten carats, some time during the last six weeks.

LeGrande stroked a lean chin thoughtfully: "I believe . . . Rodriguez? Nice bit of goods, was she, Inspector? Beautiful figure? You've come to the right place, I think. We'll see . . ." He opened a ledger, turned a page headed "April," ran his finger down a column. "Here you are. . . . Emerald, nine and three quarters carats . . . she asked a thousand on it. Couldn't see my way clear. Business is bad . . . very bad! Gave her seven fifty. . . ." He was speaking more slowly.

An obscure premonition warned the inspector. "Is the jewel here now?"

The pawnbroker shook his head mournfully. "If you had come in twenty minutes ago."

Outgeneraled again. But twenty minutes wasn't a very long time. LeGrande, an old man, was shaking like a leaf under his bright gaze, the drive of his questions. The emerald had been redeemed by the lady's brother. "I knew there was something wrong—I felt it. Such a shabby fellow. And yet he pulled the money out of his pocket, gave me the ticket—what could one do? Dressed? A brown coat and gray trousers. Yes, small and dark."

"Let me see the ticket."

LeGrande, moving faster now, went out into the shop, rummaged in a trash basket under the counter, produced two small bits of pasteboard. The Scotsman pressed them to his nostrils. The odor of Chinese lilies was distinctly perceptible. He was right. The ticket had been folded inside the compact.

He began pounding LeGrande, got another detail: "The fellow had a bundle of newspapers under his arm." This was not illuminating. Like a gift from the gods, help arrived. It came in the shape of a hesitant, "Hey, mister," from the youth with the blond hair prickling his chin. McKee turned.

"You're looking for the guy who got the emerald? I spotted him right away as kind of queer. When he first shows up outside he's giving the shop the once-over, see? Then he comes in quick, walks up to the counter, planks down cash, and is on pins and needles. As soon as he gets what he's after he walks to the door, looks up and down the street—and beats it."

"Did you notice which way he went?" McKee held his breath.

The boy nodded vigorously. "Yeah. I got to thinkin' he was acting funny, that maybe someone was after him. And what he did made me know I had the right dope. It stands to reason."

"Yes?"

"Cause why? After being in such a rush, all he does is walk along the street and go into the Aladdin."

"The Aladdin?"

"A motion-picture house across the street."

"And that was—how long ago?"

"'Bout a quarter past eleven. Don't you see? The show is almost over . . . " The helpful boy found himself talking to the empty air and into the profound countenance of his employer. Both of them stared after the tall gaunt figure disappearing rapidly along the aisle of the shop.

CHAPTER XX

BLOOMINGDALE'S STANDS at the northeast corner of Fifty-ninth Street and Lexington Avenue. Opposite are a cigar store and a long row of houses with shops on the ground floor, punctuated midway to Third Avenue by the ornate stucco portals of the Aladdin. At that hour of the night the corner is a busy one with its tangle of cars, trolleys, buses, and trucks. McKee came to a stop on the far pavement. In the middle of the street an officer was directing traffic.

He hesitated for a moment. He would have preferred a half-dozen of his own men with whom to seal up every exit from the theater—but minutes were precious. Granted that the waiter was still inside, the show was almost over, and in the rush of people coming out he might manage to slip away unseen.

The traffic policeman, one Gavagan, recognized the inspector at once as the Scotsman strode towards him. A few words were enough. "Officer, I'm after a man who went into the Aladdin a few minutes ago. You watch the alley while I go in. Grab him if he tries to get away—he's a small dark man in a brown coat and gray trousers."

Gavagan took up his post as directed, at a pair of iron gates opening on a narrow alley to the left of the theater and only used in case of fire, while McKee, approaching from the other side, looked over the empty vestibule with its flaming posters and the cashier's cubicle in brilliant light. The cashier was knitting.

He struck pay dirt at the first assay. She was an intelligent girl and, as it happened that she had noticed the man the inspector was inquiring about, described him accurately, said:

"He came in very late and he was nervous, dropped his change all over the floor. That door on the right."

The Scotsman was across the rubber-matted tiling in three strides, swung the door open, stepped from the glare into darkness that was for a moment Stygian, punctuated here and there with a red light and with a vague glow out in front. Above the last row of seats there was a curtain, which shielded the audience and most of the screen from view. Orienting himself in the gloom, he put his inquiry to the ticket chopper leaning against the wall chewing gum. The ticket chopper went away and came back with two ushers, curious under pill-box hats. Again he was in luck. One of the boys remembered the waiter perfectly. "I took a squint at him when he come in. Seemed kind of drunk. They come in to sleep it off sometimes. This way, sir."

McKee followed him to the mouth of the aisle at the left. The mechanical piano skidded into "Mademoiselle from Armentières," against a wave of titters and a scattering of applause. The Yanks were coming—across the screen. The usher started down the aisle. People were stolid heads and shoulders without detail. The usher was stopping at a row of seats sparsely filled. He stood there for a moment looking around as though in doubt, flashed his torch on a man and a woman side by side, a woman and two children farther along, drew the light towards him, held it still on a bundle of newspapers on the floor in front of an empty seat.

McKee, staring, pulled himself sharply erect. His eyes and ears, focusing simultaneously, recorded the shot first, nothing against the triumphant cadence of "Hinky Dinky Parlez Vous" but a tiny pop. It was enough. The firing of a service revolver outside the theater. Even as he dashed back along the aisle, put the transverse behind him and made for a door on the far side below a red light, he understood what had happened. The waiter, crouched and ready, had seen his head above the curtain in back as he came in. McKee opened the iron door, was on a platform at the head of a flight of steps, and the traffic man was running towards him down the alley from the direction of the street.

Gavagan shouted: "Fellow beat it out that way half a minute ago. I yelled to him to stop. When he saw me he turned and ran back there." Gavagan waved towards the dark alley losing itself in shadow and started to sprint beside the Scotsman moving swiftly down the tunnel. Without pausing in his stride, McKee said, husbanding his breath: "Go back. Call the precinct. Get men, notify the radio patrol, surround the block. He's in here some place," and raced on.

The traffic man obeyed. McKee rounded a corner flanked by a towering garage and the back of the theater and stood still. A thorough familiarity with New York prepared him for the cul-de-sac in which he found himself. The narrow passage ran smack up against a brick wall. No sign of the waiter—but he could only have gone one way. The inspector gripped the coping with his hands, flexed his knees, drew himself up, dropped into the next enclosure. A pair of tea towels hanging on a line in the light of windows in back of a brownstone house didn't tell him anything he wanted to know. Which thoroughfare was the waiter striking for? He had come from the direction of Lexington Avenue, the street to the south was quiet, Third was the best bet. McKee negotiated a low cement extension and two yards of varying dimensions, watching for a likely out between buildings. No sign of the waiter, who would of course try to put as much distance as possible between entrance and exit.

That scrambling flight through the hollow inside of a city block filled with an amazing variety of variegated shapes was not without incident. Scudding past a door, he came into violent contact with a woman who opened it carrying a garbage pail, didn't pay any attention to her scream as he catapulted gray boards, was in the rear of an A. & P. store, ran around crates and boxes, tumbled into another cubicle, dodged a whisky bottle flung from a roof, collided with a child's express wagon in front of a high wall, kicked it closer, put his feet on it and was over the barrier.

Still no sign of the waiter, but from the construction of the labyrinth he must have taken this general direction. There was nowhere else to go. The Scotsman's torch ripped the darkness aside as he fell into each enclosure. Three quarters of the way along the block he pulled up with a jerk and held it steady. Belated jonquils were a yellow flame in a neatly tended patch of earth behind an old-fashioned brick house. At one spot they were crushed and broken by an empty up-ended barrel which had been dragged into the middle of the border.

McKee made use of this stepping-stone the fellow had so kindly left, negotiated an unusually high fence, sat motionless on the top, straddling it, and studied the layout. The waiter had done for himself now. High walls on every side, no openings, and straight ahead the towering flank of a huge apartment fronting on Fifty-eighth Street. He must be, at the moment, cowering somewhere in the darkness close at hand. The Scotsman raised his torch, sent it stabbing the long narrow courtyard. There wasn't cover for a mouse, nor was there any possible way the waiter could get out of that sunken chamber, walled and floored with smooth cement—and yet he wasn't there! The first row of windows was fifteen feet above the ground, on a level with the last tier of iron platforms in which the crisscross fire escapes terminated.

Then McKee saw the ladder. It was leaning drunkenly against the whitewashed bricks and was four feet short of the lowest fire escape. To an agile and desperate man four feet wasn't much. He sent the long diffused beam from his torch upwards in a sweep, and in its ineffectual glimmer caught— there was no doubt about it—a dark blur that was a man moving swiftly towards the roof.

The Scotsman put his voice into a shout, drew his gun. Then the waiter betrayed himself. He paused for just an instant, hanging by his hands under the shock of that ringing command, suspended in midair a hundred feet from the ground. The next moment he swung himself up and leaped the parapet. As he did so his body was silhouetted clearly between two chimneys against the rosy glow of the city beyond. McKee fired—low. The waiter dropped.

But when McKee reached the apartment-house roof after a racing climb by the same route the waiter had taken, the fellow was nowhere in sight. The Scotsman fought for breath and looked around. Below him, now, windows thrown up, inquiring voices, but, what was much more important, a sprinkling of dark drops on sanded tar paper ten feet from the parapet, drops that ran in a diminishing trail to the door of the kiosk that led to the stairs. He pulled this door open and started down. Already the excitement caused by his shot had died away. The halls were silent, empty. Only an occasional splash of blood now. He lost all trace of the waiter at the bottom of the last flight of steps, which opened abruptly on a courtyard to the left of the main entrance fronting on Fifty-eighth Street. And was still using his torch on the wide pavement fifty feet either side when the radio patrol with Gavagan clinging to the running board swung around the corner and pulled to a stop with screeching brakes.

A crowd gathered in the twinkling of an eye. The patrolmen ordered them back. Without haste McKee began to issue orders. The waiter had either hailed a cruising cab or had swung himself up onto some moving vehicle, for there wasn't a single blood spot anywhere in the vicinity. The street began to fill with cars. Holding the pedestrians first on the scene in a compact knot, McKee said: "Chase those people away, Gavagan," and went on talking to a salesman who had been approaching from the west at or about the time the waiter must have left the apartment. The salesman either hadn't seen him or didn't notice him, but he was positive of the cars in the street because he wanted to cross over. First there was a roadster moving at a fast clip, a woman driving, then a yellow-and-black taxi, and a good way behind both of these, a truck. Questioned minutely about these cars (one of the radio patrolmen took notes), he perspired a lot, gave what details he could remember, and said further that there were three or four men in a group on the corner.

McKee squeezed conversation out of half a dozen other pedestrians, didn't get anywhere, proceeded to the corner where the group of suspiciously vanishing men had foregathered, didn't get anything but a fat candy-store proprietor standing in his doorway, asked a question, got an answer, and chased the fugitives into a poolroom farther along the avenue. He spotted several familiar faces in a crowd of pasty-looking, shifty-eyed men staring at him in the sudden silence his entrance produced, said, his voice mild: "It's all right, I'm not looking for any of you boys just now," and put his questions. One Baldy Lewis, a remarkably clever sneak thief, declared after cogitation, that no one had jumped on the truck but that: "The yellow-and-black taxi was parked in front of a house this side of that apartment, two women came out and climbed into it, and the guy"—the one the inspector was after—"might have got away in that."

McKee went back to the radio car, gave orders about the papers the waiter had left behind him in the motion-picture theater, the bills he had paid over to the pawnshop proprietor, and keeping Gavagan with him, mounted the steps of the house in front of which the taxi had been standing and rang the bell.

A hunched little woman with tired-eyes in a lined face and pins stuck into the breast of her black gown opened the door. The Scotsman introduced himself quietly, asked about the cab, and the woman, whose name was Mrs. Tremont, and who owned the house, said:

"Oh, yes, it was there. My sister-in-law, Mrs. Shuntag, and her daughter came to dinner with me, and they wanted to go home, so I telephoned for a car. They live in Riverdale, and it's a long walk from the subway, and my sister has a bad heart . . . so my niece said——"

"From what garage did you order this cab?"

"From Mason's over on Third Avenue."

"Have you a phone?"

She led the way to it. McKee called the garage, got the manager and the information he was in search of, dialed headquarters, turned the number of the cab over to them, put the receiver back on the hook, and left the house. The waiter must have a very grave reason indeed for being so anxious to evade the police. His capture was imperative. The chances were about fifty-fifty.

CHAPTER XXI

OFFICER KELLY, on post at the corner of 110th Street and Seventh Avenue, saw the fleeing cab first. He hadn't heard anything at all about it, but he didn't like the way the driver pulled from behind a truck, shot past the changing lights, and nearly ran down a colored man leading a white poodle on a bit of clothesline towards the confines of the park. Blowing his whistle, Kelly detached himself from the curb and stepped directly into the taxi's path. He didn't stay there—he jumped back just in time to keep the buttons from being shaved off his uniform by the near fender, and got a glimpse of the driver's frightened face and license number.

Swearing lustily, he put the number in the alarm box at the next corner and took up his post again. The motorcycle man straddling his machine in a side street twenty blocks farther along was the next one to pick the cab up. Unfortunately he was on the wrong side of the avenue. Nevertheless he pressed the accelerator, opened the throttle wide, and gave chase.

Meanwhile the little radio car for the section to the north was cruising past the empty ball park when the alarm shrilled. Picking the numerals out of the air, the man at the wheel headed down the hill—not at a snail's pace. The traffic officer at the bottom was shouting something to the motorcycle man in the snarl of traffic, when they reached the intersection of streets. The wanted car had just gone across the bridge. Both vehicles roared after it, under girders over the dark ribbon of the Harlem, picked out with red and green lights.

Halfway along that modest span is an opening to a ramp which turns sharp left. When the motorcycle flashed steadily east along the main fork, the radio car took this turn on two wheels. A stopped trolley at the foot of the little incline, a jam of people gesticulating indignantly. A woman had been hurt—not badly—by the fleeing cab. The little green Ford didn't wait for details. A dozen willing voices and twice as many hands sent them towards the dark mouth of Sedgwick Avenue, opening towards the north.

The radio car rolled plenty then on broken-down macadam badly lighted, above the bank of the Harlem where railroad trains shunted to and fro and an occasional tug steamed tranquilly past. It wasn't a crowded road. But at the shrill warning—the siren was on full—motor trucks grinding along drew sharply towards the curb, scattered cars bunched to a stop like frightened fowls. Under the arch of Washington Bridge a man and a girl in a roadster, roused abruptly from pleasanter things, stood up and pointed ahead. The cab was still invisible, but it had left plenty of evidence in its wake.

Rounding the sharp elbow above whose bank the Hall of Fame rears a stately crest, where famous men shiver in stone among the arches, they caught a glimpse of their quarry for the first time. The yellow-and-black taxi was swaying a little and moving at a dizzying pace. The officer at the wheel gave the car all he had, but the cab's motor was a better one. The distance between the two vehicles widened. Suddenly they lost the cab in a V of converging streets where an ambulance cut sharply in. But not for long.

There is a dip in the terrain there, where Fordham Road is laid like a long snake between the breasts of twin hills sloping gradually towards the river. On the right Conklin's Funeral Home is a decorous sheet of plate glass with monstrous green ferns behind it. As the radio car hurtled down the last slope, the driver put the brake on—hard. Their chase was over.

The fleeing cab, in an altercation with an advancing trolley, had crashed into the front of Mr. Conklin's Home (which was no longer decorous) and stood, hood crumpled, fenders buried deep in an avalanche of falling glass fully across the pavement, surrounded by a rapidly increasing crowd of excited spectators.

The radio men persuaded, shoved, pushed men, women, and children out of their path. The taxi was a complete wreck. There were three people inside. The driver himself slumped over the wheel, his eyes half closed, blood all over his face, and a woman and a girl in the back. The woman had fainted. The girl, hat crazily sideways on her head, was kneeling on the floor at the woman's feet and crying over and over again in a loud, monotonous singsong: "He's gone, Mother, he's gone. It's all right . . . it's all right. Won't somebody please get a doctor? Mother, he's gone!"

When Lieutenant Henry Barr left his home on Catherine Street that night to report for duty at the precinct, instead of following his usual custom, which was to take the trolley, he decided to walk, with the laudable intention of getting air down into his lungs and fat off his muscles. About a minute before the taxi crashed (he wouldn't have heard it anyhow, he was too far east), he struck across a small park which would cut off a quarter of a mile of his journey—for, although the spirit was willing for exercise, the flesh was inclined to be weak. The park, except for an occasional tightly linked group, was empty at that hour. He had almost reached the gates of the old Sailors' Home, that mellow landmark of another century, when he saw a running man leap through some bushes and start up the hill. The man had a knife in his hand. Reflected light from a street lamp drew a glimmer from along the blade. The lieutenant instantly gave chase.

Barr was inclined to be corpulent; on the other hand he knew the ground. The man dashed through a scattered clump of elms, disappeared under the walls of the building, and the lieutenant smiled grimly (for there was no out that way), simply walked to the far wing and waited. The fellow literally jumped into his arms. The struggle was short and sharp. Breathing deeply, Barr finally subdued him in the dense shadow of an old ship's prow anchored to the grass. A final desperate fling and the small dark man, without any hat and with blood soaking one trouser leg, collapsed like a jellyfish, flat on the turf, and lay still. The lieutenant picked up the knife and put his whistle to his lips.

Three quarters of an hour later, when McKee and Tannin entered the circular sweep of that big building at the edge of what used to be the Claflin estate, the district attorney's car was already there. So was the ambulance that had brought the waiter, and one of Conklin's funeral coaches into which the taxi driver and the women had been put. The two men mounted the steps, Tannin pushed the door out of the way. Right and left of the square entrance hall corridors stretched, gleaming, arid, empty of dust and of germs, full of the smell of iodoform, the sweet clinging odor of anesthetics. An interne, Lieutenant Barr, who had effected the capture, and two plainclothesmen from the local precinct were standing in a knot near the desk. Armstrong was pacing up and down the polished floor, his rubber heels making a little squashing sound as he turned. His stenographer leaned against the wall, looking sleepy.

The district attorney advanced on the Scotsman and threw out his hands. He said with triumph: "Well, we've got him. I guess this is the end! Forestalled you this time. I was dining in the neighborhood. When the call came in I rushed right over. The women are merely shocked. I let them go. They and the taxi man tell the same story. He's upstairs. Green, the waiter, is upstairs, too, in the operating room. They're still working on him. He'll be through in a couple of minutes." Armstrong's lips folded grimly.

And when McKee said nothing but simply looked inquiry, Armstrong continued: "Well, here's the story. The cab these two women engaged had just started away from that house in Fifty-eighth Street when the waiter dashed out of the apartment house next door, leaped on the running board, wrenched open the door, jumped inside, whipped out a knife, told the driver to step on it, and threatened the three of them that if they yelled or in any other way attracted attention, he'd kill them all. Nice peaceful citizen! The rest you know. Only that the driver lost his nerve and finally smashed up at the corner of Sedgwick Avenue and Fordham Road, the fellow would have got away.

"You haven't seen him yet, Armstrong?"

"No. They'd just taken him upstairs when I got here."

"Did you—get the emerald?"

And at the D.A.'s blank stare of astonishment McKee smiled. "I forgot you didn't know about that." While they waited he outlined briefly the archeologist's story, his hesitation over the name "Green," his own interview with the hat-check girl, and his trailing of the waiter to the pawnshop. At the end, grudging respect animated Armstrong's austere features. He said:

"Good work, Inspector. That was a long way to go from the bit of jade you found in the dancer's bag. Didn't have much to work with, did you? Well. We'd better have a look now." He turned towards the young doctor with whom the lieutenant was conferring about his boy's attack of measles. "Where are this fellow's clothes?" And as the interne led the way down the hall to an office at the far end: "Did he kill her for the stone, Inspector? Looks like it—looks as though we've got a real case!"

McKee only shrugged, his shining gaze inscrutable behind short thick lashes which were always puckered in the same fashion when he was thinking—or puzzled. Armstrong continued: "There's no doubt that he was desperate—hijacking that cab—whipping out that knife—by the way, it's a small machete which he must have brought with him from South America to have handy. If we could prove his ownership of the pistol that shot the dancer, we'd be sitting pretty, eh?" Armstrong rubbed his hands together. He was in high good humor.

McKee said quietly: "That's the weak point, that and the testimony of the janitor's wife in the house next door to the Sanctuary, through which Green made his escape. I'm not yet entirely convinced in my mind that . . ." Armstrong swore under his breath. He had no use for such quibbling in the face of facts. His own legal training was too sound to permit him to ignore these loopholes, however. But they might wring a confession out of the waiter. They had their hands on him now—he couldn't get away!

An attendant behind a slab produced a bundle from a locker marked "13" with profound indifference, threw it down on the counter, and returned to a moody perusal of a letter from his girl.

McKee unrolled the neatly strapped clothing. The gray trousers stiff with dried blood were not informative. He pushed them aside. Neither were the socks, B.V.D.'s, a cheap white shirt, or a green tie. But the brown coat was. He felt in the pockets, took out some change, a key to the dancer's apartment (you could tell that from the notches on the haft), another key of a very ordinary make (with which he had probably gotten into Telfair's little house in Grove Street), a box of matches.

At a wave of the district attorney's hand the interne and attendant had already withdrawn. The sergeant, Armstrong, and McKee were alone in front of the checkroom. The nursing home was very quiet. Off in the distance a stretcher was wheeled in and out of view, a bell rang some place, a nurse rustled across the hall carrying a feeding cup against the slam of a door blown by the wind.

McKee opened the matchbox. Tannin drew a deep breath. Armstrong said: "I'll be damned!" The Scotsman didn't say anything. Standing very still, they all stared down at the lump of green fire that burned inside the little wooden box and that had once rested, at the end of a platinum chain, in the dancer's white breast.

It was the district attorney who made the decisive movement. Turning away he said trenchantly: "Well, I guess that's about all we need. We'll talk to this gentleman now!" The Scotsman didn't follow him immediately. There was something else in the pocket of the waiter's coat. He drew it out. It was a small black box, about three inches long by two wide by one deep, and was made of some dull wood smooth as a pearl from countless years of handling. He took off the lid. Inside were three small dark-ish objects about the size of pea beans varying a little in weight. McKee, studying them, looked blank and then suddenly startled and incredulous. He put out a tentative finger, rolled them over one by one. From behind his shoulder Tannin murmured: "Gee! Something else? More jewels?"

The Scotsman didn't answer. Armstrong was waiting impatiently, a few feet away. An interne advanced towards them along the corridor, stripping rubber gloves from his hands, his face wet with perspiration above his surgeon's gown. "You're the police?" he asked curtly. "All right. Your man's coming out from under the anesthetic now. Nasty wound. We've fixed him up. He won't be able to talk long. Better take the elevator. First door on your right as you get out."

The district attorney went in first. McKee followed him. Tannin remained in the hall. The room into which they stepped was small, narrow, painted gray, held a white bed, a dresser, a table, a screen, and one hard chair. A nurse was standing beside the bed holding a small pus basin in front of the patient. She drew back as the two officials appeared, wiping his lips with a piece of gauze. McKee closed the door behind him.

The waiter was just ahead on a pillow, very dark against the whiteness of stretched linen, his body a small flat mound beneath the counterpane. His eyes were open, fixed on the ceiling. His sallow skin was greenish, and there were heavy shadows under his eyes. But there was a curious dignity in his stripped aspect, the small compact skull, the straight nose, sharp jaw, delicate chin. He was conscious.

The district attorney addressed him. He said in a slow monotone: "Green—we don't know what your real name is, but you killed Rita Rodriguez last night down in the Sanctuary. You might as well come clean now. We've got plenty of witnesses. And we have the emerald you killed her for. You might as well come clean—it will be easier for you in the long run. You can't get away."

This was not the opening McKee would have chosen. Standing to the left of the bureau in the gaunt room, he watched intently, almost as aloof as the man in the bed, thinking things over, weighing intangibles, drawing a thousand impressions, his senses curiously alert. The waiter neither moved nor spoke, but a change had come over him at the end of the district attorney's slow, drawled statement. He kept on staring at the ceiling, but his face, his whole body, was locked suddenly in an unspeakable rigidity. It was as though, while they stared in the silence of that bare little cell, broken only by the rustle of the nurse's starched uniform as she moved involuntarily, he was turning to stone, a petrification that nature achieves only after the passage of a thousand years.

Armstrong cleared his throat, gripped the iron rail at the foot of the bed tightly, leaned over it, as he repeated: "We've got the emerald," raising his voice as though the waiter were deaf. And indeed he might well have been for all the attention he paid, his gaze fastened persistently on unbroken white plaster. But in spite of the man's control a flicker ran across the immobility of olive-skinned features without touching eyes or lips, and that flicker rang a bell deep in McKee's mind.

Once, fishing off the coast late at night, he had heard the same forlorn and mournful cry from a floating buoy. Reaching out, he put his hand on the D.A.'s shoulder. But Armstrong was oblivious. "Better tell the truth, Mr.—er—Green—that name will do as well as any for the Grand Jury. We have you dead to rights. The woman next door to the speakeasy saw you beating it right after Rita was shot. We've got the gun the job was done with. You can't get away. Why did you kill her? Come on—speak up! What's the use of it? If you give us a statement . . ." The waiter turned his head. It was only to motion towards a bowl of cracked ice on the table beside the bed. The nurse gave him a spoonful, and for a moment the only sound in the room was a crunching of ice behind strong white teeth. It was then that McKee took the black box from his pocket.

Sighing, he tapped it, and the little repeated sound was very loud in the confined space, against the footrail. This by-play startled the district attorney. He turned with a frown. But the Scotsman was speaking to the nurse.

"When this—gentleman—was undressed and taken to the operating room, was there—anything peculiar about him? Was he—mutilated in any way?"

The girl (she was quite young and stiff with professional pride, afraid of these big men, sorry for her patient) hesitated. As for the man in the bed, he was paying attention now, his eyes wide open, glaring, the pupils contracted in the space of a second to mere pin points. He looked like a man being hypnotized, drawn out of himself by some overwhelming force as though in another moment he would put the covers aside and leap at the Scotsman.

But he didn't move. The nurse merely stood there at the bedside, looking down anxiously at the waiter, still speechless behind that terrible and staring gaze. McKee said, turning to the district attorney: "The things in this box belong to this gentleman in the very truest sense of the word. He was born wearing them. But no power on earth can restore them to him now. It's too late. They are three of his toes, sliced off some time ago" (the nurse gasped) "by a person or persons unknown. Pleasant little memento to carry about with one, Armstrong? But—eh—Mr. Green doesn't seem disposed to tell us about it now. There will be plenty of time later on. Shall we go?"

It was time. The man in bed suffered a sudden relapse, his eyes closed. He was breathing thickly. The two men left the room.

CHAPTER XXII

THE DOCTOR who had operated on Green was waiting for them in the corridor and went with them as far as the door. He said that while Green's wound was not dangerous in itself, to move him would be exceedingly risky business, and that he personally would most emphatically not advise it. McKee was oddly reluctant to leave the building. He asked some questions. The doctor smiled. "Get out of bed? Not a chance. He could no more get up on that leg and walk than he could take wings and fly."

In spite of this dictum, however, and in spite of the fact that Green's room was on the third floor, a detective from the local precinct was left on duty in the corridor outside his door. McKee sent his own car on ahead, and he and Tannin drove downtown with the district attorney. Armstrong's first jubilance had vanished, leaving behind it uncertainty and disgust. They had a half-dozen suspects, two or three well-authenticated motives, more than twenty-four hours had elapsed since Rita's killing, and there wasn't a clear case against anyone.

In addition the papers were being nasty. The story had at first attracted very little attention. A shooting in a speakeasy wasn't news. Then things began to leak out. The detention for questioning of people like Mrs. Philip Barcley, the Gairs, the beauty of the dancer herself, gave it a twist. The district attorney was thoroughly dissatisfied. Every clue they had run down was a washout. They weren't getting anywhere. He said so—with force. "Did you see the evening papers, McKee?"

Tannin blinked uncomfortably at the dark bulk of the Jewish Orphan Asylum sliding past on the left. "The evening papers" was right! There was a nasty headline in his own particular sheet: "Sixty-eight Detectives Fail to Turn up Clue in Sanctuary Murder." And it wasn't as though they hadn't been working like blazes every minute since the call had come into the radio room at eight minutes after ten the night before.

The Scotsman nodded dreamily in his corner. The evening papers didn't bother him at all. He said in a bantering tone: "Oh, have a heart, Armstrong, they've got to have something to howl about. I think the Police Department can stand it—reporters must live, and papers have to sell."

Armstrong wasn't interested in generalizations. His jaw was a razor line, his shoulders humped under a well-tailored coat. "Green must have killed her."

"Why?"

"Look at the evidence. He followed her to New York, took a room near the place where she was living, got a job in the Sanctuary because she was dancing there. He left the place in a hurry just after the shot was fired, has been in hiding ever since, committed assault to get hold of the emerald, and almost killed those two women and the taxi driver trying to get away. How did you find out those things in the box were toes?"

"I've seen mummified flesh before. Ever have a look at one of those heads the South American Indians bring down out of the jungle to sell to travelers?"

"All right, there you are, South America again. Green came from there. If you could establish that Rita spent some time there also——"

"We have. Just before I left the office we got word through the Telegraph Bureau. Her husband was employed by the Amalgamated Fruit people as a banana cowboy in Colombia from 1922 until 1925, when he died. She was with him."

Armstrong revived. "That settles it. It's as clear as the nose on your face. She and her husband probably stole the emerald from this fellow, there was a fight in which his toes were amputated and Rita Rodriguez got away. He followed her for two things: revenge and to get the stone back."

McKee remained unconvinced. "You know, Armstrong, we've got a lot of other people on our hands besides Green."

The district attorney's answer was muffled profanity. "And what are we doing with them?"

"As well," the inspector answered languidly, "as could be expected. We haven't uncovered the whole story yet. I'm sure of that. Rita was tied up in some way we don't yet know with Green——"

"Self-evident!"

"—and with her murderer also."

"Tautology."

"I'm not sure of that since I saw him up in that room. The missing link is between Green and this other person. We've got to get more information."

"Well, try and get it from those others, from Barcley and his wife, or the Gairs. As for that damned-fool girl, she talks too much and says too little. You can't break down the stories of the other two women. Mrs. Gair seems to have been an innocent bystander, and Mrs. Barcley certainly wouldn't shoot the dancer on sight when she didn't know a thing about her son's affair before she went into the Sanctuary. No, besides Green, Archer and Waring are the only other logical killers—and—well—you let them slip through your fingers. Sorry, McKee, I don't quite mean that, I know it couldn't be helped, but there it is anyhow. What do you propose to do now?"

"Dig," the Scotsman answered tranquilly, ". . . and perhaps, if your department could see its way clear to finance the expedition, send a man on a little trip down to Colombia."

Tannin grinned behind smoke from his cigar. That was telling Armstrong! The district attorney's office would have to pay for the trip. Well, the D.A. was grumbling about the progress they'd made.

Armstrong didn't exactly tell McKee to go jump in the lake, but his tone implied it. "I can't see that at all. Look here. You've isolated a number of people who, from their positions at the time the dancer was shot, might have killed her. You've got the gun that did the job. The crime is about twenty-four hours old. Now if, with all this to go on, you can't put your finger on the perpetrator, how do you expect to do it by traveling thousands of miles and going back four or five years?"

McKee's only answer was a shrug. He wanted just one decisive bit of information about the waiter, had nothing but a loosely drawn web of circumstantial evidence. Armstrong sank into himself, too. Both men realized that they were up against a problem that defied the ordinary mechanics of detection. The car slid steadily south. When the inspector and Tannin got out in front of the green lights at the station house in which their office was located, the district attorney shoved a moody "Good-night" after them, slammed the door, and drove away.

Upstairs behind his desk again, the Scotsman plunged into

a mass of reports, resetting scene after scene and matching it up with the information that was dribbling in. The man whom Gair had been going to meet on the night of the murder *was* out of town. If Rita was blackmailing Judith Pierce, his story—hers, too—was straight enough. McKee had known in that first instant that there would be a good many people who would breathe more easily with Rita dead. Women of her type, while they add to the gayety of nations, are not conducive to an orderly existence. She belonged to the great vampire brood, which sucks nourishment out of the vice and folly of its fellows. Just as in Elwell's case when the man was found dead in his room minus his false teeth and with his dressing gown bedabbled with blood, people, more stupid than criminal (and a good many of them women), heaved a sigh of thanksgiving.

And Barcley *had* come back from Canada just as he stated, on a train getting in scarcely two hours before the dancer was shot. No sign of Waring and the Hispano. No slightest indication of Gregory Archer's whereabouts. Two o'clock, three . . . at twenty minutes of four the telephone bell rang. And then the news arrived for which McKee had been waiting. It came in the flat careful voice of a man in the Telegraph Bureau identifying himself by a number, seated at that long table in the room at the top of the Police Headquarters.

That morning the waiter's fingerprints, collected in his room, and a complicated series of dots and dashes were flung through the air to the American consulate in Colombia. These dots and dashes, unscrambled, were a reproduction of Green's photograph fraudulently inserted in the passport. Green had at last been identified. He was Carlos Silva, had been, six years before, a trusted employee in an emerald mine in the Andes, was tried and convicted in 1925 for the theft of two hundred thousand dollars' worth of stones—awaiting the arrival of the representatives of a firm of Paris jewelers. The emerald had never been recovered. Silva had been released from prison the previous June, and although efforts were made to keep him in sight in the hope of recovering some of this loot, he had dropped completely out of existence. There were various other details, but the thing that held the inspector motionless, his eyes bright suddenly in a face gray with fatigue and strain, was an apparently unimportant statement at the very end. Silva had been captured in the mountains at a place called Costa de Muerte. He put the receiver slowly back on the hook. The piece of jade, the "Beach of Death." No matter how you added it up, it came back to that in the end.

His reverie lasted no more than a minute. Afterwards he made two telephone calls. One was to Donaher, rousing himself in a distant apartment at the persistent ringing of the telephone bell. All that McKee said was: "Pack a bag. Be around here in an hour." After that he talked to the commissioner.

It took a long time to convince Carey. Three hours later McKee smiled at the memory of that interview and of the subsequent telephone calls. The Cadillac raced steadily south, leaving the Holland tunnel behind. Donaher was seated beside him, bag at his feet. It was almost eight—and the ship left the Newark airport at twenty minutes to nine. But a radio message had been sent from headquarters to hold her as long as possible. The Scotsman kept looking at his watch from time to time.

Odd that it should be still early morning, but since dawn, a dawn that broke very clear but also very hot, he had been battering his head against the solid walls of official procedure. There were even moments when he had despaired.

Almost there now. Jersey City was a vague blur on the horizon, little towns sped past the windows. They sighted the airport and made it by a hair. The huge eighteen-passenger Curtis Condor of the Eastern Line, complete with stewardess, pilot, co-pilot was warming up both six-hundred-and-fifty horsepower Conqueror engines mounted outboard between the wings of the ship as they raced out on the field, stopped, sending up a shower of mud (it had rained in the night), and drew up twenty feet away from the anxious knot of officials.

The two men exchanged succinct words as Donaher sprang out. McKee said: "You're sure you understand?" And Donaher answered blithely: "Quite. I'll be seeing you," and sprang, astonishingly light on his feet for so rotund a gentleman, through the door that an attendant was holding open.

McKee didn't even wait for the ship to take off. He was already back on the highway when the drone of the plane broke the stillness of that brooding May morning with its long, diminishing roar. The end was in sight. Not for all that did it behoove them to walk less cautiously. On the contrary, the danger had enormously increased. During the drive back to New York, he went over the case thoroughly, testing this and that, adding, subtracting, trying to reassure himself. In addition to this trip of Donaher's he had done something else. Carlos Silva, alias Green, alias Mendez, was to be produced in forty-eight hours. It was the Scotsman's intention to confront Silva with the remaining members of the cast he had managed to assemble, for he was convinced that there was a connection not yet uncovered between Rita and one of these people. Consequently subpœnas were to be issued to Judith Pierce, Mr. and Mrs. Philip Barcley, Colonel Waring, and the Gairs to appear in the district attorney's office on Monday morning at twelve o'clock.

Forty-eight hours wasn't long. They were all being watched. Nothing could happen. He felt nervous and jumpy simply because he was tired. Things were clear now—up to a point. It began, of course, some six years ago, in Colombia. Rita, living there with her husband near Costa de Muerte, had in some fashion or other come in contact with Silva, who was afterwards tried and convicted for the jewel robbery. Rodriguez died, and Rita had betaken herself to other parts of the world, using her profession as a cover for a mode of life more suited to her taste.

Some eight weeks before, she had turned up in New York. Was this constant change of base an effort to throw Silva off the track? It hadn't succeeded. Once free, he had trailed her to Havana, then here, and at last into the Sanctuary. But why, if revenge was Silva's object, had he waited so long before killing her? Was it because he wanted to make sure of the emerald first?

The inspector turned his attention to what had actually happened in New York. The dancer had drawn Gregory Archer into her toils. She had pawned the stone to outfit herself for this little game and, about to marry him, and without funds to redeem it, had put the screws on Judith Pierce. Her procedure was clear enough. She wasn't growing any younger, and as the wife of a rich man she could sit back and snap her fingers at the world. Then chance had betrayed her. Instead of the girl, Gair had gone to her apartment, and Archer had been a witness of their interview. Things began to go wrong. The reasoning up to this put Gregory Archer, Judith Pierce, and, as a more remote possibility, Gair on the spot as the possible killers, provided them with motive anyhow. And he himself had already demonstrated that they had had the opportunity when he reset the scene in the Sanctuary garden.

So much for those three. But what about Susan Gair and the colonel and Mrs. Barcley? He couldn't forget the expression on Susan Gair's face, the tight look at the back of her eyes. As for the other group, their appearance in the speakeasy on the night of the murder was too entirely fortuitous to have been mere chance. These things had to be cleared up.

Back at his office he made three fruitless attempts to establish Mrs. Gair more accurately on that Thursday evening and, at the fourth, succeeded. In response to an earlier telephone call he had had a visit from two gentlemen. One was the taxi starter, Hughes, whom he had talked to from headquarters just after the alarm had come in. With Hughes was a man named Schmidt, a tubby little fellow with a red face under a checked cap which he nervously twitched off as he entered the room. Schmidt was the man who had driven Miss Pierce and Mrs. Gair to the Sanctuary on the night of the murder.

McKee listened to his story intently. It was true, as both women had stated, that they had arrived there at around half-past nine. But here a discrepancy arose. The driver went on talking. When he got through McKee told the two taxi men to step into the next room, pulled the phone towards him, called Gair's apartment and, when a maid answered, asked for Mrs. Gair.

It was Gair who came to the telephone. Making his voice genial, the inspector said: "I'm checking back over statements made in connection with the shooting of Miss Rodriguez, and I want to corroborate a few details. I wonder if you and your wife would mind coming to my office? I won't detain you long," and, at the snapped affirmative, put the receiver back on the hook with a smile.

The Gairs arrived some twenty minutes later. Gair's anger was gone, but he looked more watchful than ever. Mrs. Gair looked plainer in the light flooding through the window. They sat down. Gair said that he was very glad to hear from the police, anxious to get things settled so that he and his wife could get out to their place in the country. New York was so hot. He showed a row of white teeth in a pleasant smile. Mrs. Gair didn't smile. She didn't say anything at all; simply waited. McKee studied them both with his deceptively mild brown gaze. The girl had almost certainly communicated to Gair the fact that the police knew of his visit to the dancer's apartment on the afternoon of the night she was killed. Had he or had he not told his wife of his intervention?

If he hadn't, he was in for a nasty shock right now. Well, on any count it was coming to him. Proceeding on this hypothesis, he ignored the man, turned to the woman, checking over details on a pad.

"Mrs. Gair, circumstances have arisen . . . Would you mind telling me what you were doing on the late afternoon and early evening of Thursday?"

"You mean—before I went to Judith's?" Her eyes were wary in the shadow of her hat. "What does one do in New York to pass the time?—let me see." She consulted the tips of gloved fingers. "I looked at curtains, planned new furniture for the porch . . . then went along to Judith's apartment, we talked for a while, and after that, went to the speakeasy."

"In fact, you spent a quiet, carefree couple of hours. Is that correct? You weren't ill?"

She looked up at him quickly, startled and faintly amused as though this were an interesting facet of police procedure which merited humoring.

"I'd like awfully to help you out. But I've got a perfectly putrid memory. It's all—after the shock of that awful night—very vague in my mind."

"Can you tell me what time you arrived at Miss Pierce's?"

A birthmark sprang into sudden prominence beneath powder on her cheekbone. McKee spared a side glance for Gair. The man was trapped, sitting very still, his face stony, trying to think what to say or do to warn his wife. When she gave him nothing but a frown, McKee pressed the buzzer on his desk. The door opened. Mr. Schmidt was ushered in.

Without looking away from the two people facing him across the barrier of the desk, he said smoothly over his shoulder: "Schmidt, is this the lady you drove?" and the taxi man, fumbling with his cap, muttered: "Yes, sir." And was very hot and embarrassed.

"All right. Just tell her what you told me a few moments ago."

But the driver insisted on repeating his story to the building across the street:

"It's about half-past seven, see, Inspector, and I'm cruisin' around looking for a dinner bunch when I seen—see—a lady leaning against a elevated pillar on Forty-first Street. You know, where you turn up to catch the ramp opposite the Grand Central? The lady looked kind of all in. I slowed up, but she shook her head, and then when I was starting on again, she waves for me to stop and gets in. She says choked up like, 'Take me to 604 West Thirteenth Street.' I do. When we get there, she climbs out, pays the fare, starts across the pavement, don't get no more than halfway when she runs back to the cab, gets in and tells me to take her to another address." Schmidt gave it. It was Judith Pierce's.

"What time was it then, Schmidt?"

"It must have been a quarter past eight. Traffic was pretty heavy."

"What happened after that?"

"Well, the street was pretty quiet, and I was feeling hungry. I'd lost the theater crowd anyhow, so I et my supper, some sandwiches my old woman did up with a bottle of coffee. I finished and was lighting my pipe when the door opens and the lady I drove before comes down the steps with another woman. They tell me to take them back to 604. I guess that's the lot."

Judging from Gair's stillness and Susan Gair's rock-like posture, it was plenty. McKee said: "That will be all, Schmidt." And when the driver left the room, "Well, Mrs. Gair?"

She shook herself out of a trance with, "I don't think I quite understand what you mean, Inspector."

"You weren't looking at curtains or planning furniture for the porch late Thursday afternoon. Your husband's office is close to the place where Schmidt picked you up. You followed him to the Sanctuary, didn't you?"

"And if I did?"

She was calm now. Gair, on the contrary, controlled himself from speech which evidently at the moment he considered dangerous, paying more attention to his wife than to the inspector.

"If you did you had found out that your husband went to the Sanctuary for the express purpose of meeting the dancer. Even Schmidt, not an impressionable man, was struck by your manner. It was someone in an abnormal condition who squeezed the gun that killed Rita Rodriguez."

Then, at last, Gair was spurred into action. He jumped up, sending his chair crashing to the floor. "You know I saw the dancer earlier in the day. Judith told you that. You know——"

"Gerry! Don't make a fool of yourself! This man is trying to jump us, don't you see it?" Her voice was the lash of a whip. She turned back to McKee, very white, smiling faintly. "It was all a little adventure among friends, Inspector. I suspected my husband of being interested in Miss Pierce. Is that a new situation? There was no arrangement to meet each other at the speakeasy.

We fixed that story up after the shooting. When I got there first I thought I might be mistaken about Judith, so I decided to go and see whether she was at home. I did. She proposed going to the Sanctuary. I was still in doubt. So I went. I didn't, of course, know the truth, that Miss Pierce had deliberately used my husband to get her out of trouble. As to Judith," her smile wasn't pleasant—"I really can't say, Inspector, but neither my husband nor myself had anything to do with the dancer, had no previous knowledge of her whatever. You'll have to look elsewhere for a killer. Under the circumstances you will understand if I say that we won't talk any more until we see a lawyer? I don't intend to let anyone wreck our lives. Come, Gerry."

Mrs. Gair was a small woman, unimpressive except for that beautiful voice. Now, as she got deliberately to her feet, straightening her shoulders under her coat, she completely dominated her husband. And McKee, watching them leave the room, was a little at a loss. Was the woman telling the truth? Or did she know of some link between Gair and the dancer, and had she used his information about Judith Pierce to hide behind?

He couldn't make up his mind at the moment, was primarily interested in only one thing: Who had killed Rita? The day wore on. He followed Donaher's flight. The first stop, Camden, New Jersey, flying time forty minutes. Next, Baltimore, just under an hour later. After that, in succession, Washington airport, Richmond, Virginia, Raleigh, North Carolina, Charleston, South Carolina, Savannah, and Jacksonville. There the plane would stop for the day and Donaher would continue his trip by rail to Miami, spending the night there. What would he find at the end of the trip? Some link between one of these people and the dancer that had not yet been uncovered?

Twice during the afternoon McKee tried to get in touch with

Telfair—without success. He was still thinking about the taxi that had followed Rita and Gregory Archer away from the Sanctuary a week before her death. Telfair might be able to tell him something about its occupants. Other things pressed. Tannin came in, and together the two men checked every possible angle. Men telephoned from hour to hour. The Gairs were back in their apartment, Judith Pierce at home, the Barcleys hiding from reporters behind the handsome front of that impregnable house in Sixty-eighth Street. No trace of the colonel or Gregory Archer.

It had already occurred to both McKee and Tannin that the colonel might have resorted to an old trick. He might, knowing the Hispano-Suiza would be traced, have changed cars before the alarm had had time to do much good. At dusk McKee gave orders that sent fifty men scouring every garage and parking space within the city limits and some immediately beyond. It was almost seven when he went back to his rooms, fatigue that was gray wool smothering his brain in thick folds. He had to have some sleep. Nevertheless, before he threw himself down, full length, on the couch in the living room, he put out a nervous hand and called the Faucett Nursing Home where the man they now knew as Carlos Silva was confined to his bed. Silva and the little box containing the three toes were the heart of this problem in murder. McKee wanted to assure himself that the man was still there and everything in order. It was. The ex-thief was being tenderly watched by a precinct detective seated inside the door of his room. There was no chance of the fellow's giving them the slip. McKee put the receiver back on the hook and lit a cigarette he didn't want but that his rasped nerves demanded.

No one beyond themselves knew Silva's identity. He was down on the blotter of the local station as Green, an escaping burglar. At the hospital also his real name was a mystery. He was simply a man who had been captured after a brush with the police. Surely there was no possible leak, and with his leg in that condition he couldn't get away.

The Scotsman turned over on his side, buried his head on his arm behind drawn shades, and in spite of the heat, set about deliberately plunging himself into a void. Rest was a necessity. He slept at last. It was not a tranquil slumber. Outside the window the last traces of scorching daylight faded to be succeeded by a night no less oppressive. The night advanced. More than once the Scotsman stirred . . . to be aroused by Tannin's stentorian knock at a little after half-past ten. The sergeant was the bearer of news. The Hispano-Suiza had been discovered in a garage on 149th Street. Waring had left it there the day before with a complaint about the ignition, scarcely three quarters of an hour after he took off from the house in Gramercy Square.

To Tannin's astonishment, the inspector received this almost with indifference, pacing the floor like a caged animal, glancing over his shoulder at the windows against which rain swept in a sudden glorious downpour. He had been asleep when the storm began. It had been threatening for hours. Lightning flashed in dazzling zigzags, the gutters began to sing, thunder which had been intermittent and remote burst with a loud clap over their heads.

The thunder did something to McKee. It rolled round with a shattering impact inside his skull as though it had had its inception there, were trying to find its way out. He was standing still in the middle of the familiar room, no longer paying the slightest attention to the sergeant. The telephone was on the desk at the far side. He crossed the rug on the balls of his feet like a man walking a tight rope, forcing himself to walk it, took the receiver off the hook, dialed a number, and when a voice answered he asked flatly for the detective on duty in Room 16 in the nursing home.

Tannin stared at him mystified. The Scotsman was bent double over the phone, cradling the instrument, surrounding it, shoulders hunched, head down, unseeing eyes on the opposite wall. Ten seconds, twenty ticked themselves into oblivion. The detective was the devil of a time answering. The extension phone was only a few feet away from the waiter's door. Tannin moved closer. From the receiver a voice was faintly audible: The voice said: "Just take it easy. That's the ticket." McKee said, "Yes?" softly and listened. After a half-minute he put the receiver back on the hook without the slightest change of expression, stood upright, flicked an invisible speck of dust from his sleeve, and straightened his tie.

Frightened, Tannin cried: "What is it? What's the matter?"

McKee was perfectly calm now. He answered slowly: "That was Caulkins, the precinct man we put outside Silva's room to see that he didn't get away," and didn't say any more.

"Good Lord, Inspector, you mean the waiter escaped?"

McKee's smile was a jerk of wryness across a face cast in metal. "The last flight of all, Sergeant. Our man has taken to his heels for good. His troubles are over. He's dead with two bullets in his body. Caulkins stopped a third with his shoulder. Call Armstrong. We'll have to get up there, and after that examine alibis which will probably be good."

"You think the same person who did this shot Rita?"

"Unquestionably," McKee said and started for the door.

CHAPTER XXIII

ALL DAY Saturday from sunup until sundown the heat had been oppressive. With darkness it became almost unbearable.

The Gairs were giving a party that night. It was one of those informal affairs mushroomed up over the telephone to astonishing proportions in the space of half an hour. "Hello, Anita? You and Tim busy tonight? . . . How about coming around?. . . Splendid. . . . Mrs. Peters? 'Lo, Jan. . . . A crowd there? . . . Good, bring them along." Susan herself called Telfair at around nine o'clock.

The cartoonist hadn't seen anyone since that devastating interview in Judith's apartment the previous night. He had gone home after it, had worked like a dog for fourteen hours, damned good work, too, completing a set of illustrations that had been ordered for months and on the proceeds of which he could afford to take a trip away somewhere.

There was nothing he desired less in the world at the moment than to see either Gerald or Susan Gair. Judith would be there, of course. He didn't ask, gave an excuse instead. Susan wouldn't hear of a refusal, insisted on his coming with a vehemence entirely out of character. She was usually deliberate, almost languid in the conduct of her social life. Her main interests were her home, her husband, her flower garden, her child. Now she said: "But you must, Jim, darling. It's very exciting. There's a detective watching the place. Think how upset he'll be with all this coming and going. Gerry's got a case of champagne, some brandy, and some good Scotch."

Telfair said, "All right," and put the receiver back on the hook. Much better to face the music. It was extremely probable that he and Judith Pierce would meet again and again in the days ahead. They knew pretty well the same people, frequented the same places. Odd how much a pattern life got to be after a while. He might as well show Judith now that he wasn't at all angry, didn't care two whoops in hell with whom she was in love, but simply hated to be played for a sucker.

It was very hot. Susan met him at the door of the apartment. Her eyes were bright. By George, she looked almost pretty, with plenty of make-up on her face and powder veiling her irritated skin. Even the scar scarcely showed. The big living room was crowded. For a sophisticated lot of men and women the atmosphere was distinctly collegiate. Perhaps it was the liquor or the thunder rolling along the horizon. People yelled at him. "If it isn't the big boy! Come on in, old sock. Hello, Telfair, you're a hermit these days. Try the Scotch. Where's your glass?" A pretty girl he had never seen before sat in his lap and made him use her glass. He said, looking over her shoulder: "How would you like to pose for the Puritan maiden, sweetheart?" and she laughed, drummed her heels against his shin bone, asked reproachfully, "Am I as bad as all that? I want some champagne—give me some champagne and I'll show you . . ." And kissed him.

Laughter, noises, drifting groups never still. But the Gairs ran to a young crowd. He had never realized it before. Gerry Gair, big, upstanding, blond, was busy with a tray, in a white silk shirt and white slacks. The talk was incessant. Telfair's head began to ache. A new book, a new play. "Oh, I say—that fellow's rotten." Everything was rotten. Artists, writers, musicians, not yet thirty, their critical judgment was tempered by neither justice nor mercy. They were the ones who were going to compose the great music, write the great books, paint the great pictures.

Telfair began to get more and more bored. Judith was nowhere in sight. The Puritan maiden was lovely—although the title was dubious on two counts. He was relieved when she tired of him and began a tour of the rooms. The apartment was a duplex, and there were two ways of reaching the second floor, by the balcony outside the living room (a glorified fire escape strewn with chairs) and by a staircase out of the dining room. That was at a little before ten. The place was jammed. People kept on coming, but nobody apparently went. Telfair didn't see anyone he knew. Smoke didn't improve the heat-laden air a lot. He felt miserable, but it was necessary to be having a good time when he encountered Judith. He took a little French girl away from a big bruiser with a black mustache by the simple expedient of pulling her head back and clamping his lips on hers. He didn't encounter Judith. She was nowhere in sight.

After that he shed the brunette. He didn't like the perfume in her hair, and her demands in the way of entertainment were too heavy. He would ask Gair where Judith was, in an offhand manner. But Gair, too, was among the missing. He buttonholed a poet just turning away from a clever trick of smashing some light bulbs with a ping-pong ball thrown with his left hand over his right shoulder. "Where's Gerry, Montague?" The poet said: "Gone for more supplies. The gin's all out. But there's a bottle of Bourbon behind the garbage pail in the kitchen. Don't tell anyone else. Come on, I'll show you." Telfair hadn't examined the kitchen yet. Judith wasn't in it. He had a long pull at something that tasted like embalming fluid but had the very opposite effect, interrupted two couples in a darkened alcove, tried the balcony, retreated before a *"Please,* Mr. Hemingway," from a little girl in blue, and went on prowling.

Then his exasperation flamed. Susan had vanished also. Some party, where your host and hostess walked out on you. It was at about ten that the storm broke. Rain splashed the windows, but the booming of thunder overhead was almost drowned by the noise in the apartment. Twenty times in the next hour Telfair decided to go home—and kept putting off the decisive moment. Judith must be somewhere, but if she was here and had gone, Susan would do as well. There were two rooms on the second floor he hadn't examined. An emaciated woman with a ukulele and earrings a yard long whispered to him at the top of the stairs that Susan had passed out. "She's gone to lie down for a little while, poor darling."

Telfair leaned against the wall in the comparative quiet of the upper hall, put a lot of cigarettes end to end and waited for Susan to come out. It was a little after half-past eleven when he lost his temper and rapped on her door. There was no answer. Perhaps she was asleep. Well, asleep or not, he meant to leave his message, "Going away. See you all in the fall," and take himself off. There was no answer to his knock. He turned the knob, stepped into the room, closed the door behind him. The room was empty.

There was another bedroom at the far end of the hall. Perhaps . . . He started to turn away and stood still. Beyond the bed, French windows giving on a balcony stood partly open. Rain spattered the floor in a rough semicircle. Susan was standing just

outside. She hadn't been there a second before. He didn't recognize her at first. She had on a big floppy hat and a tan polo coat.
The hat and coat didn't go well together. All her earlier anima-
tion had vanished. She looked tired. When she saw Telfair she
stepped over the sill, said in an offhand tone that was hurried:
"Oh, it's you, Jim. You retreated, too? Rather a rowdy crowd. I
had to have a breath of air."

They looked at each other, then Susan looked away. Telfair
said heavily, "I've been searching for Judith, I'm——" and was
interrupted by a clear, "Judith Pierce isn't here tonight. She didn't
come." Something in the ringing emptiness with which she pronounced these words bit through Telfair's absorption in his own
dilemma. There was a little pause. Susan Gair took the hat and
coat off, threw them on the wide bed littered with other wraps,
and, turning her back, began to powder her face.

When she didn't speak again, Telfair said: "Really? I didn't
know. Good-night, then, Susan, I think I'll amble." But as he
left the room he was puzzled and a little wary. Susan's slippers,
the bottom of her dress where it hung below the polo coat, were
wringing wet. She had been out for a good deal more than a
breath of air. And Gair was missing, too.

Meanwhile, at the hospital in the Bronx in which Silva had
been confined, routine took its course. Death had come to it in
many forms, but never before in the shape of a bullet delivered
and received—on the premises. Detectives tearing up through
darkness and the tail of the storm to the big granite building
on the hill, built like an "E" with the middle part missing, were
presented with the corpse of the waiter—and with very little
else. Photographs were taken, curt orders rapped out, the Bronx
medical examiner did his work, the borough commander questioned half a hundred frightened people, internes, nurses, near-

by patients, the night supervisor, the janitor; the Bronx district attorney conferred with the commissioner over the telephone, the grounds were searched, in fact the hospital seethed with an activity as thorough as it was useless.

The manner in which the wounded man had been so skillfully eliminated was apparent almost at once. The waiter had been shot through the window, the bullet coming from a lavatory at right angles to the room in which he lay. McKee, driving swiftly up through the rain-swept city, made just one stop. It was to buy a paper. As he had suspected, the secret of the waiter's death lay there, smeared in a two-column spread down the left side. It consisted of an account of the wild taxi ride and the capture, in the grounds of the old Sailors' Home, of a man who had been a waiter in the Sanctuary.

Afterwards the Scotsman was to ponder the incalculable arrangements of chance. If the little student nurse who was on duty when Green was brought in hadn't had a cousin in the law department, so that she had recognized the district attorney; if she had had straight instead of curly hair, brown eyes instead of blue—the young legman on the tabloid wouldn't have fallen for her. If the day following Silva's arrest hadn't been her day off, if a friend hadn't lent the reporter a car to go riding in . . . a man's life might have been spared. But spilt milk—no, another commoner fluid—had to be written off as finished business and the case brought to as swift a conclusion as possible.

They reached the hospital. McKee forced himself out of the car in the sergeant's eager wake. All this was a farce, and yet—drain the bitter cup to the dregs, roll the dregs over his tongue. The case had been shot to pieces under him. Build another. Vital need for speed now, but not for haste. No ordinary crime, this; but he had known that from the first moment in the Sanctuary.

In the dim and silent hall the Bronx medical examiner and the borough commander took themselves wearily from a bench against the wall, produced their findings with savage brevity. One bullet had been extracted from Silva's chest. It had been fired from a .32-caliber revolver. The lavatory from which the waiter had been shot was a washout. To the left there was a staircase leading down to the courtyard by way of a little side door. This staircase was used by doctors and by people visiting patients. And although the place had been emptied of these visitors by ten o'clock, the killer had run practically no risk at any time. For it was not at all odd to see a strange man or woman wandering around the corridors waiting for admittance to a room where father, mother, son, or daughter was dangerously ill. At the end of all this the borough commander put a question: "Want to see him?" Tannin shrugged, but McKee answered "Yes," curtly.

They went upstairs. In the narrow room with the gray walls, the window was open, rain still falling softly outside. A nurse drew back the sheet. McKee stared down. The little South American was nothing below that rigid profile but a gleaming bronze bust, its smooth surface cruelly shattered by what looked like red wax coming out in two places just under the heart. The sergeant turned away with a shiver, but McKee stood there for a long moment looking down, his face almost as stony as the one flat on the mattress now, turned towards the ceiling.

Caulkins after that, the detective who had been wounded in the shoulder while on duty in the room, by the same gun that eliminated the waiter. Caulkins was farther down the hall, propped high on pillows. He was conscious, but in some considerable pain. His forehead glistened with sweat, and a faint odor of chloroform still clung to his skin. McKee asked for and received a short account of what had taken place.

He had come on duty at eight o'clock, relieving Detective Judd, had remained in the room all evening. At nine an interne came, bandaged the waiter's wound, and went away. He was followed by a nurse who took the patient's temperature, rubbed his back with alcohol, gave him water, arranged the bedclothes for the night. After that——

McKee interrupted with a question: "How were the lights in the room?"

"There were two lights, Inspector—a bulb in the ceiling and a lamp. The bulb in the ceiling was only on while the doctor was fixing him up. The lamp was lit all the time, but it shouldn't have kept him from sleeping, because it had a thick shade."

The Scotsman envisaged the scene with stony eyes. A rabbit in a trap, a helpless target in flesh and bone (such vulnerable stuff) plainly visible through the window. "Go on, Caulkins."

"At around ten the thunder and lightning got worse. The storm seemed to bother Green. At around half-past ten, I heard St. Malachi's Church clock chime once. There was a terrific fusillade of thunder. Green jerked up in bed just after the crash. He opened his eyes and mouth wide. I was sitting in a rocker near the foot of the bed. I heard the whine of the bullet when it went past my ear . . . but I was a little slow on the trigger jumping up."

McKee's smile didn't even faintly resemble mirth. "For which, Caulkins, you can thank your lucky star."

"Yes. I ran around to him. He fell over on his side, and a jet of blood shot into the air, and I felt my shoulder burn and knew I had been shot, too. I fell over him and must have passed out, because when I woke up he was dead and the covers were all messed up and sticky, the door opened and a nurse came in and screamed, and a doctor came and took me to the phone. You were calling." It was all Caulkins had to tell.

McKee and Tannin drove back to the office. Then began that business, in even more deadly earnest now, of checking up on all those people. It was a long and difficult job, and the results were astonishing. Not more so, however, than the Scotsman had expected. From the moment when that group of visitors had converged in Rita's apartment after she was killed, he had been looking for trouble. Well—there was plenty of that.

Shadowing, so lightly passed over in newspaper accounts of police activities, is a really difficult job and not always attended with success. At best it is incomplete and, when it breaks down, is a boomerang. A clever man or woman bent on losing a shadow can always manage to slip through the net. Knowing that he had been watched, he can say: "You had a man tailing me, didn't you? He can testify that I was in such and such a place at such and such a time." But walls are not made of glass, and it would take a young army to stop up every exit from a given house, exits in some cases not even known to the detective on duty.

As far as the reports of men engaged in this uncomfortable pastime that night went—McKee pulled sheet after sheet towards him and studied the results with a derisive smile. The Gairs were giving a party. Mr. and Mrs. Philip Barcley had remained at home during the early part of the evening except for an excursion Barcley made for the purpose of exercising a Russian wolfhound kept in the house. At around nine o'clock they had gone to a reception at one of New York's smartest hotels, where a Mrs. Hamilton Reich was giving a farewell supper dance on the eve of her sailing for her villa at Eze. Judith Pierce was at the movies during the crucial three hours. In fact, they were all playing tricks, tricks bound up inextricably with the dancer's death. After careful study, McKee pulled Barcley's record towards him and went over it again. Mr. Barcley's walk at around eight-thirty interested him. West on Sixty-eighth, south to Sixty-sixth, across Lexington, where he had stopped in a florist's shop to buy some orchids which Mrs. Barcley wore later to the reception. . . . A florist's shop! Not a drugstore . . . but the shop would have a phone, even though there wasn't any sign outside. McKee went to work. With the result that some half-hour later he and Tannin were speeding north through the cool darkness of the early hours of Sunday morning. Barcley had telephoned. It was a long-distance call. And it had been made to a house in Fairfield, overlooking Long Island Sound and belonging to a widowed sister, at that time in Europe, of Colonel Waring. Waring and Archer had already been traced as far as the Greyhound bus in Larchmont. The conclusion was obvious. The bus ran up into Connecticut. Fairfield was about twenty miles farther along.

CHAPTER XXIV

AND WHEN they got there the house was empty. Before they left New York it had been surrounded by the state police. Again and again during that ride, Tannin, stirring in his corner, had seen McKee glancing at his watch. He had on the way up taken a wide swing east so as to pass the hospital where Silva had been killed. As they went through gates and up an overgrown driveway where dandelions were golden buttons sprouting through gravel, he snapped his watch shut, dropped it back into his pocket. The journey had taken exactly (from the building in which the little South American's body still lay) an hour and ten minutes. Which amounted precisely to this: if Barcley had telephoned to the colonel at half-past eight (and they all knew then of Silva's confinement in the hospital in the Bronx), both Waring and Archer had been drawn sharply back into the picture. Some one of the people involved in Rita's murder had killed Silva, and these two men could just as easily have driven south from Connecticut as any one of the others could have driven north from Manhattan. They had plenty of time.

Routine work, performed mechanically. The two men got out in a circular sweep below a long white house faintly visible in starlight. A state trooper stepped forward, made his report. They had arrived at one-twenty. The place seemed deserted—at any rate, there were no lights. An admirable country home, secluded, neat. The flowering shrubs needed pruning. They went in through a pantry window. Caution was entirely unnecessary, the birds had flown: There was plenty of evidence of their having been there, traces of food in the blue-and-white kitchen, two beds in an upstairs room still unmade, but no indication of what time they had left the house.

A station wagon was missing from the garage. McKee put various agencies in movement, dropped into a chair in front of the fire in the living room, would have seemed asleep except that his eyes were wide open on tarnished andirons. Rita and her past with which one of these people was connected? The Archer yacht anchored in the harbor at Barranquilla, Colombia; the exact date was indeterminate, but sometime in the spring of 1926. And it was in April that Silva had been captured in a shack fifty miles up country at Costa de Muerte. Donaher would arrive here tomorrow. Tonight, Kingston. At seven in the morning the forty-passenger Sikorsky flying boat would leave for the longest over-water flight in the world, six hours to Barranquilla, where he would be met by a local agent of Scadta, a Colombian-German syndicate, and whirled into the mountains. But that was a long time away, and a great deal could happen here in New York while the lieutenant was busy digging up whatever fragments of Rita's history he could unearth, Rita and her dead husband and Silva and that shadowy fourth man or woman. Some one of the people was playing possum behind more than half a dozen obliterating years and a battery of lies and evasions.

He pronounced their names aloud in the silent room, making the sergeant jump. "Count them, Tannin: Barcley, Mrs. Barcley, Waring, Gregory Archer, Judith Pierce, and Gerald Gair. All of them with money, all people who have traveled, all——" The shrill ringing of a phone in the hall cut him off.

It was the Homicide Office calling. Waring had turned up at the Barcley house in Sixty-eighth Street in the missing station wagon, was waiting for the Barcleys when they themselves arrived home at a quarter of two. Waring was alone. Archer was not with him. What were the inspector's orders?

"Have them tell the colonel," McKee called languidly from his chair, "where I am." And when the sergeant came back into the room, "I'm sure he'll be anxious to see me. There are so many explanations to be made. The colonel will want to do that. He's a plausible fellow. We'll have a visit from him, Tannin, before very long. It will pass the time. Look for Archer ourselves as soon as it's morning."

As usual, he was right. Dawn was washing the world back into view behind the windowpanes, gnarled apple branches were being threaded with new leaves, a glimpse of the Sound over their crests, when a car climbed the driveway and came to a stop outside. Tannin brought the colonel in.

Waring was a changed man, or a remarkably good actor.

His face was gray, burnt out, and he dropped heavily into a chair opposite the inspector's and seemed to have some difficulty with his vocal cords, had to clear his throat twice before he could speak. He didn't hedge now, said with hoarse directness: "I have a statement to make."

McKee smiled without moving. "That's splendid, Colonel. We've been waiting to hear from you for some time."

Waring ignored the jibe, brushed it away with a wave of his hand. "It has been a terrible night, terrible, but perhaps I'd better begin at the beginning so that you will understand. I brought

Gregory Archer up here to this house on the day after the dancer was killed down in the speakeasy. I knew that he was innocent, but he was in no shape, either mentally or physically, to be
questioned by the police."

"You mean," McKee interrupted softly, "that he's a dipsoma-
niac, was in the grip of a terrific hangover and . . . might blurt
out things that would be prejudicial to him?"

"I . . . he . . . well, he's very young. He does drink too much.
But——"

"How old is Gregory Archer, Colonel?"

"Twenty-nine."

"I should scarcely call him a boy. You're his guardian?"

"Co-guardian and executor of his father's estate with the
Bennington Trust Company." You could feel wariness back of his
big spare frame.

"And when does Gregory Archer legally come into control of
his heritage?"

"When he's thirty."

"Had he married in the meantime without the consent of the
trustees . . . what?"

"The bulk of the estate would have gone to various charities.
He would have been left with the interest of a small residue to
live on."

"In case of his death, who would benefit?"

Waring looked as though he were going to protest what he
evidently considered meaningless questions, changed his mind.
"The aforementioned charities and myself."

"Nothing would go to his mother?"

"Claire was left amply provided for when her husband died.
Barcley himself is a wealthy man."

McKee abandoned this subject abruptly. "You say that Archer

had been drinking and that you wanted to get him back on his feet. How did you go about it, Colonel? You didn't cut off his supply completely, did you?"

"I'm not a fool."

"I see. You rationed him after you got here. And yet the whisky glass on the tray beside the bottle down in your library in the house in Gramercy Square was clean. You didn't consider that he needed a touch before starting out on that journey?"

Suddenly the colonel was shouting in the stillness of a room broken only by the laced call of birds beyond the windows. "Isn't this all very absurd? I came here at a considerable trouble to tell you something and you won't listen. He's gone. He got away. We don't know where he is now. We're worried. When I came back to this house at seven o'clock tonight after going over to town for some food, he wasn't here."

And his bloodshot eyes were cold as he watched the effect of this, red veins mottling his fleshy cheeks. The Scotsman, rousing himself lazily, asked a number of questions. To which Waring replied that when he entered the upstairs bedroom Archer wasn't in it; that he hadn't the slightest notion where he'd gone, that he himself had driven back to the city in a Ford station wagon belonging to his sister——

"After," McKee murmured, "you had that telephone call from Barcley telling you all the news. You wouldn't get an evening paper here, naturally. Wouldn't know about what was going on. You wouldn't care to repeat the substance of that telephone talk?"

All trace of emotion suddenly vanished from Waring's face. He rose without haste, picked up his hat and stick, and said: "I have told you the truth about Gregory. I can do no more. You don't seem inclined to help us find him. Very well, we will have to take what steps we can ourselves."

That was at twenty minutes to six on the morning of May twenty-fourth.

Fairfield County is one of the richest in the state of Connecticut. Great estates lie flung over the tumbling hills in every direction. New York has invaded it here and there, but an occasional oasis lingers where the country people relax only among themselves or with "city folks" who have lived there for a long time. The colonel and his sister were old residents, and Gregory Archer had spent a good many summers with them in that remodeled farmhouse within sight of the shore. Archer had to be found. Tannin worked hard that Sunday morning gathering information, as a result of which McKee, in an entirely different suit of clothes which had been sent up from New York, took a stroll at a little after eleven when the air was still full of the lingering sound of church bells.

Beyond the post office was a field where daisies were tight buds in high grass and, opposite this field and before you come to the Inn, there was a very impressive building of white stucco with four pillars and a stained-glass window either side of the front door. This was the establishment and home of Mr. Edward Bell, among other things an ardent fisherman.

A stranger, if he wanted to see Mr. Bell, would have gone up steps between these pillars. McKee didn't. He strolled around to the side, nodded carelessly to a tall, weedy individual doing, in spite of the Sabbath, some excellent spadework in a garden, and said: "Nice-looking potatoes you've got there. Ed at home?"

"Yeah, he's looking for a call—go on in."

McKee pushed open a small door to the left of commodious garages, found himself in a large room with an organ in one corner, two handsome ferns in jardinières on a wide sill, Axminster rugs, three overstuffed chairs, and a sofa. There were doors at either end. He went through the one on his right, was in a small bar office. The office was empty. He thrust his head down some cellar stairs, didn't hear anything, and tapped on another door beyond. A voice drawled, "Come ahead," and the Scotsman obeyed the invitation.

There were two men in the room into which he stepped. It was a strange place. There was a great deal of plate glass running from floor to ceiling, and behind the plate glass a number of handsome and imposing caskets were ranged in rows. McKee picked Bell out unerringly, small, dark, neat, with a chubby face, a man of sixty-eight who didn't look a day over forty. He was in the act, with the help of his assistant, of pushing a newly arrived coffin into its niche, had in fact paused a moment before to examine the fluted satin interior with a glance of admiration.

He sprang like a soldier to attention at McKee's entrance, but McKee said: "I'm a friend of Greg Archer's. I've often heard him speak of you. I was passing and I thought I'd look in." Bell relaxed, put a half-smoked cigar back between his teeth, and held out his hand. "Pleased to meet any friend of Greg's. You're Mr. . . . ?"

McKee ignored the question, put his shoulder against a narrow strip of wall, felt for a cigarette, and asked with interest: "How's business?"

He had struck the right note. Bell's face creased itself into lines of satisfaction. He said confidentially: "Looking up. Getting better. We had two last week, one yesterday, and we're expecting another now at any moment. Look out for that corner, Elmer. That-a-baby." The casket slid smoothly into place.

McKee discarded his cigarette, offered the undertaker a cigar, lit one himself, and pursued his inquiries. Bell and Archer were fast friends and ardent fishermen. If anyone would know his whereabouts, this man ought to. And in the country things get around. He explained that Archer had promised him a spot of eeling; had said he would be at the house on the shore this week, but that when he arrived Archer wasn't at home. "Although I'm sure he was in town yesterday."

Bell was at first hurt and then informative. "That's right. I thought he might be up, because I did see the colonel around a couple of times, met him in the drugstore yesterday evening, but I didn't get to speak to him. The eels are running good now. Lemme see where you might find Greg . . ." There was a chap named George Buckley who did for the colonel's sister, looking over the place while she was away—he ran a little trucking business, but did odd jobs on the side. George had a boat. He lived over at the station. "Turn left at the railroad bridge, dead-end street, little red house on the right."

McKee shook hands cordially with the undertaker and left the shop. The words "drugstore" and "colonel" had sent a little tingle along his spine. Sending Tannin to cover that end, he went in search of George Buckley. He left the Cadillac at the station and walked down a narrow lane. Insects sang loudly in the grass. Trees were waving masses of green against a pale sky. He thought of a lot of things. The persistence of Archer's flight, the way he was being helped by his people. And yet it wasn't such a bad idea, would never have done in the case of a poor man, but with shekels to grease the wheels, put gas in the tank, buy faithful help, he could vanish indefinitely, holding the case in status quo until such time as pursuit slackened and fresh crime and violence engaged the attention of the authorities.

There was no one in the little red house. It was locked up tight. A lean-to at the back that served as a garage was empty. The Scotsman shopped around the neighborhood. Cottages stood back under trees, in straggling yards. George lived with his father (his mother was dead), and the old man "took a drop." They didn't get on very well together—which didn't matter, but what did was: George had not been home the night before and had gone off in his truck at about nine o'clock, and, "might have been trekking out to that camp of his that he's building up in the hills."

After that McKee drove across to the state troopers' barracks in record time. Clear as crystal now what had happened. Barcley had found out by inquiry at the garage where the Hispano was cached (this was afterwards verified) that the police were on Archer's trail. He had phoned Waring, and that interesting young man's base had been shifted—with considerable skill. In the barracks McKee asked questions, bent over a map. No one knew quite where the camp was situated except that it must be out Redding way. He didn't wait for Tannin, who was still gathering information about the colonel. A half-hour later, with a trooper who knew the country beside him on the seat, he left the village behind. That ride was memorable—in more ways than one.

At first the going wasn't bad, a dirt road between fields with farmhouses dotting it. Then at an intersection they turned sharp left into a narrow lane ribbed with rock that the Town Council had the impudence to call Bayberry Avenue. Bayberry Avenue dropped straight into a narrow valley between high hills that shut out the light on either side. The farther you went the worse it got.

Presently the Cadillac dropped to a walk, nosing around blind turns, branches slapping the windows; was at one moment threading the lip of a precipice with a sheer drop of a hundred feet to a rocky gorge below (the upper reaches of the Saugatuck), at another, negotiating a stretch of marsh in green gloom, where rotten planks were a makeshift bridge. Their gait was now about ten miles an hour and fast at that.

McKee controlled himself with an effort. All this backing and filling and dragging information from people who didn't want to give it had taken time. And time, from the beginning, had been of extreme importance in the progress of this case. Everybody involved was fighting for it—the police included— but they had a different end in view. It was almost four o'clock when they left the barracks, and here in the valley dusk was beginning to sift down. He went on thinking. Rita and her wide-flung web! She had overstepped herself on that last night. Her greed was too much for her. She wanted Archer, and she wanted the emerald. Archer had brought Waring and Mr. and Mrs. Barcley to the Sanctuary, and the desire to regain the stone (for which Rita had resorted to blackmail) had brought the Gairs and Judith Pierce. Silva was already on her trail—and Silva was dead.

He turned to the more immediate problem. If those sub-pœnas were to be of any use at all, the whole cast would have to be assembled tomorrow morning—and that wasn't very long away. Impenetrable shields of green hemmed the car in, ash, oak, maple, ironwood, and slim white birches looming through gray-ness, all choked with underbrush. More than once they passed a camp buried in the trees. Each time, after a brief scrutiny, the trooper shook his head. But as twilight deepened, even he be-gan to lose hope. He said: "I haven't been out this way in a year. The road empties into another valley farther along. We ought to reach Buckley's place soon." And they did. And it was up a mountain side.

They came quite suddenly on a dilapidated farmhouse, minus one wall, crouched under two mangy pines in the shadow of a

cliff, and a woman washing clothes in the last of the light directed them with a fling of her thumb straight, apparently, into the
skies. "George Buckley's got a camp there." They couldn't take a
car. It was what she said as they turned away, squeezing soapsuds
out of gray flannel against a washboard, staring at them with
dull eyes, that sent the Scotsman bounding towards the path:

"I ain't seen him in quite a spell. He must be using the other
road."

The trooper objected to running. He objected still more to
climbing, but climbing, and running and talking at the same
time were too much for him. He did manage to gasp out, in that
precipitous journey up the flank of the hill, that ". . . maybe you
could get in from the east, but it would be a long trek across
country, past the Devil's Den and Chickawaw."

Branches lashed their faces treacherously out of dusk, vines
tangled their feet. But presently the trees began to thin, they
were almost at the top, and now you could see, in the faint af-
terglow, a wide moor with a glimpse of something that might be
the Sound on the horizon. They were on the cabin almost before
it was visible.

Buckley had chosen well. The view in daylight ought to be
magnificent. It was perched on the shoulder of the young mountain and half buried in laurel. But it was closed, shuttered and
lifeless. They broke in. Ship lamps of bright brass hung on the
walls of the big central room. The trooper lighted one (it was
full of kerosene). They went through the place rapidly. The cabin
contained, besides, two small bedrooms and a tiny kitchen, complete with an oil stove and ice box. The stove gave them valuable information. It had been used a short time before; the metal
shield of one burner was still warm. But that wasn't what interested the inspector most.

In the fireplace in the living room there was a half-burned log. The hearth was very neat, but off to one side a scrap of whiteness had escaped the flames. McKee picked it up, to stand very still, turning it over in his fingers. It was half of a small envelope such as druggists use, empty and with the edges charred. The trooper looked his curiosity, but the Scotsman merely said, pocketing the exhibit, "We've got to get out of here—we've got to get back to town."

They didn't even bother to close the door behind them.

CHAPTER XXV

"GEORGE HAS a boat." That was what the undertaker had said. As to where the boat was now, that was easily answered. It was in the yacht basin at Compo Beach, a thirty-foot cabin cruiser, and a trooper was over there now watching it. Nevertheless McKee was uneasy on that journey back to town. This futile trip with failure at the end had consumed almost three hours. And the cabin in the hills was only a mile across country from the Sound.

He took time to ruminate with wonder on the determined effort to keep Archer away from the police. Barcley, Mrs. Barcley, Waring, and now George Buckley had all assisted in the little game of hide and seek. It couldn't go on forever. The two men had quitted the shack in the woods only a short time before they themselves entered it. They couldn't have gotten very far. Back at the barracks his heavy brooding erupted into action. Men were sent scouring the roads, beating the fields. Tannin was waiting for him with information.

As far as the question of drugs went, Waring had gotten a prescription filled the night before. It consisted of pills, a comparatively harmless mixture of morphine and atropine. "I went to see a doctor, boss. He says they give it to people in pain, or to nervous women, anyone who's upset and has got to be quieted." So much for that. McKee fingered the scrap of paper that he had picked up from the fireplace thoughtfully, turned to the various reports that had come in. One commanded his sudden attention.

At six o'clock Mr. Buckley, senior, who "took a drop," returned home from a day's jaunt obviously the worse for over a gallon of hard cider. (There was a two-gallon jug in the back of his car— more than half empty.) Interviewed by a trooper watching the house, he said that he didn't know where his son was and cared less. He was goin' eelin'. And he did, in a rowboat, with the remainder of the cider and some worms for bait, intoning a ribald song and splashing up the river. The trooper let him go and kept on watching the house.

McKee was across the floor of the little room at the back of the barracks in two bounds, studying a map hung on the wall. The Saugatuck emptied into the Sound. It was dark. The old man could easily have turned around and gone downstream. He didn't wait for anything more. Instantly they were in the Cadillac speeding east.

The yacht basin at Compo Beach is a horseshoe curve bitten out of mud flats and opens on an inlet into which the river runs. Summer cottages flank the approach. At the entrance there is a booth in which a town constable sits watching all nonresidents who attempt to go in. The trooper sent to keep an eye on Buckley's boat was with him.

As Tannin and McKee loomed out of the night both men assured the inspector that Buckley hadn't turned up. The booth was about a hundred feet from the yacht basin. The Scotsman fairly raced along pebbly shale to the steps and the landing float. Speedboats, sailboats, a yawl, two small yachts, some canoes, half a dozen rowboats, but to the left, where Buckley's cabin cruiser should have been, there was nothing but a stretch of black water. The boat was gone.

The Scotsman's fury and haste vanished as abruptly as they had arisen. He stood motionless on the edge of the float swaying gently under the surge of the incoming tide, and while the constable and trooper stared aghast he murmured to Tannin: "'One if by land and two if by sea.' What we really wanted was a Paul Revere. They've been too clever for us again. This thing was well planned. Waring turned Archer over to Buckley after that telephone call from Barcley, Buckley promptly took him out to the cabin in the woods. As soon as it began to get dark they went across country to the Sound. Buckley's father in the meanwhile, obeying orders, rowed over here, got the cruiser away, and has by this time picked them up."

"They can't . . ." the sergeant was profane . . . "keep this up indefinitely."

McKee answered, his voice a mere thread: "Tomorrow will be a new day. All these people expect to clear themselves then, to be done with the police. I should say offhand that they are expecting to travel. That boat of Buckley's has speed and staying power. The Barcley yacht is anchored off Brielle about seventy-five miles from here. That's nice, that's fine. I think we'll see this time that we're in the right place at the right moment."

And on that, abruptly he left the shore. The drive back to New York was accomplished in complete silence. The sergeant was very tired. Back at the office he dropped into a chair, chewed a dead cigar morosely, and listened to McKee's questions and answers into the telephone. It was the slow, dogged creep and feel of this inquiry, the fret of detail, that bothered Tannin. A chase he could have entered into with zest.

The Scotsman on the contrary was oddly jubilant and alert. Donaher almost in Colombia, word from him soon. He called the commissioner, Armstrong, and the Marine Division of the Detective Bureau, turned to the reports that were waiting, skimmed these, paused at one dealing with the activities of the Barcleys and the Gairs early that afternoon. Barcley and the colonel had gone to the Gair apartment. He meditated this with a slow smile. Easy to see what that was about!

Gerald Gair had been quite definite in his statement as to his own and other people's whereabouts in the Sanctuary the night Rita was killed. He had stated, for instance, that Mrs. Barcley was alone at her table, that Waring had already left it, that he himself had just gotten up to go to the telephone booth when the dancer dropped. Now they were making a deal. Roughly it would run to Gair's, "I feel now that I was mistaken. The colonel and Mrs. Barcley were together when the shot was fired," and to Waring's, "Mr. Gair was sitting near us. He couldn't have had anything to do with it, because I had him in plain view all the time."

In other words, they would erase their previous testimony, and the police would be left holding the bag—a situation by no means new. It was just this that was bungling the case up now, the necessity for proof. Hour after hour McKee turned papers, studied notes, reassembled the various groups like a child rolling marbles in his palm. Monday morning now. At six, when dawn was graying the east, he sent out for coffee and sandwiches, to glance at the calendar with a frown as he consumed them. His morning at the line-up. Tannin went to bed. McKee went down to headquarters.

A stream of men converging from all parts of the city, on all sorts of errands. The elevator, the line-up room, chairs ranged side by side in dimness. (Beyond the windows it was full day, but here night still prevailed.) The room was already crowded. Detectives checking in, the aisles on the right jammed with waiting prisoners. A platform at the front with steps on either side. Klieg lights beat down on this platform with a merciless glare. The voice of the examining officer, majestic out of an amplifier, Jove-like, level, pouncing without menace. Assistant Chief Inspector Mulligan, in an elevated chair hidden from gaze by the blanketing of shadows, as he examined the flotsam and jetsam that the night had washed up.

McKee watched a bank robber make his impudent plea, withdrew, half slept, his brown eyes hooded. The bank robber's place was taken by an automobile thief, three confidence men, a janitor's assistant, a colored boy of about nineteen. Mulligan's voice bit through the silence.

"Where did you get this gun?"

The Scotsman sat up abruptly. He was to say later, "It was in my mind; I couldn't be sure, of course, but it had to be somewhere." Now he simply stared. Theodore Quinillan would have made his fortune on the stage. The question was repeated. "Where did you get that gun?"

Quinillan on the platform blinked in the glare, ran a red-tipped tongue around pale lips in dark flesh, was innocent with the peculiar pleading guile of his race, took a step forward, was ordered back, threw up his hand cried: "Before God, boss, I picked it up in the alley. I was just standing there when she dropped it. She threw it away. She didn't want it no more. She was a white lady, that was all I could see. She just walked off. I swear before . . ." McKee didn't wait to hear any more. He was already moving past some empty chairs and swiftly down the aisle.

In the Ballistics Bureau, Stutz was peering through a micro-scope at a fragment of shell when the Scotsman spoke to him. The lieutenant got up with a smile of pleasure. It changed to a frown of concentration when McKee said: "I've got a hunch. There's a gun been taken from a Negro in the line-up. They gathered him in last night in Harlem."

"Still on the Sanctuary murder, Inspector?"

"Still on the Sanctuary murder, Lieutenant."

Stutz got busy. As a matter of course all weapons brought into headquarters are discharged on the pistol range and the results filed away for references. They simply hadn't yet gotten round to this particular weapon. Stutz picked it up. It was a thirty-two Colt, and Silva had been shot with a thirty-two.

"I'll give her the works."

Four slugs still cumbered the chambers, little messengers of death; in this case, as Stutz pulled the trigger and fired, they buried themselves one after another in a target less vulnerable than the complicated structure called man. Before the echoes died the ballistics man retrieved them and continued with his investigation. The bullets that had killed Silva were here, tagged and dated. He got one out, placed the test bullet beside it, bent over the table. In the Scotsman's mind the conclusion was foregone, nevertheless a little thrill ran along his spine when Stutz raised his head at last, said (and no man could be more careful):

"The bull's eye, Inspector. You're right. This is the gun that killed the waiter."

With a swift, "Thousand thanks, old man, I'll see you later," McKee started out of the room. That was at about a quarter of nine. The meeting in the assistant district attorney's office was for twelve.

CHAPTER XXVI

MULTUM IN parvo. So much in so little. So many people poured into so confined a space. Lives all tied up in a knot because of a woman's beauty and her greed. They were about to be untied. The assistant district attorney's office had not about it any appearance of drama that morning. Sunlight bright outside the windows, tall towers rearing themselves against the sky. Within, gleam of mahogany, efficiency-plus in the very latest equipment, a desk like a battleship, other desks, a stenographer waiting, chairs in a row, the commissioner already there, Armstrong, a plainclothes-man at the door admitting the various actors.

Mr. and Mrs. Barcley arrived first, punctual to the minute. Mrs. Barcley wore a gray suit trimmed with fur. In spite of clev-erly applied make-up, her face was lined and old in the shad-ow of a small hat. Barcley, for all his alertness, looked tired, too. Waring was on their heels. He had recovered most of his aplomb. The Gairs were next. They bore themselves well and with no more stiffness than a rather disagreeable job warranted. There was a low murmur of casual greetings as they all sat down. The girl was last. Her eyes were very bright as she came in. Su-san Gair happened to be busy with her purse as Judith Pierce dropped into a chair beside Gair, so that she didn't turn her head. Anyhow Armstrong was on his feet explaining the formalities. Precise words had a meaningless ring to them coming from behind his thin lips. ". . . in order that we may have your signed statements, so that by sifting the evidence we can establish the identity of the murderer of Rita Rodriguez . . ." He kept glancing at the door, showed openly his relief when it opened and Inspector McKee walked into the room.

Something of the showman about McKee. Tall, lean as a rake, he nodded to the commissioner, to Armstrong, seated himself slowly behind an empty desk, fingered some withered flowers in his buttonhole absently, took them out, turned to the stenographer, said: "May I have a glass of water, Miss Stillson?" And when in the midst of a dead silence she brought it to him from the cooler, he arranged four white sweet peas with elaborate care. Armstrong was staring at him with a frown. Carey was watching, slim, interested, thoughtful behind lightly folded arms. McKee said to the district attorney: "We'll come to these later." And the hearing was resumed.

One by one their previous statements were read to each man and woman in the room with a windup of "Is this correct?" Just as McKee expected, Gair wished to change his testimony. He was apologetic. In the confusion following the dancer's death he had made certain statements which he felt were not . . . He went on with it: "Mrs. Barcley and the colonel were talking together when Rita was shot."

Then Waring rose and eliminated Gair from the picture with the same regret at having been mixed up in his statement to the police on that first night. Armstrong glanced at McKee. The Scotsman shook his head. The girl was last. Not a single question asked about her eventful journey across that ten feet of space between the kitchen and the mahogany barrier at the front of the garden just before Rita died. The stenographer put down the sheet of paper. McKee leaned forward, arms out across the desk, one hand playing with the glass of water, and began to speak.

"We will leave the dancer for a moment and go back to Carlos Silva who was shot on Saturday night in the middle of a thunderstorm. Our knowledge of this man is somewhat vague. But we have a few interesting mementoes." He took in succession various objects from his pockets, spread them out on the blotter in the most leisurely manner. The first was the emerald, burning brilliantly in the sunlight, the second was the black box with its gruesome little burden, the third was the bit of jade. He went on in his unhurried voice: "This much we can say positively: Silva knew the dancer in South America. He stole a valuable collection of emeralds from the mine in Colombia, of which he was a trusted employee, was caught and imprisoned. What happened to the rest of the stones we don't know, but this one which was in the dancer's possession belonged to the collection. If we could establish the link between a third person, a third person who was mixed up with Silva and also with Rita Rodriguez in that exceedingly profitable little adventure . . . would you all be prepared to establish and swear to your whereabouts in the fall of 1925 and the spring of 1926?"

He had certainly succeeded in getting their combined attention. Every shade of astonishment, incredulity, and at last indignation was painted on various faces. Gair, Waring, and Barcley protested at almost the same moment. They had been requested to come here to verify statements made in the Sanctuary on the night of the murder. This was going a bit too far. No one of them, and the women nodded assent to this, had ever heard of Silva.

"And yet," McKee said dreamily when the outburst had died,

"the same killer disposed of both Rita and the little Colombian. Well." He ignored the men now, sitting tense and enraged, glanced very deliberately first at Claire Barcley, then at Susan Gair, and lastly at Judith Pierce. "The gun that killed Silva has turned up. It was thrown away last night in Harlem in the alley of a tenement in which a colored cook lay dead. These flowers are from her funeral wreath. She has lived out for years, has a long record of service behind her. Some woman who employed her at one time or another went up there with a wreath of white sweet peas and took advantage of that out-of-the-way spot to get rid of an extremely damaging piece of evidence." He paused. There wasn't a murmur in the room.

The Scotsman sighed, leaning back in his chair. He went on in a listless voice: "Unfortunately this colored cook has no relatives, and it will take time to dig up the list of her various employers. So for the present, if no one has anything more of interest to communicate . . ."

They couldn't believe that it was over, had braced themselves for an ordeal with a fortitude that was not apparently going to be required. It left them confused, up in the air. Not a single question about Gregory Archer, about the various suspicious details that had cropped up during the investigation, not even a word as to the future—that was perhaps the worst. Simply a request that the individual statements be signed, which was done stiffly. And then the room cleared and the district attorney and the commissioner and McKee were alone.

It was a long interview and not satisfactory to Armstrong. Carey, watching the Scotsman narrowly, was sure he had something up his sleeve, a card he wasn't at the moment ready to play, perhaps because he didn't have enough evidence. He was silent, too, in the face of the district attorney's protest about Donaher's useless flight to Colombia. That was being made for the purpose of gathering the truth about Silva in order to make him speak— and Silva was dead.

McKee dwelt at some length on the third visitor to Rita's apartment on the night of her death. The girl had confessed she was there, had mentioned that sound in the living room after she entered and before the police arrived. Silva was at that time hidden in the bathroom watching her movements, so it must have been someone else. As for Archer, McKee said with a shrug that he was being taken to the yacht anchored off the Barcley estate on the New Jersey coast, where no doubt his father and mother and the colonel would join him as soon as they considered it safe.

"And what," Armstrong demanded bitterly, "are we to do while we're waiting for him to turn up? Sit and twiddle our thumbs until somebody breaks down and confesses?"

"Keep," McKee answered, "those signed statements nice and safe. I have a notion we're going to need them—when Donaher gets back. There are half a dozen things I want to check up on. I'll be in touch." And with that he was gone.

A lull then. Monday afternoon, Monday night, Tuesday morning. The police knew a good many things, surmised others. The river police had failed to locate Archer. No trace of the thirty-foot cruiser anywhere along the coast. It had slipped under cover and was waiting for darkness to make a run for it. The yacht was still anchored off Brielle. She couldn't move ten feet without being instantly hailed and boarded. So that with that particular trap baited all they had to do was wait. Which the Scotsman proceeded to do with masterly decision.

Not so the people involved in Rita's death. After having answered those subpoenas by appearing in the assistant district attorney's office, they evidently considered themselves free to return to a normal existence. The Gairs had gone to their country place; Judith Pierce moved about the city—she went shopping, she visited friends. From hour to hour McKee received the most precise information about the girl. On Tuesday afternoon he had a long telephone call from Armstrong.

The district attorney had succeeded in tracing the man in the taxicab waiting outside the Sanctuary for Rita on the Tuesday night before her death. And at once the Barcleys and Waring were drawn sharply back into the limelight. For Claire Barcley, in the absence of her husband and worried about her son (he was spending a great deal of money), had hired the Bascomb detective agency (a rather shoddy firm but working under a state license) to trail Gregory Archer and Rita Rodriguez. Bascomb had come forward. And the substance of Bascomb's information was that he had discovered that Archer and the dancer were on the eve of marriage and that the Barcleys and Waring had gone by appointment with Rita herself to the Sanctuary in an attempt to buy her off.

Armstrong began to argue it exactly at the other end of the wire. "If, McKee, Waring was the man who dropped the cigarette ash behind the screen in her dressing room—and there was a man there—it would indicate that the interview came off, that the dancer refused to give Archer up, and that one of the three of them, Barcley, was in the speakeasy, too, took that way of wiping Rita off the slate in order to get the fellow out of her clutches."

McKee sighed and droned into the transmitter: "Gair was the man in her dressing room. He was on the trail of those letters of Judith Pierce's. And if that's the solution, why was Silva killed?" The district attorney said something forceful between his

teeth and slammed the receiver back on the hook. The Scotsman brewed himself a cup of maté and returned to the perusal
of a brochure on handwriting. It was getting dark now. Buckley
would soon be moving out of his hideaway. From time to time
the Scotsman stirred, sipped, and turned a page, his eyes on the
text. "In Graphology to know how to distinguish peculiarities of
character is the most difficult as it is the most important . . . We
write not only with the hand but with the brain . . . writing is . . .
an outburst of the heart, an exponent of life and character more
reliable than the delineations of the countenance . . ."

At a few minutes after seven Telfair walked in. His countenance at least was an open book. He was elaborately calm, with
bloodshot eyes and a face haggard from lack of sleep, and he
had quite obviously come to find out what the police were doing
about Judith Pierce, because the papers were singularly uninformative as far as the Sanctuary murder went.

The inspector murmured, "Whisky in the kitchen if you want
it. Sit down," and went on studying the list of signatures, to
lean back with a yawn after a minute, push papers aside, and
gaze thoughtfully at the cartoonist. "You had a visit from Susan
Gair yesterday afternoon, didn't you?" And when Telfair merely
nodded, his jaw tight, "She is furious about her husband getting himself all tangled up with the dancer on account of Judith
Pierce, isn't she?"

Telfair tried to keep his voice level. He said slowly, "I can't say
I blame her, McKee. Men don't do that sort of thing for nothing.
I think—Miss Pierce might have chosen someone besides the
husband of her best friend to . . ."

"To help her out, you mean?"

"No, I don't," Telfair cried, "I mean to . . ."and was suddenly
brutal under the lash of his own pain.

"You may be jumping at conclusions that are absolutely false."

"You know all about it, I suppose, McKee."

"I know a good deal." The telephone rang. He took the receiver off the hook, listened, put it back on again. "The Barcleys and Colonel Waring left the Sixty-eighth Street house in a black Lincoln limousine at a little after 5:30 this afternoon. They've just passed Spring Lake. They'll reach Brielle at about eight. Sometime tonight there'll be a loving reunion between mother and son. It will be interesting to observe. Of course——" The phone rang again. It was the man watching the Gair house out in the country. Susan Gair had taken a train for New York.

The Scotsman was not surprised at this, either. He said: "Her husband didn't arrive home from the office, so she's coming to New York in the hope of surprising him with Miss Pierce in her apartment. She won't do that because——"

"Why?"

"Because Miss Pierce left it to take a ride in the subway about half an hour ago. There's a man watching every move she makes."

Telfair started to say something—and stopped. McKee was absolutely right. Judith had gotten herself into this mess, now let her get herself out—or she could go to Gair for help.

The inspector returned to his scrutiny of the signatures. "Claire Barcley," he murmured aloud. "If I'd never seen her I'd know that she was the product of a select finishing school, was about fifty (notice the Spencerian slant taught in our most exclusive establishments thirty or thirty-five years ago), had a narrow emotional range (the precision with which the letters are formed), was extremely self-willed (the regularity of the stroke), and subject to an occasional attack of fury (the crossing of the *t*'s)."

And in the fact of Telfair's incredulous stare, he proceeded to

MCKEE OF CENTRE STREET · 217

relate some interesting facts about Barcley and Waring, to be interrupted a third time by the ringing of the telephone bell. He picked up the instrument. It was raining now, drops spattered the windows. Telfair dropped back into bitter thoughts, roused himself as the Scotsman slammed the receiver into place and leaped to his feet with a glance at his watch. It was twenty minutes to eight.

"What is it?" the cartoonist demanded, his thoughts, as always, reverting to the girl. This time they were strictly relevant, for McKee said, his brown eyes stern in deep sockets, "The men following Judith Pierce lost her in the subway. She's got to be found. She's got to be found right away or it may be too late!"

CHAPTER XXVII

Tannin was probably the one of the three who suffered most from the outward circumstances which followed that last telephone call. He was very carefully checking reports in the office just before it came in. There was a cable from Donaher that looked like good news. The lieutenant was bumming a ride back from Colombia in an old ship that one of the transatlantic flyers had used, and hoped to make New York sometime late Tuesday night or early Wednesday morning. The sergeant grinned at the shameless waste of expense contained in the last words, "No seats. Front gas tank damned uncomfortable."

It was the one thing that arrested McKee's attention when they met in the rain on the wharf on the East River, to which Tannin repaired when McKee said after he finished giving orders, "Meet me there in ten minutes."

The sergeant did. He found McKee busy in the shelter of a clump of piles under an overhead light with a time table and the stump of a pencil with which he kept figuring on the margin. The last train for Brielle and all shore points left at seven-thirty. The girl had taken that. Which would bring her into Manasquan (the nearest station) at about twenty minutes of nine. It was now almost eight. The Cadillac was too slow on a night like this, for the roads were skiddy; so would an ordinary craft have been. But the launch commanded by a lieutenant of the Marine Division was exceptionally fast and, taking into consideration the fact that the yacht was anchored off Brielle and that that was the only way that any one of them could escape, the open water was their one best bet. The sergeant gave Donaher's message and then permitted misery to overwhelm him. By water! The world was made of water, was full of it slanting out of the air persistently from the east. Waves sent a long black wet shape that looked like a half-submerged whale and was a fast launch bobbing up and down sickeningly at the end of the pier. Tannin shuddered as he jumped down on a gleaming deck, dotted with men in oilskins, and made for the cabin. Hell of a night for a boat ride. Even the lake in Central Park would have been too much of a hazard. He stumbled down some steps, fell on a hard narrow bench, stared without any favor into Telfair's face three feet away, was swung violently against paneling. They were off down the harbor, streaking for the Jersey coast.

It seemed to the sergeant that he and the cartoonist sat opposite each other swaying like drunken marionettes for endless hours against a wild song composed of the creaking of timbers, the noise of the motor, and the heavy smashing of waves. Out on deck, close to the rail, McKee was a crouch in marble, face set sternly ahead, dashing water from his eyes, beaten by the wind, unmoving, eyes and ears beyond reach of his surroundings, counting each hurrying minute as though it were a full day, adding, subtracting, calculating possibilities, estimating the final ounce of a killer's necessity.

He urged the slim launch forward with his will, picked up lights, discarded them. Not yet. The journey would take almost two hours. Judith Pierce on the contrary could make it in a little over one. She was going to Brielle, of course, had given the man watching her the slip in the maze of subways under the Grand Central. The Barcleys were on their way there, too, with Waring, and Gregory Archer and his faithful henchman, Buckley, were possibly even now aboard the yacht anchored out in the bay in front of the Barcley estate. As for Gair . . . he shrugged irritably underneath an oilskin dripping spray. These people were going to have a little private session from which the police were to be rigidly secluded. Either the killing of Rita Rodriguez and Carlos Silva was to take on the character of a permanent mystery or an even more sinister denouement was being planned.

He scowled at a tug as they scuttled past, at a trail of barges wallowing low against the faint brilliance of an excursion boat beating south. If he could only have clapped them all in jail until Donaher got back. It was not the first time that he felt the galling need for evidence, for proof; for slow careful substantiation of endless detail had tied him hand and foot.

Meanwhile in the cabin Telfair listened stupidly to hammering heartbeats, knew that nothing else in the world but Judith mattered, not her guilt or her innocence, or what she'd done or was likely to do, not even whether she cared for him or for someone else—just Judith herself, the curve of her cheek, the turn of her head.

He wanted to see her once again, tell her this—that was all he did want at the moment, all there was room for inside of him. The sturdy little craft surging ahead put mile after mile behind her heels. Plunge down, rise again, past river mouths, wide harbors, endless towns invisible in darkness and rain.

McKee stood steadily by the rail peering through the murk.

Once he descended into the cabin for a brief conference with the marine lieutenant, who became immediately surrounded by a pool of water. The lieutenant was consulting a map. He said: "Will the yacht be carrying lights, Inspector?"

"Yes, I think so. It must all have an appearance of the usual, the crew must not be allowed later to talk. These men who hope to board the yacht have probably done so by this time, will want everything straight for the record. How long now?"

"We ought to sight the beacon on the point in twenty minutes. Perhaps five after that. The tide is with us."

Both men were turning to leave the cabin when Telfair leaped to his feet, fell over the sergeant, and grasped McKee's arm. He stammered out in a haze, "I thought . . . what about Judith? I thought we were going after her."

McKee turned. "Listen, Telfair. Miss Pierce gave the man following her the slip. We're on our way to Brielle now. Will be there in a few minutes. Miss Pierce took a train at the Pennsylvania Station and arrived there probably about an hour ago. She could only have gone to have a talk with the Barclays. The house is being watched back and front. In addition I warned men to be on the lookout at the local station. Don't worry, keep your nerve."

Nevertheless as he ascended again on deck he was far from feeling as confident as he made his voice sound. In the partial shelter of a tarpaulin, binoculars poised, the lieutenant peered ahead. They had picked up the beacon, were rounding the point.

Under the heel of a ketch beating for shore, muffled cry of the man at the wheel, sharp heave to starboard . . . on again.

A rather lonely stretch of coast, this, bordered for the most part by big estates. Isolation in this part of the world costs money. Nothing much to get in their way. They were traveling pretty well inshore. (Farther out a division of marine police bottled up the yacht's exit.) Small pleasure craft were all tied safely away for the night.

The lieutenant shouted in McKee's ear, "Clearing. Shift in the wind." And astonishingly he was right. As though a giant tap were being turned down by some kind hand, the steadily beating pressure of stinging wetness subsided to the mere push of the boat's thrust through the waves. Nine o'clock, five minutes past nine, a half-dozen false alarms, then behind thickness of flying spray the lieutenant caught, or thought he did, the riding lights of a craft anchored a quarter of a mile off-shore, between them and the shore, a little to the south. His cry, a mere breath behind poised binoculars, was a veritable shout to McKee, who had been waiting for it for a long time.

The lieutenant snapped the glasses away from his eyes, went aft and gave sharp orders. The Scotsman remained where he was, staring steadily ahead. They were slackening speed now. The yacht was no more than three hundred yards away across wild leaps of gray water, her long white hull faintly visible, bits of brass gleaming dully here and there. Then her bulk towered as the cocky little speedboat whipped across her stern and swung around close to her flank.

Down in the cabin Telfair stared steadily at the sergeant without seeing him. Tannin, hunched into a ball, was being violently ill. Suddenly the engines died and the stillness over their heads was broken by the scream of the siren, the shouting of men through megaphones. Both men leaped to their feet, scrambled for the companionway, were out of the cabin moving along the rail. They boarded the yacht.

The captain, aroused apparently from sleep, was waiting for them on deck. He managed to combine a sense of outrage with incredulity and a sharp request for their credentials. McKee, with Tannin beside him, Telfair and a detective bringing up the rear, produced his shield, slipped it back into his pocket, and said in a polite voice:

"That being settled—Gregory Archer is on board. He came with a man named Buckley. I want them both." Captain Christiansen was a Swede with a wife and family in the Bronx. Jobs were hard to get. He was the yacht's captain. He had his orders. Nevertheless these were the police. The fight went out of him. He succumbed because there was nothing else to do, washed his hands of the whole business with what dignity he could summon. Calling a steward, he gave directions in a curt voice.

The steward said: "This way, sir," and the Scotsman, followed by Tannin, his ruddy face a cheese, his legs made of licorice, and by Telfair, went through the door down a short flight of steps into a saloon, past mirrors, turned to the left, moved along a narrow corridor paneled in fine woods, and came to a stop before a cabin door. The steward knocked.

A voice inside (New England, thinnish, a man's voice) drawled: "Yes?"

"Captain's order, Mr. Buckley. Open up. Some gentlemen to see Mr. Archer."

The man inside the cabin must have known the game was up, but he attempted a last stand. "Mr. Archer's asleep. No use . . ." It was Tannin, animated perhaps a little by the memory of the horrid ride, who lunged at the door, threw it swiftly out of the way. But the inspector was first over the threshold.

Buckley engaged his eye for the fraction of a second, a big fellow with a stolid face under a coarse shock of black hair standing on end. Then they were all looking at the bed (two beds in the room, a dressing table between, very luxurious, as became this little floating pleasure house). The sergeant's first feeling was one of disappointment. Archer's head was half buried in the pillow, but there was enough of him visible. Thin blond hair, narrow bleak face, scanty lashes closed, mouth open above a sloping chin with a dimple in it. Archer needed a shave. He was asleep.

As they stood there he woke up. It was a peculiar awakening. Eyes wide open, pupils a mere pin point, unwinking, even in the flooding light. The vacancy of the steady stare gave him the appearance of being blind.

McKee's voice was a thrust, low-pitched but reaching: "Mr. Archer?"

Archer turned his head, looked at the Scotsman, looked back at the ceiling and—giggled. Neither more nor less. It was rather a shocking sound in the stillness of the confined space broken by the creaking of the ship and the slap of waves somewhere outside. The convulsive mirth was a mere flicker. He sat up sharply in bed, a jackknife bending, face, limbs, torso crafty beneath the covers he clutched. "Didn't," he cried loudly. "Can't say I did. Can't prove it. That for proof!" He snapped his fingers.

Telfair and the sergeant were both completely absorbed in the astonishing and curious spectacle. They didn't see McKee move back, turn around. All three men were standing in such a way that they were invisible from the corridor. So that when the cry rang through the cabin, although it was not very loud, it sounded to them like a veritable clap of thunder.

Mrs. Barcley was standing just over the threshold, and if she saw them, she had no eyes for anyone but the man in the bed. All she said was: "Gregory" then moved swiftly across the floor to stand motionless at the foot of the bed, her back turned, staring down.

And then Waring and Barcley were in the cabin, and the colonel was as cool as a cucumber and Barcley was flushed and upset, his thin face working, his ease, his geniality, wiped away. He too, was almost indifferent to the presence of the police, was at his wife's side, his hand on her arm, repeating presently the curt instructions McKee issued. "Claire, dear, we must all go back to the house. Claire . . . listen. We must go back in the launch to the house. It's all right. He's perfectly safe. Gregory is to come, too. Listen, my dear . . ."

Telfair could still hear his voice as he followed McKee up the stairs and out on deck. The inspector on that journey to the shore seemed to be in a good deal of a hurry.

CHAPTER XXVIII

AFTER THAT things were plain enough to Telfair, but they were like things heard and experienced in a dream. They scarcely touched consciousness, which was a stiff layer stretched rigidly above his fear. He wouldn't examine his fear, knew that he couldn't do that and remain calm. And there was need for calmness now. McKee was very calm indeed. They crossed in the launch to the shore. A number of men loomed out of the darkness in the extensive and ornamental grounds surrounding the long low house on the hill above. They went through a garden and up steps. They went across a terrace and into the house. Some of the men went with them, some of the others were sent away.

McKee stood very tall and straight in the middle of a paneled room that had a lot of books in it and asked questions, addressing most of these to two detectives from the Homicide Squad who had followed the Barcleys and Waring down here earlier in the evening. He spoke slowly:

"You, Albright, stationed yourself out in front after the Barcleys entered the house at a little before eight. Then . . . ?"

"Nothing for a while, Inspector. Mr. and Mrs. Barcley and the colonel went in and lights came on. About ten minutes of nine a taxi came up the drive, stopped at the front door. A girl got out. I knew it was the Pierce girl right away, because I was tailing her last week. She went into the house. The taxi drove away. She was inside about a quarter of an hour when a motorcycle man came over with orders to grab her if she showed. But as she was inside anyhow, and there was a man on the back——"

"I understand." McKee turned to the second detective. "You're sure, Brown, she didn't slip out that way?"

Brown shook his head. "Not while I was watching. At about half-past nine, three people came out. I couldn't see very well, but I made sure against the windows they were the Barcleys and Waring. They started across the lawn and down the hill. I followed. They went into a boathouse at the shore over on the left. It was pretty dark. They were in there a long time. I heard voices and tinkering noises and I figured they were trying to get some sort of launch started to get out to the yacht. Then, after about half an hour, they did get it started. I knew our men were out there. I stayed down on the beach ready to grab anyone who came back."

"All right. Search the house, the outbuildings."

The two detectives tramped away. McKee began to pace the floor, hands in his pockets, his head bent, concentrating on a problem of minutes. There was no question at all as to *why* the girl was there. She had come on the same errand that had sent her to the penthouse the morning they themselves paid it a second visit—to get the letters for which Rita was using black-mail. The letters had been lost in the shuffle after the dancer's death. One thing was clear: if the Barcleys had the letters—and this went for Waring, too—they might have summoned the girl down here to propose a bargain. The meeting in the district attorney's office was over, the case apparently closed. But they could never feel quite safe as long as they weren't sure of two things: first, whether Judith Pierce, crossing the space beyond the mahogany barrier in which Archer was standing just prior to Rita's death, had seen anything incriminating; then, secondly, if she had, whether she would keep still about it permanently.

All this was beside the point at the moment. She had been alone in the house for a full half-hour after the Barcleys had left it, while they were down in the boathouse trying to start the launch. And where was Gair? There was one thing McKee could do and do immediately: ask the Barcleys and Colonel Waring some questions. They didn't know they had been closely watched, might deny even now that they had seen anything of the girl at all that night.

Telfair could have taken a lesson in composure from the group of people who presently filed into the room. Archer had been dressed and pulled back to some semblance of normality. He looked weak and ill as he came in between Waring and George Buckley, but that was all. Barcley held his wife tightly by the arm, supported her to a chair. They all sat down.

And at once McKee's vague hope of trapping them in a lie died stillborn. Claire Barcley, putting her husband aside, admitted everything: "I telephoned Miss Pierce. I asked her to come down here. I suggested this place because we had been—rather annoyed by the police in New York."

"Why did she come, Mrs. Barcley?"

Did a glance flash from one to the other? He couldn't be sure. She said languidly: "We have all been subjected to anxiety and annoyance over this case. My husband and I are going away. We wanted to have everything cleared up with the most absolute certainty before we went, thought that Miss. Pierce would feel the same way."

"She was still in the house when you left it to go down to the shore?"

"Yes. We telephoned to a garage in Manasquan for a car to take her back to the station. There was no car in. They said they would send one as soon as they could. She said she would wait." She was still explaining this when a detective came into the room and announced that a car from a local garage had just driven through the gate.

Telfair, who had been listening, absolutely motionless, to this drive of questions that didn't lead anywhere, got up on that and made his way stumblingly to an open French window and through it out into the air. He had no plan of any kind, was scarcely conscious of where he was going or what he meant to do—but he had to do something.

Darkness and the roar of the surf. The night was full of the sea, smelt of seaweed and sand and fish and slime and salt. Far off to the left, where the garages were, lights shot to and fro and voices were faint and echoing across the gardens. Men were beating about the tangle of shrubbery near the lodge. Within its walls McKee was still asking those people questions. The grounds in front were being gone over. The shore then. He turned towards it blindly and curiously, after a minute or two, found himself going uphill instead of down.

The sky had been steadily breaking up after the storm, and at this moment the slow moon sailed out from behind a fling of clouds and made painted magic of the landscape. In its sharp and sudden light, objects were almost discernable as in day. Telfair stood still. Far out, the sea; behind him and to the left, the house; ahead, the water was a wide curve biting into the hilly shore. He stood at its highest point. Everything but this narrow strip on the extreme right had been already explored. There didn't seem to be anything here to . . . He stared down steadily at the precipitous drop clothed with pines and running in a sharp point out into the ocean.

Then he saw a lot of things all at once: broken branches and trampled shrubs, as though someone had gone down what was almost a small precipice at his feet; but more than that, buried in pines at the bottom on the edge of the shore, the roof alone betraying it, there was some sort of house.

Telfair didn't stop to think. No time for thinking. He followed the faint trail, sliding down ground tilted at a forty-five degree angle, slippery with needles between small tree trunks at which he grasped with his hands to break his fall. He reached the bottom abruptly, fetched up against a boulder, barked his shins, went down on a loose pebble, fell headlong, got a gash along his jaw, wiped blood away, and continued to race forward. The pines fell back now; dead ahead, in a frame of bright ripples that was the moon on the water, a low octangular building, some sort of ornamental summerhouse, reared a dark bulk.

As he ran the remaining twenty feet he had the sense to shout, sent cry after cry ringing into the darkness. From somewhere far off there was an answering shout as he reached the building, banged furiously and without result on a small stout door. The door was locked. He was hammering on it with bleeding fists when help arrived. Telfair didn't even recognize the Scotsman at the head of a little army. They broke down the door, were in a cement chamber smelling of damp, with a spiral stair leading to the room above. The troopers leaped for the staircase. Telfair started to follow and stood still. Because McKee was standing still, sending his torch slowly around the basement of the really beautiful and secluded pagoda among the pines. There was very little in it, some folding chairs, faded with age, an old canvas hammock flung against the wall, and, standing near the hammock, a lawnmower, very bright and new, with its green paint and glistening blades. The Scotsman started to walk towards this slowly. He didn't say anything until he stood directly above the canvas hammock; then he did say in a muffled voice: "Stand where you are, Telfair." He dropped down on his knees, pulled a flap of canvas aside, and his voice changed.

"Thank God," he said simply. And then Telfair was beside him down on the floor. It was Judith beneath the canvas hammock, crowded close against the wall, and Judith was alive. He made sure of that first in one desperate heartbeat, then lifted her into his arms, smoothing her face, her hair, listened to her slow breathing, while a deep and shuddering joy shook him from head to foot.

Broken planes of nightmare fell away. It was all very simple for Telfair after that. They got Judith into the upper room, a beautifully furnished apartment with wide windows opening on the sea. McKee went away, came back. Telfair was oblivious of the passage of time, of various reports made to the inspector. Gerald Gair's car had been found parked in a deserted lane a half-mile away. There was no sign of him. After a while Judith was able to talk. (It was late then; the moon had sailed a perceptible distance up into the sky.)

Her story merely deepened the Scotsman's frown, for it confirmed Claire Barcley's. Judith had come down here for a conference. They hadn't threatened her in any way. Had told her they were leaving, that the house would be empty. But she knew the car for which the Barcley's had telephoned would be there soon.

She was watching for it at the window when something frightened her, some sound. She turned too late. The door of the room was opening. Somebody leaped at her from behind, pinioned her arms, pressed a cloth over her mouth. She knew the cloth was saturated with chloroform because she had had an anesthetic once before . . . and that was all she could tell them. She hadn't caught even a glimpse of——

A detective interrupted her at this point, springing quickly up the staircase. All he said was, "Donaher, Inspector. Just drove over here from the Newark airport. Got your call." McKee, who had been going to ask Judith about the all-important letters, turned abruptly and vanished. Telfair didn't care. He was perfectly willing to obey orders now. They were all to go up to the house. There was a less difficult route than that by which he had approached the pagoda, along the shore fifty feet and up through the gardens. Judith was able to walk now. His happiness was scarcely even dimmed by a faint withdrawal on her part as she gathered strength. It was as though during that brief journey she was bracing herself.

And then they were back in the big room lined with books. Their arrival didn't even create a stir. On the couch Archer had fallen asleep. Claire Barcley sat almost as she had been sitting when Telfair left the room. Her husband was beside her. Waring drowsed in a big chair beside the empty fireplace, and Buckley sat stolid and unwinking in the face of events for which he didn't even try to find explanation or excuse.

Telfair was completely immersed in Judith. She was still suffering from shock and the dose of chloroform, but had pulled herself together marvelously. Her hands were folded in her lap, and she stared straight ahead at a lovely piece of Ming porcelain on a table under a window. It was a long time before there was any interruption, but the cartoonist was quite content. People did get tangled up in these bad dreams sometimes, but it was all over now. Death was like that. Almost any death that was close to one. It took months to get over it.

The opening of the door found them all strangely immobile. He himself didn't feel any particular interest. McKee came in slowly, as though he were tired. He didn't sit down, stood there just inside the room, his shoulder against a bookcase, holding some papers in his hand. Behind him two detectives were dimly visible in the hall.

"I'm not"—his glance passed over them all in turn, lingering on Claire Barcley—"going to bother you now with a long resume leading up to the murder of Rita Rodriguez and the subsequent killing of Carlos Silva in the hospital in the Bronx. I have felt from the beginning that the solution was intimately bound up with the emerald robbery perpetrated by Silva in Colombia. And the moment I came on the box containing the three toes amputated from Silva's foot in a fight, I knew that he had been double-crossed and that a brain more nimble than his had planned the theft. The possessor of this brain managed to have Silva caught and imprisoned down in Colombia. This unknown man was a lover of the dancer's. He got away with the emeralds, leaving her behind—not, however, before she managed to get hold of one stone, probably in a final scene between them before he departed to the new life this wealth opened up. He vanished. But Rita was shrewd. The moment she heard that Silva had been captured at Costa de Muerte, she put two and two together. After that she started a leisurely pursuit of this man.

"And at last in New York she found Gregory Archer.—Wait!" He threw up his hand, for Claire Barcley was on her feet, her eyes wild. In the single instant of silence the noise of the surf

on the shore below came clearly into the room. There was another movement: two big sturdy men stepped over the threshold, ranged themselves beside the inspector. He went on slowly:
"Just when or where she saw the man she was in search of with
Gregory Archer in New York, I cannot tell you. At any rate she
did." And then McKee turned. His voice sounded tired. "Barcley,
I arrest you for the murder of——" Claire Barcley's scream cut
across the mechanical formula. She stumbled, would have fallen,
only that McKee, who had been expecting this, caught her in his
arms. And over the uproar that surged up and filled the room, he
cried—it was the only thing he could think of in that frightful
moment: "At any rate, your son is innocent."

He didn't go on with that brief summary until Claire Barcley
had been taken away. Barcley himself, alias Mr. Philip Hamilton, sat on quite easily next to the empty chair his wife had oc-
cupied. There was no evidence of strain about his easy posture,
no attempt at denial, scarcely even any fear. It was as though
he, instead of the others—instead of Waring, for instance, his
face flushed, with hands balled into fists, staring incredulously,
torn between rage and disbelief—might, have been the spectator
rather than the principal in this final moment.

In fact, when he spoke it was in the voice of a man who has
played a game of billiards and who has lost every cent in his
pocket but whose only emotion is one of physical fatigue. His
eyes were fastened on the papers McKee still held in his hand.
The Scotsman nodded impersonally.

"Yes, your handwriting. We sent a detective down to Colombia. He got the story of a Mr. Hamilton's infatuation with the
dancer, got Mr. Hamilton's signatures, six years old, for food and
drink at the clubhouse outside Bogota. Hamilton vanished just
after the theft was committed. Have you anything to say?"

Barcley's eyes met his. He spoke slowly: "I don't suppose it would do any good. Besides, I'm too tired now. Perhaps—later?" And stifling a yawn, he got up deliberately, almost before the detectives either side of him made a move, and with that easy graceful stride walked between them out of the room. A quick finish then. Orders issued. Archer, who had viewed all this with the stupid gaze of a puzzled child, was taken away to bed by his henchman; Waring, who wanted to ask a lot of questions, was dismissed with a shrug, and the Cadillac was ordered round.

It wasn't until they were alone, the three of them, Judith Pierce, Telfair, and the Scotsman, that McKee said: "And now, Miss Pierce, what about those letters?" The girl glanced up at him, looked away and didn't move. And then he spoke again, and his voice was stern: "Barcley gave them to you, didn't he, here, tonight? He picked them up in Rita's apartment after he killed her, picked up also the pistol with which Gerald Gair threatened Rita on the afternoon of her death when he went to her apartment to get the letters. Gair left the pistol behind him. You've all been very stupid and have caused us a great deal of trouble. You and Mr. and Mrs. Gair, running around watching each other— on the night of Silva's murder, for instance. Think of how Barcley used you and the knowledge he had. He read the letters, kept the gun and used it to kill the waiter. But he didn't throw it away at once. Because it was valuable and might be of assistance in incriminating someone else. When he went to the Gaits' house on Sunday afternoon to bargain with Gair about testimony given in the Sanctuary, he took occasion to drop it somewhere.

"The papers were full of descriptions of the pistol. Susan Gair knew her husband had one like it. She found the pistol. What happened then? When she went up to Harlem to visit an old colored cook who had been employed by her mother, she threw it away in the alley."

Judith Pierce fell back against the cushions with a long breath and covered her face with her hands. But the inspector was not yet through with her. "Mrs. Barcley telephoned you to come down here, offering the bait of these letters which her husband told her he had found in Archer's apartment. But it was Barcley who called Gair at his office, who told Gair to drive to that deserted amusement park above Manasquan and wait there until someone turned the extremely incriminating documents over to him.

"Do you know what they intended to do in the end? No? I'll tell you. But first you had to be wiped out. Because, you see, you were the only witness to the actual murder."

The girl took her hands away and stared at him whitely. "But . . . I wasn't!"

McKee's smile was thin. "He thought you were—which comes to the same thing in the end. I am in doubt about a good many things still, but not as to what happened that night in the speakeasy. When Barcley walked in there in pursuit of his wife, he hadn't the slightest idea in the world of who Rita was. He recognized her while he was still seated at the table and understood everything at a glance. She was striking at him through Archer; was about to have an interview with his wife. That would have been the end. He was confronted with two alternatives. Either to lose the life of security he had built up or to kill her. Knowing his past, I believe that he went constantly armed, always fearful of the emergency which confronted him then. What took place? He walked the length of the room and stepped behind the barrier. There was no one there. He was alone, to all intents and purposes, the restaurant beyond, crowded and in the shadow, except for Rita in the middle of the dance floor, her body a bright shaft in the spotlight. He drew the gun and fired. When he turned round he was no longer alone. Archer had come in, and you yourself were crossing towards the aisle at the far side.

"Archer was drunk. He had a pistol in his hand. In the grip of a jealous rage he had gone to the Sanctuary either to shoot the dancer or to threaten to shoot himself. Barcley was an opportunist. He was quick to see the chance this afforded him—could easily deal with his stepson. He had taken good care to keep him under the combined influence of drink and an opiate ever since, while passing him from hand to hand, playing on his mother's fear and the colonel's self-interest. You were another kettle of fish. You hadn't spoken, but you might. Very well, we return to my point. You had to be eliminated before he could feel really safe.

"After leaving you here in the house, he returned while his wife and the colonel were trying to get the launch started, chloroformed you, and (it was a comparatively simple matter) carried you down to the pagoda. Desperate people will take long chances. He hadn't time to dispose of you then, would have returned later. But there was an added element of safety then that he couldn't bring himself to pass up. And there he overstepped himself.

"If you were dead and your body rose to the surface within a reasonable length of time, those letters would have been found in your pocket. And Gair, waiting to keep the appointment with a man who never came, would have had some difficulty explaining his whereabouts when you disappeared. Miss Pierce, hadn't you better give me the letters now?"

And then when she still didn't move but sat there like a little figurine carved in ivory, McKee walked to the fireplace, where logs were laid, bent down and put a match to the kindling beneath. He turned away, blew out the match, walked to the window. And suddenly Telfair knew.

It was Gerald Gair the dancer was blackmailing all the time, Gair who had gone to the Sanctuary that night to get his letters. Susan Gair followed him, and after the murder was committed, Gair, finding himself in a tough spot and afraid of his wife, told Judith the truth and appealed to her for help. The dancer had not brought the letters with her to the Sanctuary; therefore they must be in her apartment, because she had told him that afternoon after he paid that she was going to get them from the bank. Judith had stolen the purse in order to gain admittance there. Not finding the letters, she had regained possession of it again to see whether the purse contained any further clue to their whereabouts. Could as peaceful an emotion as friendship have sent her plunging into the whole adventure?

Telfair's new-found peace receded, leaving him very cold and detached. All of it couldn't quite go. For Judith was safe. Had he found her only to lose her again? And to a man like Gerald Gair! He understood Gair's character as he had never done before. The man was charming, easily attracted, unreliable, without even strength.

Telfair stood looking at the girl fixedly. She got up out of the chair, walked with little steps to the hearth, stood there for a moment looking down into the flames, put her hand into the pocket of the tweed coat, stained with moisture and crushed leaves, took two folded sheets of paper out and tossed them straight into the middle of the blaze. Then she turned round. Her eyes met his. There was a question in her eyes.

Telfair said very slowly and distinctly: "I don't want to worry you now. You've had enough. After all, — have no right——" He stopped. For the Scotsman, without looking at them, was walking out of the room, and over his shoulder, as he went, he said in a tired voice: "Don't be a damn fool, Telfair. The car will be around in ten minutes. I'll wait for you at the door."

On an afternoon in late August almost three months to a day since the alarm announcing Rita's death had come blurred and breathless into the golden bowl at the top of Police Headquarters, McKee sat at his desk and watched a flight of pigeons alight a roof in sunlight across the street. His brow suddenly cleared, and he sank back in his chair. There was beauty in the world, although sometimes it was difficult to find. He had had a long and tiring week in court. That morning the jury had brought in a verdict of wilful murder against Philip Hamilton, alias Philip Barcley. He had just been working on the last notes, supplementary evidence that had been brought out during the trial. Now as the door opened he pushed a sheaf of papers into an envelope and pressed down the fastener. It was the sergeant who came in. McKee said: "Don't sit down. We're taking a little trip." Tannin looked resigned. "Where to?"

"Pier Number 59, North River, for the purpose of seeing Mr. and Mrs. James Telfair off on a trip to the Continent."

"A ship?" the sergeant frowned, then a grin ran all over his freckled face. "Well, so's I don't have to stay on it that's O.K."

Before he went, McKee pulled the envelope labeled *Sanctuary Murder* towards him. Below *Sanctuary Murder*, Hamilton's name was written in full and the words, *Indicted May Thirty-first; brought to trial, August Eighth,* then *Verdict.* He scribbled, *Guilty, first degree* after *Verdict,* threw the pen aside. There were two other items to be filled in later. They consisted of *Sentenced in Su-*

perior Court by Judge McDermott, with the month and day left blank, and a still further word, *Executed* . . . The answer to this was not yet forthcoming.

McKee dropped the envelope into the drawer and closed it with a bang. Finished business—or almost. At the moment he had other, pleasanter things to do.

THE END

DISCUSSION QUESTIONS

- Did any aspects of the plot date the story? If so, which?

- Would the story be different if it were set in the present day? If so, how?

- Did the social context of the time play a role in the narrative? If so, how?

- If you were one of the main characters, would you have acted differently at any point in the story?

- Did you identify with any of the characters? If so, which?

- What skills or qualities make McKee such an effective sleuth?

- Did this book remind you of any present day authors? If so, which?

- How has police work changed since this novel was written?

Charlotte Armstrong, *The Chocolate Cobweb*. When Amanda Garth was born, a mix-up caused the hospital to briefly hand her over to the prestigious Garrison family instead of to her birth parents. The error was quickly fixed, Amanda was never told, and the secret was forgotten for twenty-three years … until her aunt revealed it in casual conversation. But what if the initial switch never actually occurred? **Introduction by A. J. Finn.**

Charlotte Armstrong, *The Unsuspected*. First published in 1946, this suspenseful novel opens with a young woman who has ostensibly hanged herself, leaving a suicide note. Her friend doesn't believe it and begins an investigation that puts her own life in jeopardy. It was filmed in 1947 by Warner Brothers, starring Claude Rains and Joan Caulfield. **Introduction by Otto Penzler.**

Anthony Boucher, *The Case of the Baker Street Irregulars*. When a studio announces a new hard-boiled Sherlock Holmes film, the Baker Street Irregulars begin a campaign to discredit it. Attempting to mollify them, the producers invite members to the set, where threats are received, each referring to one of the original Holmes tales, followed by murder. Fortunately, the amateur sleuths use Holmesian lessons to solve the crime. **Introduction by Otto Penzler.**

Anthony Boucher, *Rocket to the Morgue*. Hilary Foulkes has made so many enemies that it is difficult to speculate who was responsible for stabbing him nearly to death in a room with only one door through which no one was seen entering or leaving. This classic locked room mystery is populated by such thinly disguised science fiction legends as Robert Heinlein, L. Ron Hubbard, and John W. Campbell. **Introduction by F. Paul Wilson.**

Fredric Brown, *The Fabulous Clipjoint*. Brown's outstanding mystery won an Edgar as the best first novel of the year (1947). When Wallace Hunter is found dead in an alley after a long night of drinking, the police don't really care. But his teenage son Ed and his uncle Am, the carnival worker, are convinced that some things don't add up and the crime isn't what it seems to be. **Introduction by Lawrence Block.**

John Dickson Carr, *The Crooked Hinge*. Selected by a group of mystery experts as one of the 15 best impossible crime novels ever written, this is one of Gideon Fell's greatest challenges. Estranged from his family for 25 years, Sir John Farnleigh returns to England from America to claim his inheritance but another person turns up claiming that he can prove he is the real Sir John. Inevitably, one of them is murdered. **Introduction by Charles Todd.**

John Dickson Carr, *The Eight of Swords*. When Gideon Fell arrives at a crime scene, it appears to be straightforward enough. A man has been shot to death in an unlocked room and the likely perpetrator was a recent visitor. But Fell discovers inconsistencies and his investigations are complicated by an apparent poltergeist, some American gangsters, and two meddling amateur sleuths. **Introduction by Otto Penzler.**

John Dickson Carr, *The Mad Hatter Mystery*. A prankster has been stealing top hats all around London. Gideon Fell suspects that the same person may be responsible for the theft of a manuscript of a long-lost story by Edgar Allan Poe. The hats reappear in unexpected but conspicuous places but, when one is found on the head of a corpse by the Tower of London, it is evident that the thefts are more than pranks. **Introduction by Otto Penzler.**

John Dickson Carr, *The Plague Court Murders*. When murder occurs in a locked hut on Plague Court, an estate haunted by the ghost of a hangman's assistant who died a victim of the black death, Sir Henry Merrivale seeks a logical solution to a ghostly crime. A spiritual medium employed to rid the house of his spirit is found stabbed to death in a locked stone hut on the grounds, surrounded by an untouched circle of mud. **Introduction by Michael Dirda.**

John Dickson Carr, *The Red Widow Murders.* In a "haunted" mansion, the room known as the Red Widow's Chamber proves lethal to all who spend the night. Eight people investigate and the one who draws the ace of spades must sleep in it. The room is locked from the inside and watched all night by the others. When the door is unlocked, the victim has been poisoned. Enter Sir Henry Merrivale to solve the crime. **Introduction by Tom Mead.**

Frances Crane, *The Turquoise Shop.* In an arty little New Mexico town, Mona Brandon has arrived from the East and becomes the subject of gossip about her money, her influence, and the corpse in the nearby desert who may be her husband. Pat Holly, who runs the local gift shop, is as interested as anyone in the goings on—but even more in Pat Abbott, the detective investigating the possible murder. **Introduction by Anne Hillerman.**

Todd Downing, *Vultures in the Sky.* There is no end to the series of terrifying events that befall a luxury train bound for Mexico. First, a man dies when the train passes through a dark tunnel, then it comes to an abrupt stop in the middle of the desert. More deaths occur when night falls and the passengers panic when they realize they are trapped with a murderer on the loose. **Introduction by James Sallis.**

Mignon G. Eberhart, *Murder by an Aristocrat.* Nurse Keate is called to help a man who has been "accidentally" shot in the shoulder. When he is murdered while convalescing, it is clear that there was no accident. Although a killer is loose in the mansion, the family seems more concerned that news of the murder will leave their circle. *The New Yorker* wrote than "Eberhart can weave an almost flawless mystery." **Introduction by Nancy Pickard.**

Erle Stanley Gardner, *The Case of the Baited Hook.* Perry Mason gets a phone call in the middle of the night and his potential client says it's urgent, that he has two one-thousand-dollar bills that he will give him as a retainer, with an additional ten-thousand whenever he is called on to represent him. When

Mason takes the case, it is not for the caller but for a beautiful woman whose identity is hidden behind a mask. **Introduction by Otto Penzler.**

Erle Stanley Gardner, *The Case of the Borrowed Brunette.* A mysterious man named Mr. Hines has advertised a job for a woman who has to fulfill very specific physical requirements. Eva Martell, pretty but struggling in her career as a model, takes the job but her aunt smells a rat and hires Perry Mason to investigate. Her fears are realized when Hines turns up in the apartment with a bullet hole in his head. **Introduction by Otto Penzler.**

Erle Stanley Gardner, *The Case of the Careless Kitten.* Helen Kendal receives a mysterious phone call from her vanished uncle Franklin, long presumed dead, who urges her to contact Perry Mason. Soon, she finds herself the main suspect in the murder of an unfamiliar man. Her kitten has just survived a poisoning attempt—as has her aunt Matilda. What is the connection between Franklin's return and the murder attempts? **Introduction by Otto Penzler.**

Erle Stanley Gardner, *The Case of the Rolling Bones.* One of Gardner's most successful Perry Mason novels opens with a clear case of blackmail, though the person being blackmailed claims he isn't. It is not long before the police are searching for someone wanted for killing the same man in two different states—thirty-three years apart. The confounding puzzle of what happened to the dead man's toes is a challenge. **Introduction by Otto Penzler.**

Erle Stanley Gardner, *The Case of the Shoplifter's Shoe.* Most cases for Perry Mason involve murder but here he is hired because a young woman fears her aunt is a kleptomaniac. Sarah may not have been precisely the best guardian for a collection of valuable diamonds and, sure enough, they go missing. When the jeweler is found shot dead, Sarah is spotted leaving the murder scene with a bundle of gems stuffed in her purse. **Introduction by Otto Penzler.**

Erle Stanley Gardner, *The Bigger They Come.* Gardner's first novel using the pseudonym A.A. Fair starts off a series featuring the large and loud Bertha Cool and her employee, the small and meek Donald Lam. Given the job of delivering divorce papers to an evident crook,

Lam can't find him—but neither can the police. The *Los Angeles Times* called this book: "Breathlessly dramatic ... an original." **Introduction by Otto Penzler.**

Frances Noyes Hart, *The Bellamy Trial*. Inspired by the real-life Hall-Mills case, the most sensational trial of its day, this is the story of Stephen Bellamy and Susan Ives, accused of murdering Bellamy's wife Madeleine. Eight days of dynamic testimony, some true, some not, make headlines for an enthralled public. Rex Stout called this historic courtroom thriller one of the ten best mysteries of all time. **Introduction by Hank Phillippi Ryan.**

H. F. Heard, *A Taste for Honey*. The elderly Mr. Mycroft quietly keeps bees in Sussex, where he is approached by the reclusive and somewhat misanthropic Mr. Silchester, whose honey supplier was found dead, stung to death by her bees. Mycroft, who shares many traits with Sherlock Holmes, sets out to find the vicious killer. Rex Stout described it as "sinister ... a tale well and truly told." **Introduction by Otto Penzler.**

Dolores Hitchens, *The Alarm of the Black Cat*. Detective fiction aficionado Rachel Murdock has a peculiar meeting with a little girl and a dead toad, sparking her curiosity about a love triangle that has sparked anger. When the girl's great grandmother is found dead, Rachel and her cat Samantha work with a friend in the Los Angeles Police Department to get to the bottom of things. **Introduction by David Handler.**

Dolores Hitchens, *The Cat Saw Murder*. Miss Rachel Murdock, the highly intelligent 70-year-old amateur sleuth, is not entirely heartbroken when her slovenly, unattractive, bridge-cheating niece is murdered. Miss Rachel is happy to help the socially maladroit and somewhat bumbling Detective Lieutenant Stephen Mayhew, retaining her composure when a second brutal murder occurs. **Introduction by Joyce Carol Oates.**

Dorothy B. Hughes, *Dread Journey*. A bigshot Hollywood producer has worked on his magnum opus for years, hiring and firing one beautiful starlet after another. But Kitten Agnew's contract won't allow her to be fired, so she fears she might be terminated more permanently. Together with the producer on a train journey from Hollywood to Chicago, Kitten becomes more terrified with each passing mile. **Introduction by Sarah Weinman.**

Dorothy B. Hughes, *Ride the Pink Horse*. When Sailor met Willis Douglass, he was just a poor kid who Douglass groomed to work as a confidential secretary. As the senator became increasingly corrupt, he knew he could count on Sailor to clean up his messes. No longer a senator, Douglass flees Chicago for Santa Fe, leaving behind a murder rap and Sailor as the prime suspect. Seeking vengeance, Sailor follows. **Introduction by Sara Paretsky.**

Dorothy B. Hughes, *The So Blue Marble*. Set in the glamorous world of New York high society, this novel became a suspense classic as twins from Europe try to steal a rare and beautiful gem owned by an aristocrat whose sister is an even more menacing presence. *The New Yorker* called it "Extraordinary ... [Hughes'] brilliant descriptive powers make and unmake reality." **Introduction by Otto Penzler.**

W. Bolingbroke Johnson, *The Widening Stain*. After a cocktail party, the attractive Lucie Coindreau, a "black-eyed, black-haired Frenchwoman" visits the rare books wing of the library and apparently takes a headfirst fall from an upper gallery. Dismissed as a horrible accident, it seems dubious when Professor Hyett is strangled while reading a priceless 12th-century manuscript, which has gone missing. **Introduction by Nicholas A. Basbanes**

Baynard Kendrick, *Blind Man's Bluff*. Blinded in World War II, Duncan Maclain forms a successful private detective agency, aided by his two dogs. Here, he is called on to solve the case of a blind man who plummets from the top of an eight-story building, apparently with no one present except his dead-drunk son. **Introduction by Otto Penzler.**

Baynard Kendrick, *The Odor of Violets*. Duncan Maclain, a blind former intelligence officer, is asked to investigate the murder of an actor in his Greenwich Village apartment. This would cause a stir at any time but, when the actor possesses secret government plans that then go missing, it's enough to interest the local police as well as the American government and Maclain, who suspects a German spy plot. **Introduction by Otto Penzler.**

C. Daly King, *Obelists at Sea*. On a cruise ship traveling from New York to Paris, the lights of the smoking room briefly go out, a gunshot crashes through the night, and a man is dead. Two detectives are on board but so are four psychiatrists who believe their professional knowledge can solve the case by understanding the psyche of the killer—each with a different theory. **Introduction by Martin Edwards.**

Jonathan Latimer, *Headed for a Hearse*. Featuring Bill Crane, the booze-soaked Chicago private detective, this humorous hard-boiled novel was filmed as *The Westland Case* in 1937 starring Preston Foster. Robert Westland has been framed for the grisly murder of his wife in a room with doors and windows locked from the inside. As the day of his execution nears, he relies on Crane to find the real murderer. **Introduction by Max Allan Collins**

Lange Lewis, *The Birthday Murder*. Victoria is a successful novelist and screenwriter and her husband is a movie director so their marriage seems almost too good to be true. Then, on her birthday, her happy new life comes crashing down when her husband is murdered using a method of poisoning that was described in one of her books. She quickly becomes the leading suspect. **Introduction by Randal S. Brandt.**

Frances and Richard Lockridge, *Death on the Aisle*. In one of the most beloved books to feature Mr. and Mrs. North, the body of a wealthy backer of a play is found dead in a seat of the 45th Street Theater. Pam is thrilled to engage in her favorite pastime—playing amateur sleuth—much to the annoyance of Jerry, her publisher husband. The Norths inspired a stage play, a film, and long-running radio and TV series. **Introduction by Otto Penzler.**

John P. Marquand, *Your Turn, Mr. Moto*. The first novel about Mr. Moto, originally titled *No Hero*, is the story of a World War I hero pilot who finds himself jobless during the Depression. In Tokyo for a big opportunity that falls apart, he meets a Japanese agent and his Russian colleague and the pilot suddenly finds himself caught in a web of intrigue. Peter Lorre played Mr. Moto in a series of popular films. **Introduction by Lawrence Block.**

Stuart Palmer, *The Penguin Pool Murder*. The

first adventure of schoolteacher and dedicated amateur sleuth Hildegarde Withers occurs at the New York Aquarium when she and her young students notice a corpse in one of the tanks. It was published in 1931 and filmed the next year, starring Edna May Oliver as the American Miss Marple—though much funnier than her English counterpart. **Introduction by Otto Penzler.**

Stuart Palmer, *The Puzzle of the Happy Hooligan*. New York City schoolteacher Hildegarde Withers cannot resist "assisting" homicide detective Oliver Piper. In this novel, she is on vacation in Hollywood and on the set of a movie about Lizzie Borden when the screenwriter is found dead. Six comic films about Withers appeared in the 1930s, most successfully starring Edna May Oliver. **Introduction by Otto Penzler.**

Otto Penzler, ed., *Golden Age Bibliomysteries*. Stories of murder, theft, and suspense occur with alarming regularity in the unlikely world of books and bibliophiles, including bookshops, libraries, and private rare book collections, written by such giants of the mystery genre as Ellery Queen, Cornell Woolrich, Lawrence G. Blochman, Vincent Starrett, and Anthony Boucher. **Introduction by Otto Penzler.**

Otto Penzler, ed., *Golden Age Detective Stories*. The history of American mystery fiction has its pantheon of authors who have influenced and entertained readers for nearly a century, reaching its peak during the Golden Age, and this collection pays homage to the work of the most acclaimed: Cornell Woolrich, Erle Stanley Gardner, Craig Rice, Ellery Queen, Dorothy B. Hughes, Mary Roberts Rinehart, and more. **Introduction by Otto Penzler.**

Otto Penzler, ed., *Golden Age Locked Room Mysteries*. The so-called impossible crime category reached its zenith during the 1920s, 1930s, and 1940s, and this volume includes the greatest of the great authors who mastered the form: John Dickson Carr, Ellery Queen, C. Daly King, Clayton Rawson, and Erle Stanley Gardner. Like great magicians, these literary conjurors will baffle and delight readers. **Introduction by Otto Penzler.**

Ellery Queen, *The Adventures of Ellery Queen*. These stories are the earliest short works to feature Queen as a detective and are among the best of the author's fair-play mysteries. So many of the elements that comprise the gestalt of Queen may be found in these tales: alternate solutions, the dying clue, a bizarre crime, and the author's ability to find fresh variations of works by other authors. **Introduction by Otto Penzler.**

Ellery Queen, *The American Gun Mystery*. A rodeo comes to New York City at the Colosseum. The headliner is Buck Horne, the once popular film cowboy who opens the show leading a charge of forty whooping cowboys until they pull out their guns and fire into the air. Buck falls to the ground, shot dead. The police instantly lock the doors to search everyone but the offending weapon has completely vanished. **Introduction by Otto Penzler.**

Ellery Queen, *The Chinese Orange Mystery*. The offices of publisher Donald Kirk have seen strange events but nothing like this. A strange man is found dead with two long spears alongside his back. And, though no one was seen entering or leaving the room, everything has been turned backwards or upside down: pictures face the wall, the victim's clothes are worn backwards, the rug upside down. Why in the world? **Introduction by Otto Penzler.**

Ellery Queen, *The Dutch Shoe Mystery*. Millionaire philanthropist Abagail Doorn falls into a coma and she is rushed to the hospital she funds for an emergency operation by one of the leading surgeons on the East Coast. When she is wheeled into the operating theater, the sheet covering her body is pulled back to reveal her garroted corpse—the first of a series of murders **Introduction by Otto Penzler.**

Ellery Queen, *The Egyptian Cross Mystery*. A small-town schoolteacher is found dead, headed, and tied to a T-shaped cross on December 25th, inspiring such sensational headlines as "Crucifixion on Christmas Day." Amateur sleuth Ellery Queen is so intrigued he travels to Virginia but fails to solve the crime. Then a similar murder takes place on New York's Long Island—and then another. **Introduction by Otto Penzler.**

Ellery Queen, *The Siamese Twin Mystery*. When Ellery and his father encounter a raging forest fire on a mountain, their only hope is to drive up to an isolated hillside manor

owned by a secretive surgeon and his strange guests. While playing solitaire in the middle of the night, the doctor is shot. The only clue is a torn playing card. Suspects include a society beauty, a valet, and conjoined twins. **Introduction by Otto Penzler.**

Ellery Queen, *The Spanish Cape Mystery*. Amateur detective Ellery Queen arrives in the resort town of Spanish Cape soon after a young woman and her uncle are abducted by a gun-toting, one-eyed giant. The next day, the woman's somewhat dicey boyfriend is found murdered—totally naked under a black fedora and opera cloak. **Introduction by Otto Penzler.**

Patrick Quentin, *A Puzzle for Fools*. Broadway producer Peter Duluth takes to the bottle when his wife dies but enters a sanitarium to dry out. Malevolent events plague the hospital, including when Peter hears his own voice intone, "There will be murder." And there is. He investigates, aided by a young woman who is also a patient. This is the first of nine mysteries featuring Peter and Iris Duluth. **Introduction by Otto Penzler.**

Clayton Rawson, *Death from a Top Hat*. When the New York City Police Department is baffled by an apparently impossible crime, they call on The Great Merlini, a retired stage magician who now runs a Times Square magic shop. In his first case, two occultists have been murdered in a room locked from the inside, their bodies positioned to form a pentagram. **Introduction by Otto Penzler.**

Craig Rice, *Eight Faces at Three*. Gin-soaked John J. Malone, defender of the guilty, is notorious for getting his culpable clients off. It's the innocent ones who are problems. Like Holly Inglehart, accused of piercing the black heart of her well-heeled aunt Alexandria with a lovely Florentine paper cutter. No one who knew the old battle-ax liked her, but Holly's prints were found on the murder weapon. **Introduction by Lisa Lutz.**

Craig Rice, *Home Sweet Homicide*. Known as the Dorothy Parker of mystery fiction for her memorable wit, Craig Rice was the first detective writer to appear on the cover of *Time* magazine. This comic mystery features two kids who are trying to find a husband for their widowed mother while she's engaged in sleuthing. Filmed with the same title in 1946 with Peggy Ann Garner and Randolph Scott. **Introduction by Otto Penzler.**

Mary Roberts Rinehart, *The Album*. Crescent Place is a quiet enclave of wealthy people in which nothing ever happens—until a bedridden old woman is attacked by an intruder with an ax. *The New York Times* stated: "All Mary Roberts Rinehart mystery stories are good, but this one is better." **Introduction by Otto Penzler.**

Mary Roberts Rinehart, *The Haunted Lady*. The arsenic in her sugar bowl was wealthy widow Eliza Fairbanks' first clue that somebody wanted her dead. Nightly visits of bats, birds, and rats, obviously aimed at scaring the dowager to death, was the second. Eliza calls the police, who send nurse Hilda Adams, the amateur sleuth they refer to as "Miss Pinkerton," to work undercover to discover the culprit. **Introduction by Otto Penzler.**

Mary Roberts Rinehart, *Miss Pinkerton*. Hilda Adams is a nurse, not a detective, but she is observant and smart and so it is common for Inspector Patton to call on her for help. Her success results in his calling her "Miss Pinkerton." *The New Republic* wrote: "From thousands of hearts and homes the cry will go up: Thank God for Mary Roberts Rinehart." **Introduction by Carolyn Hart.**

Mary Roberts Rinehart, *The Red Lamp*. Professor William Porter refuses to believe that the seaside manor he's just inherited is haunted but he has to convince his wife to move in. However, he soon sees evidence of the occult phenomena of which the townspeople speak. Whether it is a spirit or a human being, Porter accepts that there is a connection to the rash of murders that have terrorized the countryside. **Introduction by Otto Penzler.**

Mary Roberts Rinehart, *The Wall*. For two decades, Mary Roberts Rinehart was the second-best-selling author in America (only Sinclair Lewis outsold her) and was beloved for her tales of suspense. In a magnificent mansion, the ex-wife of one of the owners turns up making demands and is found dead the next day. And there are more dark secrets lying behind the walls of the estate. **Introduction by Otto Penzler.**

Joel Townsley Rogers, *The Red Right Hand*. This extraordinary whodunnit that is as puzzling as it is terrifying was identified by crime fiction scholar Jack Adrian as "one of the dozen or so finest mystery novels of the 20th century." A deranged killer sends a doctor on a quest for the truth—deep into the recesses of his own mind—when he and his bride-to-be elope but pick up a terrifying sharp-toothed hitch-hiker. **Introduction by Joe R. Lansdale.**

Roger Scarlett, *Cat's Paw*. The family of the wealthy old bachelor Martin Greenough cares far more about his money than they do about him. For his birthday, he invites all his potential heirs to his mansion to tell them what they hope to hear. Before he can disburse funds, however, he is murdered, and the Boston Police Department's big problem is that there are too many suspects. **Introduction by Curtis Evans**

Vincent Starrett, *Dead Man Inside*. 1930s Chicago is a tough town but some crimes are more bizarre than others. Customers arrive at a haberdasher to find a corpse in the window and a sign on the door: *Dead Man Inside! I am Dead. The store will not open today*. This is just one of a series of odd murders that terrorizes the city. Reluctant detective Walter Ghost leaps into action to learn what is behind the plague. **Introduction by Otto Penzler.**

Vincent Starrett, *The Great Hotel Murder*. Theater critic and amateur sleuth Riley Blackwood investigates a murder in a Chicago hotel where the dead man had changed rooms with a stranger who had registered under a fake name. *The New York Times* described it as "an ingenious plot with enough complications to keep the reader guessing." **Introduction by Lyndsay Faye.**

Vincent Starrett, *Murder on 'B' Deck*. Walter Ghost, a psychologist, scientist, explorer, and former intelligence officer, is on a cruise ship and his friend novelist Dunsten Mollock, a Nigel Bruce-like Watson whose role is to offer occasional comic relief, accommodates when he fails to leave the ship before it takes off. Although they make mistakes along the way, the amateur sleuths solve the shipboard murders. **Introduction by Ray Betzner.**

Phoebe Atwood Taylor, *The Cape Cod Mystery*. Vacationers have flocked to Cape Cod to avoid the heat wave that hit the Northeast and find their holiday unpleasant when the area is flooded with police trying to find the murderer of a muckraking journalist who took a cottage for the season. Finding a solution falls to Asey Mayo, "the Cape Cod Sherlock," known for his worldly wisdom, folksy humor, and common sense. **Introduction by Otto Penzler.**

S. S. Van Dine, *The Benson Murder Case.* The first of 12 novels to feature Philo Vance, the most popular and influential detective character of the early part of the 20th century. When wealthy stockbroker Alvin Benson is found shot to death in a locked room in his mansion, the police are baffled until the erudite flaneur and art collector arrives on the scene. Paramount filmed it in 1930 with William Powell as Vance. **Introduction by Ragnar Jónasson.**

Cornell Woolrich, *The Bride Wore Black.* The first suspense novel by one of the greatest of all noir authors opens with a bride and her new husband walking out of the church. A car speeds by, shots ring out, and he falls dead at her feet. Determined to avenge his death, she tracks down everyone in the car, concluding with a shocking surprise. It was filmed by Francois Truffaut in 1968, starring Jeanne Moreau. **Introduction by Eddie Muller.**

Cornell Woolrich, *Deadline at Dawn.* Quinn is overcome with guilt about having robbed a stranger's home. He meets Bricky, a dime-a-dance girl, and they fall for each other. When they return to the crime scene, they discover a dead body. Knowing Quinn will be accused of the crime, they race to find the true killer before he's arrested. A 1946 film starring Susan Hayward was loosely based on the plot. **Introduction by David Gordon.**

Cornell Woolrich, *Waltz into Darkness.* A New Orleans businessman successfully courts a woman through the mail but he is shocked to find when she arrives that she is not the plain brunette whose picture he'd received but a radiant blond beauty. She soon absconds with his fortune. Wracked with disappointment and loneliness, he vows to track her down. When he finds her, the real nightmare begins. **Introduction by Wallace Stroby.**